CHASING MOONFLOWERS

PAULINE CHOW

GHASTLY GOINGS-ON PRESS

For my parents

Thanks for keeping our history alive through stories, language, and deliciously cooked meals. There are many ways home.

PRAISE FOR CHASING MOONFLOWERS

A dazzling blend of fantasy intrigue and historical drama. Chow deftly moves from the intricacies of real events to graphic horror scenes that would feel at home in a Stephen King novel.

— KIRKUS REVIEWS (STARRED REVIEW)

"*Chasing Moonflowers* is a mysterious, cosmic, folk horror with elements of the weird nestled in a web of politics and the occult, exploring power, choice, and the way both changes our relationships to others.

Atmospheric and enticing, this is a book you'll want to read by a the dim, quivering light of a lantern in a garden."

— AI JIANG, IGNYTE, NEBULA, AND BRAM STOKER AWARD WINNING AUTHOR

"Packed with unexpected twists, moments of revelation, and a tension and attraction that translate to a powerful read, *Chasing Moonflowers* is hard to put down and nearly impossible to predict."

— MIDWEST BOOK REVIEW

"Ling is an unforgettable protagonist, courageous yet authentically vulnerable, demonstrating the interplay between power and humanity. Chasing Moonflowers is both chilling and enchanting, definitely a book that deserves to be read slowly and savored."

— Angela Yuriko Smith, A two-time Bram Stoker Award winner and HWA Mentor of the Year

"A once in a lifetime book."

— Librarian, NetGalley review

"A riveting novel that keeps readers looking over their shoulders while unwilling to put it down."

— Readers' Favorite

"*Chasing Moonflowers* is an intriguing blend of mystery and horror, set against a backdrop of political tension and cultural transformation. A story that feels both timeless and unnervingly fresh!"

— Christopher O'Halloran, Author of *Pushing Daisy*

"Magic. Monsters. And eyes in jars. Chasing Moon-flowers is a creepy, haunting, and hopeful journey of a girl who wants to save her family. A rich and beautiful story set in a time and place I want to know more about."

— KATHLEEN PALM, AUTHOR OF INTO THE GRAY

"Fans of *Sinners* seeking new stories combining the supernatural with consciousness-raising narratives would do well to add *Chasing Moonflowers* to their TBRs.

Chow effortlessly blends horror, adventure, history, and colonial critique, producing a life-giving elixir for anyone who wants entertainment and enlightenment in equal measure"

— PATRICK BARB, AUTHOR OF NIGHT OF THE WITCH-HUNTER

"An exceptional read that will transport readers into 1920's Hong Kong and a world of vampires and magic."

— JORDAN FRANCIS, POET OF *SAILING IN DARK WATERS*

"If you enjoy complex female leads, folklore-laced thrillers, or tales of rebellion against monstrous systems this book's for you."

— LITERARY TITAN

Author's Note

Hong Kong and the Kowloon Walled City have undergone significant transformations over time.

In 1842, following the First Opium War, Britain gained control of Hong Kong. During the peak of British trade in the 1870s and 1880s, over 6,500 tons of opium passed through the port annually. The colony's economic growth often bypassed the local residents. On May 30, 1925, police brutality in Shanghai ignited the Canton-Hong Kong Strike, a large-scale labor movement and boycott targeting British businesses.

For 16 months, workers organized a sustained and targeted response. Approximately 250,000 workers left their jobs and returned to mainland China, bringing commerce to a halt. The pressure on business operations forced the British to negotiate, resulting in agreements to raise wages, improve working conditions, and abolish child labor. The strike concluded in October 1926. Decades later, in 1997, Hong Kong was returned to China and became a Special Administrative Region. Hong Kong's identity continues to evolve.

The Kowloon Walled City (KWC), once home to roughly 35,000 residents on 6.4 acres of land, was demolished in 1994. Originally a Chinese military fort, the site was never ceded to the British. Both governments largely ignored it, allowing the area to grow unchecked and ungoverned. While often portrayed in media as a chaotic and lawless enclave, KWC was also a thriving community that provided affordable housing, services, jobs, education, and entrepreneurial opportunities for the local population. It stood as a symbol of resilience and resistance to colonialism. Today, the site has been rebuilt into a park featuring open spaces and remnants of the old city.

This book uses Cantonese, a regional variety of Chinese in Southern China, written out in the romanized system of Jyutping without tone numbers. It's common in Cantonese to start and end phrases with "ah" to soften, emphasize, or alter emotional tone. This is the reason that "Ma" (媽) appears as "Ahma" (阿媽) throughout the book.

道高一尺,魔高一丈

Where good flourishes, evil can flourish even more.

- Ancient Proverb

ONE

June 27, 1925

Ling inventoried the containers of preserved animals in her uncle's seaside medicine shop. Counting withered caterpillars, broken tiger teeth, and shriveled seahorses, she recited the ways death remedied maladies of the mind, body, and spirit. Life valued sacrifice.

She unfurled herbs from butcher paper as a breeze brought in the evening hour. Her uncle's shop was wedged between three other sellers near Woyi Ping Tsun pier. Fishermen called out their summer catches from the bustling waterfront. A scattered cloud of amber flyers blew up into the air, bearing the manifesto of the workers' strike on the wind. Sudden gusts carried the message out to sea. Dissent circulated everywhere.

Beneath the noise of passengers waiting in a queue for the ferry, voices spoke to each other. Ling tilted her head toward the thick tarp separating her from a furtive conversation nearby. What she heard made the hairs on the back of her neck stand up.

"Please print a notice in the papers that she is missing!" Desperation seeped from the woman's words.

"I cannot." The voice sounded like her uncle's. Ling glanced at the front of the stand. The doctor had abandoned his post at the counter. "It's dangerous if they trace the politics back to us."

"But you must help Cili!" the lady cried. She spoke with a Northerner's accent.

Ling's stomach dropped. She knew this girl. Cili was a new student at her brothers' primary school. She had seen her last week, pink-cheeked with red bows in her hair. This news was heartbreaking.

"We can organize a search," her uncle said over her muffled sobs. "We must stay strong and cautious." Ling was concerned. She trusted his judgment, but it was unlike her uncle to turn someone away. What could be more important than finding a child?

When they stepped out from behind the narrow space between the stands, Ling scurried back to her spot. She glimpsed a lady with bobbed hair, her face puffy and slick with tears. Ling diverted her eyes to the mugwort she'd been tallying. Dried, broken, and crumbled into a million pieces, these leaves promoted relaxation and eased mental anxiety.

Why was the woman asking Dabak, a traditional medicine doctor, about a newsletter? He wrote scripts, not political dissent. Did Dabak have something to do with the strike? Her uncle slipped back into his seat and began to pore over his medical texts.

Ling viewed her distorted reflection on a jar of herbs. She examined her own elongated copper eyes and high-bridged nose, faintly echoed on the curved surface. The features mapped back to her father. She wanted to love these reminders of him. However, the shape of her face made people question her lineage. To them, different brewed distrust.

Her uncle cleared his throat. "Did you catalog the new items?"

Ling turned her head, staring up with glassy eyes at her uncle. Should she ask him about the secret conversation? What fliers had the woman referenced? She wanted to talk about Cili, not the shop. Stuttering, she grabbed at the nearest item within reach. "Dabak...um...uh."

Her uncle leaned forward. "Well?" He scrutinized her work area, which she hadn't yet cleaned up.

"This." She lifted the first package at the end of the counter, catching only the name written on it. "I wanted to ask you about its contents."

Dabak stroked his chin. "It is a delivery to Lady Tun."

"To the house on the peninsula?" She turned the bulky bag, noticing its lightness. Feeling a sense of repulsion at the sight of the patient's alias, she covered her mouth. Lady Tun was a creepy woman who took an unsettling interest in children.

Rumors swirled about the woman, who lived alone. She'd been the wife of a lieutenant who staked a claim on his outpost. Lady Tun chose to live on the mainland even after her fellow Englishmen had relocated across the water. The ghosts, the local's epithet for the occupiers, had all moved their homes to the island. With the influx of opium, the ghosts still haunted the village. "It says here, the patient requires it by midnight."

Dabak frowned. "Yes. I was too caught up in..."

What was he working on? She'd already finished recording today's sales in the ledger, a task he had trained her in last week, but he seemed occupied by something else.

He sighed. "Never mind...it shall has to wait until the morning."

She pursed her lips. This was alarming. Never had her uncle ever been dismissive about his customers. Something was wrong. With her uncle, conversations usually flowed between English and Tangwa. Now, he was lost in thought.

"Dr. Shaw." She addressed her uncle by his profession. Otherwise, he was Dabak, her father's older brother. "I can deliver the package," she blurted out, to her own surprise. The pain on her uncle's face stirred her boldness. She wanted to help.

"No. Absolutely not." His eyebrows flexed, deepening the wrinkles on his brow.

The sea churned behind him as a strong wind whistled across the tin roof. It sang a song of adventure.

"You said to never disappoint the customer." Ling placed her hands on the counter.

"I did say this. However, exceptions exist. This time, we must delay." Dabak ran his hand through his hair.

Ling was eager to make her case. "But—"

"It is not wise." He plucked the package from Ling's hand with finality and deposited it into a pile of herbs.

The horn sounded from the last commuter ship. It would soon be departing for the island. Ling's eyes darted to her uncle. He had to go.

"Young lady, look at me." His eyes darkened. "Promise me you will not go to the peninsula. It is not a place for children."

The comment infuriated her. Her twentieth birthday was in a few weeks. She was no longer a child. "Do you think I'll get lost like Cili?" she retorted without thinking.

His eyes widened. "Lady Tun is difficult. Stop worrying. Cili is an... unfortunate situation." As he spoke, Dabak filled his briefcase with books and medicines for her Aunt Marcella. Some saffron colored papers had been haphazardly stuffed in between medical texts.

She couldn't let the subject go. "What happened to Cili? She's the twin's classmate."

The whole region was on edge. Locals had been fleeing the island, refusing to continue working for the ghosts. Workers were on strike, protesting unsafe conditions. Regardless of the tumult, however, a missing child should've risen above politics. How could this not be an emergency? As far as Ling could tell, no one was canvassing the neighborhoods, combing the marshes, or patrolling the cliffs. The seaside communities should've been up in arms, shouting the missing girl's name.

Dabak pressed his mouth into a thin line, securing his case with a lock. The ship sounded another warning.

"I am sorry. I must depart for Marcella. She's been having extra troubles. Tomorrow, I will explain. Keep an eye out for your mom and your brothers." He pushed over a tin of salve. "Infused with the protective qualities of bay leaves." Then he patted her on the shoulder and sprinted to board the ship.

Ling hadn't seen her aunt in a long time, though she had made quite an impression. Aunt Marcella had stunned Ling at their first meeting with a full-hearted embrace. At the wedding banquet, Aunt Marcella's red silk wedding dress had complimented her soft eyes and golden hair. However, after the couple returned from their European honeymoon, she had changed; Aunt Marcella spent hours staring vacantly at the gardens instead of frolicking in them as before. The trip had triggered a deep sadness. Ling didn't know why.

"Doctor!" A crew member shouted as Dabak's feet pounded against the wooden planks. The crew knew him well. Every night, he sailed home on the last ship without fail, and they watched for him expectantly before casting off.

Her uncle had sown seeds of curiosity in Ling. His

warnings sent her spirit ablaze. She inhaled the scent of the salve. It was an herbal mixture of citrus, peppermint, and mugwort. Bay leaves added a slight bitterness to the concoction. The scent reminded her of warnings parents gave their young ones.

"Be good, little children."

"Don't play close to the jungle. Wicked creatures prey on the weak."

Untamed wilderness surrounded the foothill villages of Kowloon, impenetrable to the occupying forces. While foreigners tumbled unhindered into the island ports, they did not venture far outside of them. Ancient lore persisted in these marshes, jungles, and mountains of the nine dragons—the namesake of this area. People vanished in more than one way in the countryside, but it wasn't always because of mysterious creatures. The source of the most peril, as is often the case, was people.

Ling squeezed Lady Tun's medicine. The shape of the package was odd, bulging and lightweight. Why did she require this at such a late hour? It was so out of place that Ling ached to discover the reason. A forbidden urge to venture into the unknown overtook her. Despite her uncle's warnings, she made a hasty decision and stuffed the package into her bag. She respected her uncle, but hated to break promises to important patrons. And after all, what harm could come from a frail old lady who lived alone at the edge of the ocean?

Two

Ling contemplated the myriad of theories about Lady Tun on her way home. Was she a mean witch who hexed children who came too close? Or simply an old woman waiting for a visit from the grim reaper? Too old to take children's tales seriously, Ling nonetheless felt the thrill and danger of the mystery.

The road home took her past the mansions along the bay. Her best friend from school, Emma, lived inside one of these homes, a lemon yellow house. However, while they lived reasonably close to one another, their lives couldn't be farther apart. In between Emma's neighborhood and hers, the missionaries had constructed a marble building as a school for younger grades. Here, the twins started their studies at the proper time, unlike her.

Continuing onward, Ling passed a wall erected with hand-chipped stones. The barrier divided the lands of the ghosts and those of local rule, enclosing the area around an abandoned fort. In between the military structures, factories, schools, and restaurants sprang up overnight. The armory had been converted into residential apartments.

With no sovereign nation assuming jurisdiction, the Kowloon Walled City was run by groups committed in an uneasy truce.

A week ago, her town had been a quiet, rural village. But now, new families flooded the farmlands. Tents and signs organized around the stone wall suggested a season for rebellion. The winding paths also increased her travel time. Laborers had departed their posts on the island in households, factories, and shipping companies in support of a greater cause. After foreign forces had killed unarmed protestors in Shanghai, locals were demanding better hours, higher wages, and an end to child labor.

The school yard was empty. She was too late to pick up her brothers. While it wasn't her responsibility to fetch them, she loved to catch them by surprise when she could. They sometimes played jacks or jumped rope after school. Watching Gou and Kit laugh made her days complete.

Passing the playground, an eerie feeling descended on the courtyard lined with flowering trees. Ominous white blooms popped up out of waxed leaves. The colors reminded her of a scene of mourning. Hot wind carried a heaviness from the mountains, thickening the air and weighing down her steps. As she approached her house, Ling shrank into herself. The two-bedroom structure had been haphazardly constructed, unlike the artful Venetian decor of her father's old ship.

Inside, her brothers sang. Lights glowed from the kitchen window as smoke poured from the crooked metal chimney. She had never imagined her life to have contracted so tightly.

When she opened the door, her mother was not there. Her brothers were sitting at the kitchen table two bowls in front of them, swinging their legs while humming an off-key melody:

Three blind mice.
Three blind mice.
See how they run.
See how they run.

"Mom left food for you," Gou said, jumping up to greet her. "She agreed to an extra shift." A third bowl sat with a cover on the table. Ling's stomach grumbled.

"Be back before eleven," Kit parroted Ahma in a fake high-pitched voice.

Ling pursed her lips. This complicated things. To deliver the package to Lady Tun, she would have to wait until her mother returned. Ling never liked when Ahma was out during twilight, especially when it meant leaving her brothers alone. Her mother's sacrifice felt like she was running away. Ling felt that Ahma was disappearing into responsibility, so she wouldn't have to face the bleakness of their situation. It was up to Ling to stay grounded.

"Ahma only left a short time ago." Kit read Ling's face. "Don't worry. We're safe." He lifted up a slingshot. "I have this to protect us!"

"Our warrior." She ruffled his hair. Then she plucked three stones she had collected from the sands out of her bag.

Kit's eyes sparkled as Ling lined them up on the table. He rolled a smooth stone in between his hands. Then he pulled one back in the slingshot, making his fiercest face. "I can battle all the ancient beasts: dragon, bird, tiger, and tortoise."

He loved mythological stories, and like her, he always had his head buried in books. The world's common origin grounded her. Without these tales, her dreams floated back out to sea, where she had been born and raised during the first decade of her life.

"Your weapon doesn't work on people." Gou waved his hands in front of Kit's face.

"I wouldn't want to meet you in the woods," Ling assured him. She put on a brave face, but the idea of her kid brothers lost in the wilderness sent shivers down her back. It was just as possible for her siblings to go missing.

Kit relaxed and rested the slingshot in his lap. With a pleased look, he scooped another mouthful of rice and chicken into his mouth. "I've been practicing behind the trees at school. I can knock pods off from the panpo trees."

Ling blinked twice. She had gathered those seeds around his school during the fall; they didn't grow on school grounds. This was the first time she'd heard of either of them leaving the school yard. "When did you play in the woods by yourself?"

"No, there are...oh...um..." Gou mumbled with a mouthful of half-chewed dinner. The question quieted both of them.

"It's okay, you're not in trouble, but you must be careful. Do you know that Cili is missing?" She enunciated their classmate's name, watching her brothers' expressions change from mischievous to frightened.

The boys glanced at each other, then nodded in unison.

Kit replied. "She wasn't in school yesterday or today. But the day before..." Under the table, he fidgeted with his hands.

Ling moved toward the table. The woman, probably Cili's mother, and her uncle had spoken the truth about the girl's disappearance.

"Cili...she..." Gou said.

"Shh." Kit lowered his head, rubbing his fingers over the leather strap on the slingshot.

"If you know something, it can help find her," Ling said, hoping she spoke the truth. She glanced at the old oak steering wheel leaning against the back corner. In times like these, she wished her father was around to advise them.

She knelt next to Kit and touched his arm. He blinked rapidly as he scrunched his nose. Lowering her voice, she reassured him. "It's not your fault."

"Cili told us," Kit swallowed, "about sweets at the edge of the marsh."

"Licorice and cookies." Gou smiled as if the treats conjured in front of him.

"Sweets? From who?" She bit her lip. There had been too many new people coming into their town.

Kit looked into her eyes. "We told her not to go."

The dread in their eyes set a knot in her stomach. "Who told her to head there?"

Kit shook his head. Gou gobbled up his food and left the room, dragging his school bag with him.

The space fell dead silent, except for the crickets outside. Something twisted inside of her, making it hard to breathe. Reluctantly, Ling abandoned her inquiries. The thought of their missing friend had distressed them too much; she would get nothing more from them.

She didn't want to leave her brothers alone to deliver the package to Lady Tun, so she ate and waited for her mother to return.

At bedtime, Kit asked Ling to tell the story of creation. The stories were ancient; they had existed before Imperial Kings, before invasions by the Manchurians, before the poppy plague. Tales of primordial creatures brought a certain comfort in these times when strangers whispered offers of treats from the marsh.

Ling jumped into the story:

After the wars between the Gods of Fire and Water, Nuwa repaired the sky. She used bits and pieces of her human face and serpent body to heal the wounds in the air, waters, and earth. When she was done, the Goddess was lonely. She gathered substances from the earth, crafting noblepersons from yellow mud, animals from white sand, and demons from red clay. With a sprinkle of dark sky, she formed the four mythical beasts.

When Ling ended the tale, Gou had burrowed under the blankets, asleep. Kit's eyes were still half-open. He waved Ling to his side.

"Did she make us?" Kit asked, his eyelids drooping.

"Perhaps she did," Ling said.

"The snake woman said we could have more sweets." Kit mumbled.

A tingling feathered Ling's scalp. Had he really just identified Nuwa as the culprit in Cili's disappearance? Kit had a wild imagination, but something inside of her said he hadn't fabricated the revelation. She squeezed his arm gently, hoping for clarification.

A small hand reached out from under the covers, dropping something cold into Ling's palm. Her fingers rubbed over a pattern etched into the material.

"What is this?" Ling held up the piece of round metal. It reflected silver in the moonlight. The edges were rough and uneven. At its center, the word for snake had been engraved. But it wasn't the modern word *se* (蛇). It was the script from thousands of years ago:

"Snake" in ancient bone script.

"Caramels and taffy." His eyes rolled backwards as they closed.

She gasped. Her brothers had never tasted those soft candies, only longed for them in shop windows. "When did you have them?"

His body slumped in relaxation, fully asleep.

"From who?" Ling hissed. She wanted to shake him awake, but in sleep, he looked peaceful. Who had spoken to them? What had been offered? In sleep, Kit and Guo looked so very calm and peaceful. She placed the coin on their desk, planning to ask more questions in the morning. It seemed to her that whatever had taken Cili wasn't yet finished.

THREE

Ling sprang up in a panic, startling awake. Her loaned copy of *Camilla* hit the floor with a thud. Moonlight shone over the books and other supplies that lined Ling's bedroom shelves. While waiting for her mother to return, she had read more of the novel. The story was supposed to keep her awake. Instead, the elegant violence had mesmerized her and lulled her into a doze. Her worries returned to Lady Tun again. What if Lady Tun bad-mouthed their services? Could the business thrive with a soured reputation? She had to deliver that package no matter the hour. In the morning, Dabak would thank her for her initiative.

The moon sat low in the sky. Shortcuts through the marsh or Walled City would give her the time to deliver Lady Tun's medicine by midnight. Sweat gathered on her nose as she pulled on her trousers and stuffed her hair into a cap. She yanked her bag over her shoulder. This outfit transformed her into a boy, at least from a distance. This was a safer way to travel at night.

She tiptoed into the common room. Ahma had

returned while Ling had dozed off; the snores from the other bedroom marked the distance to the front door. Her twin brothers shared the larger room with Ahma, while Ling slept in the smaller one next to shelves of pickled lotus roots and the carcasses of pregnant mice. The arrangement provided her privacy, at least.

As soon as Ling stepped outside, a putrid smell bloomed. Rain mixed with rotting vegetables. Turned meat that hadn't yet been scavenged by wild dogs. The odors of a neighborhood where no one had enough. She dipped her finger into the protective balm from Dabak. Rubbing the menthol under her nostrils, she warded the appalling smells away. Then she touched the salve to her forehead, shoulders, and wrists, the key points to shield her from unwanted evil. There were menaces which existed beyond the visible threats.

Passing the line of makeshift homes, she dodged grimy puddles and jumped over potholes. This neighborhood existed in a no-man's land between the historical villages and the old fort walls. The Walled City offered a power vacuum where only ambition ruled.

Her body slid between the unnatural spaces. Even worse than the smells, darkness brushed against the back of her neck. The shadows felt malicious on her skin, and she quivered inside. The bravery she had drummed up in her mind hadn't yet traveled to her heart.

Rubbish overflowed everywhere. Garbage service in Kowloon was fickle, run by the Red Society that collected weekly protection fees from merchants, shopkeepers, and businesspeople. Their demands had started back when they were a group of imperial rebels, taking refuge in the lawless parts of Kowloon. They had fought to restore the Ming Dynasty, because the Manchurian kings had suppressed science and hoarded resources. Absent other masters, the Red Society was the closest thing to a municipal government.

Now, a foreign ruler raided the native treasures, and people flocked to the former garrison. The location provided a perfect vantage point over the bay and foothills. If one could withstand the risks, the walled city offered unheard of freedoms and opportunities.

Approaching the entrance, Ling brushed against the tents that lined the walls. Dampness coated her skin. Lights flickered on from the higher floors in the stacked buildings above. Machines behind the stone walls buzzed and creaked, like the Walled City's heartbeat. She was having second thoughts about her venture. Was a short cut a bad choice? If she didn't return, who would search for her?

Decay permeated from the mortar. Under the moonlight, the boulders spoke to her. Ling gritted her teeth, letting herself through the entrance. After a few steps, she was startled by a different smell – inexpensive tobacco. She gasped and scurried into a divot in the wall. She hid in the shadows, observing as someone smoked.

The assured boy had hair falling around his face. He took a drag from his cigarette with confidence, revealing a reptile tattoo on his arm. She studied the scaled tail, wrapping from his muscular forearms to elbow. A symbol to show off, unlike the secret inked on her own inner arm. Who was he? He pushed his hair aside, and familiarity fluttered inside her stomach. She recognized that it was Enlai, the last person she wanted to see. In the two years since they had last spoken, he had grown taller and picked up a tobacco habit.

Her fears that her hiding place was inadequate were confirmed, as his eyes flickered in her direction. A smirk raised the corner of his mouth. He moved in her direction, until a *gwai* interrupted his stride.

"Hey there, friend," said the stranger in a suit. Foreigners weren't called ghosts merely for their pale complexions. They had earned the distinction with their shifty actions.

"Wait a second." Enlai tried to go around the meddler, still gazing into the dark space where Ling held her breath, but the man grabbed his bicep. He whispered into Enlai's ear.

"If you insist." Enlai scowled. He flicked his half-smoked cigarette to the ground and followed the man through a door.

Ling breathed again, slipping back into the street. Enlai hadn't crossed her mind in a long time. The burn of his betrayal still stung. He had apparently gotten everything he'd wanted. Well, good for him. He'd exchanged their friendship for ambition. Ling wanted nothing to do with him.

With the moon still rising, Ling decided to take a different route through the marsh. The thugs didn't patrol the swamplands. They feared the monsters hiding in the reeds. But she would rather take her chances with nature than Enlai's new pals.

Ling slid into an orchestra of frogs and bugs. Thanks to her many trips hunting herbs, she recognized where to step to keep her shoes dry. The warmth of the swamp wrapped around her ankles. Stars spread out overhead. Cries of the city fell away.

About halfway through the wetlands, Lady Tun's shack became visible in the distance. Candles in its two windows glowed like eyes. Waves crashed against the rocks echoing through the dark. The sound deafened Ling's other senses. A porch jutted from the structure's middle like an open mouth, ready to devour visitors. Ling conjured an image of the rusted rectangular house, trying to see past the mist-shrouded, predatory shape facing her now.

The scent of sugared cookies carried her forward, the stars lighting up the cobblestone path.

"See, Dabak. I am competent enough to make the deliveries." A thrill ran through her. She was so close to completing a task no one thought she could do.

Then a faint sob broke through the waves. It sounded like a cat. Without hesitation, Ling peeked over the edge of the rocks. Down below, the tide had receded, exposing footprints in the sands at the bottom. She was alarmed. Why would anyone go down there? It was dangerous.

She could so easily become one of the missing, falling into the waves or getting lost in the maze of homes inside the Walled City. Her own precariousness mixed with the dangers her brothers faced.

Ling shook her head. Cultivating terrible ideas would only scare her further.

As she approached the shack, Ling tiptoed around the back. One could never be too careful. Was Lady Tun expecting her uncle? A gust scattered the smells of chocolate and dried fruits through the air. The sweetness clashed with the earthy, fetid environment of the marsh. Ling hugged the shadows to inspect the trays on the open kitchen windowsill. Her mouth watered as she peeked over the ledge, marveling at the frosted cinnamon rolls, cut-out gingerbreads, and powdered-sugar dusted scones.

A grunt from inside drew her retreat. Ling released her grip and crouched on the ground. She looked through holes in the exterior wall. A dark silhouette slithered on the edges of the room. It maneuvered furtively like a thief. Her heart leapt into her throat.

Ling snuck to the front, a sense of danger percolating in

her veins. She must finish her task. Climbing up the porch railing, where straw dolls and crooked charms dangled over the door, she extended a shaking hand with the package. There was no need to knock; she could leave it here, surely. Coiling its string around the door handle provided a little relief.

While curtains flapped, Ling retreated over the railing. Was Lady Tun in the middle of a clandestine visit from someone? Ling listened to the rhythm of the steps as she crouched behind overgrown weeds. The cadence didn't belong to a middle-aged woman. Crickets and spiders skittered over her legs. A small tickle started inside her ear. It told her to stay put.

She held steady, waiting for the commotion to settle. What was happening? As if answering her question, the structure rattled with the noise of shattering glass and objects crashing to the floor. High-pitched shrieks splintered the silence.

Ling's breath sounded very loud to her. A cold bead of sweat trickled down her neck.

Come out, come out wherever you are.

Messages stung her thoughts like nettles.

Ceot loi ba, Ceot loi ba.

Strange syllables drifted into her mind.

Yog-sothoth, yog-sothoth na'khul.

Pain shot through her eyes. She could hear something sharp scraping against the walls. The points where she'd rubbed the protective ointment suddenly throbbed. Her whole body heated up as footsteps stomped toward the porch and then flung open the door.

"We shouldn't be strangers," said a hushed voice.

Ling closed her eyes, wishing fervently to be invisible. She hoped the voice wasn't addressing her. Her frantic mind conjured images of Carmilla's victims' tragic endings. Was she to be torn apart or drained? She prayed harder than she had ever prayed. *Please God don't allow... this creature... to see. My family needs me. Please.*

With no reply, Ling opened her eyes. Against the light spilling out from inside, she could see spindly fingers reaching around the door. The nails scratched into the wood, searching for something. Not her.

Stepping out into the moonlight, a figure grabbed at the suspended package wearing a defiant expression. It was frighteningly odd. Gold decorations studded a leather jacket. It had a human torso and blotchy skin, but its sunken cheeks and disfigured ears appeared as shriveled roots. Patchy clumps of hair covered the back of its head. It wasn't human.

"Yesss..." It spun quickly, its red eyes flashing at her. Lifting the package with blackened fingers, it examined the edges with satisfaction before slicing through the paper with clawlike nails. Roots, herbs, and petals tumbled next to its feet.

Despite her fear, Ling's stomach tightened at the sight. *The medicine, all those precious herbs.*

Then a screeching woman ran from the shack, hurling herself on top of the figure. Thrusting an object into its chest, she ripped and tore at her target. But the monster didn't panic. The creature extended its arm leisurely, folding its gnarled fingers around the flailing lady's head. Its long nails dug easily into her flesh. Blood flowed from the punctures, soaking the floor planks in an instant.

The woman's body went limp and crashed down the steps to the porch. As her body rolled out onto the path, the moon lit up her face. It was Lady Tun. Ling trembled in the grass. The woman lay lifeless in a soiled emerald dress. Dirt and leaves caked her yellow hair. Crimson tears streamed from her green eyes, set in a wrinkled face.

Bile rose in Ling's throat, and she could not prevent herself from dry heaving in revulsion.

The creature banged its chest. It stomped down the porch steps, bending to sniff at Lady Tun's body, and then turned toward Ling's hiding place. Its white skin glimmered as it stalked toward her. Ling's fist tightened around the little jar of salve. There was no way out. A fire blazed in Ling's chest. Why had she put herself in such a precarious circumstance?

Then Lady Tun exhaled.

Ling clenched her jaw.

The creature turned to the lady, flashed its sharpened teeth and then grabbed its victim by her legs. As the creature dragged her back up to the front of the house, Lady Tun's skull bounced against the stone steps. Once on the porch, the creature sank its teeth into the woman's flesh. Its fingers dug into her skull. As the Lady struggled feebly for air, the creature took large gulps of her.

After drinking, the creature pulled out an apparatus from the pocket of its heavy jacket. In the moonlight it appeared like a metal icepick. It inserted the tip into Lady Tun. As the creature torqued its elbows, the smells of death pushed a foulness into Ling's throat. She tried not to breathe as the life drained out of Lady Tun's body.

It was horrible. The blood reeked of a thousand deaths. Human blood, Ling knew, had a memorable flavor. At a young age, she had once been healed with blood. Pig's blood was bitter. Snake's blood was spicy. But human blood formed a sweet film on the tongue. Ling fought not to remember the taste.

The murderer held up disembodied eyes.

It yowled with a deep sorrow. "Not them. These are not him."

It dropped the eyes, then kicked her body. The corpse

landed hard and rolled to the railing. Watching the scene in horror, Ling felt something tugging at the bag strapped across her shoulder. She glanced to the side, afraid of another monster. To her small relief, there was nothing, only bugs in the shadows. Ling looked up at Lady Tun's empty, cold expression. Two hollow holes gazed out, angry.

FOUR

Lady Tun was eyeless, and her mouth was stuffed with blue petals. The night was quiet again. Ling had a strange urge to relieve the discomfort of her bloated cheeks. While the threat turned its attention elsewhere, Ling was trapped. She recited the names of the herbs in the medicine cabinet stored at Dabak's apartment in her mind. The recitation calmed her.

From the corner of her eye, she saw that the shadow crept out of the window onto the roof, like a spider. It howled and jumped, vibrating the building until near collapse. The figure then lept down and landed hard on the path. It lifted its disfigured hands and cursed the woman of the house. Then it sprinted toward the cliff and disappeared into the waves. A trail of iridescent blue flowers laying in its wake.

Ling's legs shook as she got to her feet. Pins and needles crawled up her legs from crouching for too long. A briny scent soured the overturned and crushed sweets, which were now scattered over the grass. Lady Tun's layered garments were torn to pieces, exposing gray flesh and, to Ling's fascination, scales. Ling shuddered. What type of skin condition caused hardened and dark scales? Bending over, she placed two fingers against Lady Tun's icy wrist. She was unsurprised that there wasn't a pulse.

As Ling withdrew her fingers, she saw a ring on Lady Tun's finger. Sculpted serpents were twisted in brushed silver, encircling a polished black gem. The stone was darker than night; looking at it felt like diving into a bottomless trench. As she turned over Lady Tun's hand, mesmerized, the carved snakes seemed to slither and hiss. Ling snapped her arm back, but not before catching a swirl of movement inside the gemstone.

See with me, a voice murmured.

Lady Tun's lips hadn't moved.

Ling stared into the moon, waiting for a sign. The only thing that came to her was a strong discomfort. It felt like something foreign was forcing itself into her body in a way she did not understand. She snapped out of her trance when the corpse's body groaned. Ling dropped the arm in an instant. The woman's overfilled mouth was bursting with flowers. Their iridescent petals containing various hues of blue. Some appeared indigo and others tinted with a light cerulean. Were these from Dabak? If so, she didn't recognize them.

Plucking out a few specimens, she deposited them into her bag. The petals were the size of violets, but they had serrated edges. She backed away, afraid to turn her back to the deceased until she was far enough away from the dreadful scene. Lady Tun's vacant stare gripped Ling's mind even as she escaped into the wetlands.

Llll mgr'luh ya.

Ling shook her head. She never lost control of her thoughts. The foreign words agitated her. The very world around her seemed hostile. The soft grasses now chafed her skin. Cattails wiggled like bloated fingers. Who was communicating with her? She refused to let Lady Tun take up residence in her mind. She pushed out the words that continued to circle her mind like birds on the wind.

Should she tell someone about what she had seen? No one would believe her. Worse yet, the police would blame her, call her a destitute troublemaker and expel her from school, maybe even arrest her. Had she imagined it? The voice didn't fade or cease. It continued, persistent, until it finally said her name.

Shiu Yiling.

See, taste, feel...

Ling recoiled as if struck. Her left foot splashed in the muck, soaking her shoe, and sending swampy water to her knees. This was really happening. She had been in the marshlands for too long. The coldness seeped into her bones. Images of Lady Tun's torn face continued to torment her. She fled, with foulness nipping at her heels.

Weaving through the trees, she tried to outrun the voice. "Why are you following me?" she shouted into the haze.

The wind fluttered over the tall grasses. Thin fingers of sunlight reached into the sky.

Ling could see farmers starting their day. They walked from nearby villages, where lineages could be traced back to the Tang Dynasty. The era of great poets, artists, and explorers. Could her bloodline also have come from bygone adventurers? Her parents had not known their grandparents.

Ling waved, not wanting to be rude, and pointed to the ocean.

"Good luck this morning," another hollered. "Watch out for the tigers!"

The good-humored warning gave Ling pause. Beasts existed in various forms. What had killed Lady Tun? It wasn't human, nor any natural beast.

By the time Ling lumbered to her front door, the rooster was crowing. Relief flooded her as she spotted the statue of the Guan Gong, the ceramic guardian placed at their front door, warding off uninvited spirits with a broad sword. She appreciated his vigilance at the exterior of the house, especially now.

In her room, she put down her bag. It felt heavier, which was odd because she had gathered nothing. On the journey home, she had ignored everything except the speed of her legs. Ling rummaged inside, finding moss-covered rocks in the largest compartment. These weren't hers. To her dismay, a sticky fluid covered the inside of the bag.

In a smaller pocket, she found two round items crammed inside. When she touched them, unfamiliar faces flashed in her mind. She saw a young child, similar in age to her nine-year-old brothers, cut across the forehead. From behind her, a grandma bared her teeth.

Ling had never seen this child or woman in her life. Pulling down on the string, light from a bare bulb flooded the room. She gulped. Two detached eyes stared up from her palm. Was this a sick prank? Touching them again sent electrical jolts through her skin, displaying again memories that weren't hers. The purple irises shifted back and forth, sending shocks with every movement.

Ling's mouth twisted in disgust, and let the eyes drop onto the bed.

"Lady Tun?" Ling asked the obvious question.

The eyes tilted with their veiny coils, stirring from side to side like small sea creatures stranded on a beach at low tide.

It was an answer – like someone shaking their head no, but without the head. Who could the gruesome orbs belong to? The child from the vision? How had they gotten into her sack? "Are you the voice inside of my head?"

Again, the eyes responded with a shake.

The disembodied body parts dragged themselves across her bed, grotesque and pathetic. They looked more wizened by the minute. Blistered veins spidered from the irises. The eyes were dried out. An idea sprouted in Ling.

The medicine shop kept saline solution to preserve foods like alligator skin for soup. She used a napkin to scoop the eyes into a jar, then perched them on a shelf next to dried dates. A new addition to her inventory. Where had they come from? How did they move on their own? But the real question was—did Ling really want to find out?

FIVE

A harsh, jangling melody echoed throughout Ling's dreams. She was clawing away from the jeering bells and crooked metal strings when someone jostled her awake. The music disintegrated into the far gentler sound of Kit's and Gou's giggles. With one eye, she peeked at the jokesters. Sunlight illuminated their freckled noses and dewy skin. Her brothers' faces were comforting this the morning.

Behind them, what remained of their father lived on her walls. His star charts, brass candle holders, and gifts from abroad lined the shelf above her bed. It was quite a collection, although her father's nautical compass had been stolen. A vacant space endured on the ledge.

"Dearest sister, what were you singing...?" Gou bounced at the foot of the bed.

As soon as Ling looked around the room with both eyes in the morning light, disappointment sank in at the realities of her life. The cluttered room brimmed with contradictions. Her cheongsam hung next to her Catholic school uniform. Traditional herbs were crammed alongside

Western medicine texts. Opposite worlds she was still trying to integrate in her life.

"We tried to wake you, but you were stuck," Kit said, knitting his brow.

It is true. I was trapped in a nightmare.

Ling sighed. She wouldn't share her distress. The twins were also prone to disturbing dreams, and she didn't wish to worry them. "I did not sleep well last night."

"The mice one. The creepy lullaby," Kit said in a lilt. "*Three Blind Mice.*"

A chill ran down her spine. She wanted to hide under her blanket, in a safe place where monsters didn't exist. Her thoughts reverted to last night, turning over the horrible memory like a ghoulish trinket. Who was the killer? Lady Tun couldn't have been the figure's first victim. Had it harmed Cili? Were there other missing children?

"Are you ill?" Kit fidgeted with his fingers. His cheeks glowed soft pink with worry.

As tempting as it was to feign illness, Ling knew she had to face the problem or at least find an ally. Staying at home and catastrophizing didn't bode well for her future. According to a proverb, a suspicious mind invented spirits — 疑心生暗鬼.

Was this all imagined? Inventing the voices from yesterday?

"I'll get up," she said from under the covers. Dabak's Oxford education would help her figure out what to do next. She had to show him the eyes. They, at least, were solid evidence. Otherwise, her narration of the murder would sound hysterical, and he would consider her unfit to treat patients. She hoped he wouldn't be too upset at her for going against his wishes.

"Are you sure you're not sick? You have raccoon eyes." Gou taunted her, snickering. He reached under her pillow, pulling out *Carmilla*. "Ma says you stay up late reading garbage."

"That is not nice." Kit shoved his brother in the arm.

Gou lost his balance and fell into the wall. The tinny boom of the impact hurt Ling's head.

"Excuse me." Ling sat up and reached over to tickle Gou's toes. "Gentlemen."

"Monkeys...Ma Lau..." From the kitchen, Ahma blended languages. "Zou can. Breakfast."

"Better go before the food gets cold." Gou leapt from the bed, snorting.

"Ma added ginger in yours." Kit thumbed through the novel, eating up the pages. Like Ling, he could be fed on ideas alone. "*Kaphyut gway* are nobility?"

"Apparently, vampires can be civilized in the West."

There was something fascinating about the Western versions of monsters. Vampires such as Carmilla could masquerade as ordinary people. In Tang stories, creatures that fed on human blood hopped around with the intellect of a bug. She had taken their existence as a metaphor. But as of last night, she concluded that these works of fiction were officially real. This idea agitated her nerves.

She turned her attention back to the twins. The twins had outpaced each other in different areas. Gou had grown two heads taller since the spring. She suspected he stole extra food to keep up with his appetite. Kit's appetite was for books, like Ling's, and she had been excited at the thought of one day sharing the inventive ghouls and paranormal spirits from world literature with him. But for now....

She snatched the book out of Kit's hand. "You're not ready for this."

Kit pouted and dragged his attention toward the shelves.

"Are you getting out of bed?" Gou asked. "You'll miss school."

"You are a worry wart." She was losing her patience. Swinging her legs onto the floor, she flicked the tip of Gou's nose. "Better to concern yourself with your own studies."

Kit stared wide-eyed at the shelf. Ling's heart fluttered. Had he noticed the eyes?

"Enough." Ling opened the wardrobe with a clatter, trying not to wince. "And Kit, you must leave too." Her fingers grazed a box that stored her father's things. She had saved pictures, stamps, and her childhood drawings for his return. She reached in and pulled her father's journal out of the stack. This was how she consulted with him while he was away. "Make haste. I must prepare for school."

The twins didn't budge.

"If I don't get to the pier soon, I cannot bring back treats for you." Ling pouted, awaiting their decision.

She chose a clean blouse as they whispered to each other.

"Fine," they both shouted in unison and left the room.

She loved them, but with their departure she could finally hear her thoughts. Wrapping a cloth around the jar of eyes, which was distressingly real, she put it next to her father's journal inside her school bag. Ling opened her door and picked up an insulated container of hot water. Even though conversations with her mother were few and far between, she left fresh boiled water every morning outside her bedroom door. Using a bowl on her desk, she wiped down her body and face. As she ran the scratchy cloth over her skin, she heard Gou hum a nursery rhyme from the kitchen while Kit sang.

Three Blind Mice.
They have no eyes.
They have no eyes.

Hearing only a small portion of the new words, she wondered how these lyrics had come to be. What a strange song to teach children. Could there be something medical in the mention of eyes? The different rendition conjured a reference to a forbidden medical text called the *Bencai Caomou,* in which human parts were believed to contain medicinal value.

"What are you singing?" Ling asked as she walked out, looking into her brothers' starry eyes.

They spooned *juk* from their bowls, tilting their heads from side-to-side, too busy eating to reply. Ahma stood silently at the stove. Ling shrugged and sat down to her breakfast. Inside her bowl, a dollop of soy sauce bled from the center of the creamy rice porridge. At the back of her throat, she could swear that she tasted blood. The horridness of last night's delivery reared in her memory. Did anyone have to know? Perhaps she could tell Ahma, but she couldn't say anything in front of her brothers.

Ahma finally shooed the boys out for school then checked the burners, accentuating a small hump between her shoulders. The time she spent leaning over embroidery and vats of soapy water had reconfigured her mother's form. Year-by-year, her mother slouched further. To the twins, Ahma had always looked this way—exhausted and shrunken. But Ling could remember her mother's elegant posture. A woman teeming with an excitement for life. Should she tell Ahma about the incident of last night? Or should the burden be Ling's alone to bear?

This morning, Ahma smiled as she moved away from the stove. "Good news! My coworker Beatrix is betrothed to a barrister who promised to review your father's case. The barrister says the courts would favor us. We can finally recover your father's promised salary."

Ling's heart leapt. Money would free them from so many things. Ahma would no longer have to work with shady manufacturers inside the Walled City. They could move back to the island where her brothers had a real chance to become self-sufficient men, not errand boys for thugs, throw-aways at the factories, or servants to the ghosts.

However, Ahma and Ling had been optimistic before. Three years after the disappearance of her father, the family had needed to sell their boat for parts. The possibility of a payment from the shipping company for her father's labor contract had lingered like a forbidden fruit.

"Ahma, sik la?" Ling didn't see a bowl on the table for her mother.

"One of the girls is celebrating a birthday today. There should be cake," Ahma said, while investigating a rip in a pair of pants. She was sitting on a bench by their only window.

Ling didn't believe her. Her co-workers, all women, struggled just as she did. All of them fled from harsh conditions. Most worked multiple shifts to support fathers and husbands who gambled and lingered at bars and dark dens. Among the sordid stories, Ahma focused on the few celebrations.

"Your hair looks nice pulled back." Ahma's chair squeaked as she threaded a hole. Despite the gray hairs on her temples, she still had a youthful face.

"Mm goi." The compliment warmed Ling. Ahma always fought for her. Ling needed her mother's help to get through this tragedy. The news of Lady Tun's death would soon be public knowledge. Fear simmered under Ling's skin as she mustered an explanation for last night.

She cleared her throat. "I have to tell you something." It came out more ominous than she expected.

Ahma furrowed her nose.

Lady Tun's dying protests rang in Ling's ears. She stared at the coals burning inside the stove. Steam tumbled out of a copper kettle.

"Always daydreaming like your father," said Ahma, cutting thread with her teeth.

A twist formed in Ling's stomach. She wasn't like her father. Unlike him, she kept her word. Ten years ago, he had promised to return. There was no trace of him since the departure of his voyage. Would a father just disappear into the sea?

In their last conversation, Ling had told him about the waterlogged faces in her dreams. These dark visions had persisted since he left. While the visitors in her dreams carried her father's name, his face was never amongst the dead. Could he still be alive?

Regardless, Ling shouldered the responsibility of keeping the family together and thriving. Ahma worked, but Ling represented the brighter future for them all. She had to become a doctor, lift their lineage back up.

"What did you want to say?" Concern laced Ahma's voice.

Ling bit her lip and opened her bag, placing the books on the table before lifting out the covered container with the eyes.

"What is that?"

"Let me..." Ling unraveled the edges of the cloth.

"Is that the book?" Her mother's voice was stern.

Ling blinked. Did she mean father's journal?

Ahma didn't give time for Ling to respond. "This is the banned book Sister March wrote a note home about?" Ahma picked up *Camilla*, investigating the cover and reading the first page. "Why must you rot your intellect? Concentrate on schoolwork. Get into medical school. The family needs you to do this."

Ling nodded, lowering the jar back into its wrapping. If her mother didn't approve of vampires in fiction, then the truth of last night would only provoke her. Her mother didn't have a superstitious bone in her body. She thought spirits were symptoms of a degenerate mind. Ahma wouldn't believe what Ling witnessed; even worse, she might force Ling to lie about it. She would focus on the fact that Ling had disobeyed her uncle and snuck out in the middle of the night. Waiting was Ling's best move.

Ahma's nostrils flared, indicating that she was no longer in the mood for discussion.

"Best not to bring it to school." Ahma stood up in a huff, taking her sewing to her room. Ling sighed. She would have to return the book to her teacher, who had secretly lent it to her, another time.

Then a ship's horn blew in the distance. Ling shot up from the table. The commuter boats would arrive at the docks in fifteen minutes and then after anchor, the passengers would disembark in another ten. If Ling ran, she could make it to the docks before the first customers reached their stands.

She repacked the jar and her father's journal. As she touched the leather-bound cover, a memory of her father sang strange notes in her mind. The image of him leaving their village blended with the discord of last night. Her head spun, twisting her into a disoriented state.

Six

September 1923
The Guianas

A thunderous boom sounded across a field of decapitated stems and shook the grass. Xie crouched, shielding his body from stray bullets. Sugarcane leaves shaded his cheeks. God chose to shine even hotter onto the plantation during harvest month. This was paradise for a few, and hell for many. He wiped sweat from his face with an already-soaked cotton sleeve. Shouts erupted from leagues away. Bullets always seemed closer to the hunted. Hot metal fragments could rip through a man's intestines and scatter him into pieces, but only if he tried to run away.

His voyage from the Fragrant Bay had started as a potentially lucrative venture. He was to teach the art of sailing as a private citizen, a commission which both the Tang and English armies frowned upon. His loyalties were seen as mixed, not secure. But to Xie, it had been an advantage to be employable by both sides. He signed the contract to sail to San Francisco. He hadn't sought field work. Only when a gun was pointed at his head did he press his thumb to the signature line. But however it had started, his ego and hubris had brought him here.

None of Xie's previous life had survived this hellish eight years. Even the parts he wanted to retain had hardened. His dreams had faded.

He squatted, gripping a handful of plants and chopping low to the ground, severing the stem. Liquid streamed from the sliced ends like spilt blood. He glanced at the men to his right and left. Their arms moved with the same mechanical swiping motions. On this island, he was only good for harvesting.

There was a strange satisfaction to this rhythm of work. The form was so instinctive now that he could live inside his head for hours. He daydreamed more than he rested.

Today, in his home country, was the time of the Autumn Festival. Chickens and pigs were slaughtered to celebrate the living. A butcher would then cut the skin, tendons, and bones for roasted meat, dumplings, and stews. He remembered enjoying them with his daughter and pregnant wife on the deck of his ship.

That life had been more than enough. But greed had disguised itself as ambition. If only he had paid attention to the signs. Bad omens for grown men were bad dreams for an nine-year-old girl. He thought of the night before he had left. He shouldn't have told his daughter to go back to sleep and keep the images to herself. The universe had provided him with sight, but he had preferred to keep his eyes closed.

Between the rows of plants, the world was dark and unwelcoming. The jungles, riverbeds, and beaches were all owned by the family with the house on the hill. They owned everything but the sea. Xie wanted to disappear, but the brutal overseer would find him. The men from the *K. Hooper* had become property. A few people had escaped before, but the punishment for running away was harsh and scalding, dealt either by whip or withholding rations. A simple bullet ended the contract.

Calluses lined his fingers and the inside of his hands. He was slow but usually steady. This kept him from overheating. The drivers usually ignored him, preferring to harass the younger and newer arrivals. But today, he felt the drivers' cold stares. The counters went through his bundles of sugarcane with extra care, tallying up a final score.

His time was almost up, which wasn't necessarily good. The owner never paid out a contract.

Seven

Ling hurried down the road. Fragrant smoke drifted up from the neighborhood temple. Her world awoke with sandalwood incense. Just before the marina, Ling admired the large homes, as always. The grass-covered lawns were built for foreign officers. Camphor trees provided a shaded canopy all the way to the docks. The windows of Emma's three-story structure were decorated with stained glass angels.

Her lungs burned as the cobbler, fruit seller, and newspaper stand owner greeted her. Competitors had thinned their profits in Hong Kong and at Kowloon's main port. But here, the stand was the sole provider of herbal teas and medicines. Textile workers, secretaries, and businessmen all needed to battle dampness from the sea. And with the strike, locals and migrants flocked to their business in unprecedented numbers. How long would the increased demand last?

Ling caught her breath, smelling the aroma of marigold tea leaves.

Without looking up from his reading, her uncle said,

"Good morning. There are fresh baked biscuits for you in the back."

Her favorites. She often craved decadent and superfluous flavors. While gauging the boats' distance from the docks, she squeezed behind the counter.

"Good morning, Dabak. Er—I mean Doctor Shaw." Ling squeezed the handle of her bag. She desperately wanted to show him the eyes and apologize for everything going wrong.

"It's fine." He cleared his throat. "Have you seen Lady Tun's package?"

Ling swallowed her words. Maybe she could feign ignorance, pretend nothing had happened. "What is the medicine for?"

She was eager to skip the horrible parts and go straight to the herbs. Part of her thought learning about the ailment could explain the attack and the aftermath. Why had the murderer stuffed petals into Lady Tun's mouth?

"It's not the proper time to talk about patients. Passengers will arrive soon. Please straighten up and ladle tonic into the containers. A wet cough has spread among the travelers."

Ling paused. The doctor spent most of his time aiding working men and women and healing their disorders. When wealthy patients complained, Dabak replied with a quote from a famous general: "Know yourself and know your enemy, and you will never be defeated."

No one questioned him twice.

"Did Lady Tun come to you about the cough, too?" Ling grappled for information.

He shook his head. "She's had her condition for a long time." He slipped a notepad into his breast pocket then pushed his eyeglasses up his nose. To Ling's alarm, the lenses magnified his nervousness.

"If her condition is chronic, then why ask for a delivery at such a late hour?" She rearranged the teas on display.

Her uncle tilted his head. "We'll have to ask her...but for now..." He glanced at her sideways, shooing her to the back.

She ducked behind the cloth separating the preparation area. Her newest school uniform hung next to the aprons, so she didn't have to walk through the neighborhood in a plaid skirt.

The gold emblem stamped on the jacket signaled her allegiance to Western education. For her family, attendance at St. Mary's Catholic Preparatory School was a source of pride. Dabak's marriage had migrated their family into another class. The school had gifted Ling a resident scholarship. This was an opportunity most kids weren't provided at birth.

Her education trained her to function in a forming society, one established by conquerors and those submissive to their demands. Yet, her classmates rejected her. She was too local for some, and others saw her as complicit to the ghosts. Growing older made her feel more and more like a piece of bamboo, hollowed on the inside.

After tying an apron around her waist, she lifted the lid of the first pot. The apples, dates, and flower rhizomes boiling inside turned the water a deep red. Many patients requested this crimson elixir which cured deficient yin energy. Over another fire, an earthy rose scent emitted from *Ching Bo Leung*, a drink for expelling toxins. She ladled honeyed green tea into glass cups. Travelers loved the warm treat.

After preparing a few dozen servings, sweat dripped from her forehead. She started to feel dizzy from the heat and rested for a minute. Listening to customers chat in the front with the doctor, she ate two buttery biscuits, homemade by Aunt Marcella. She basked in the hints of citrus in the baked treats.

Ling traced the flowers on the cookie tin with her fingers. To her trained eye, they seemed fantastical; the embossed print was impractical. Real roses, violets, marigolds, and lilacs didn't grow together in the wild. Roses needed full sun. Violets thrived in partial shade. The contradictions clashed beautifully.

At her feet, she spied packages of medicine. Flipping through the butcher-paper-wrapped bundles, she read the names scrawled on the front. Choi, Eng, and Gesner were familiar ones. Each was the size of her hand, stuffed full, and carrying dried herbs. A larger package was addressed to Lady Tun. Like the one she had delivered last night, it was oddly shaped. What medicines did Dabak prescribe to her? She was tempted to open the parcel to investigate, knowing that Lady Tun would never use them, but fragments of conversation filtering in from outside caught her attention:

When will the next typhoon hit the island?

Did the doctor think the strike would end soon?

Did he trust the Executive Council with the future of the region?

Had he been consulted when the Walled City oracle had fallen ill?

The doctor stammered lukewarm responses to these dangerous questions. He tried at every turn to maneuver the conversation to a neutral topic. Only at home did he freely give political opinions. He never discussed patients and, to Ling's chagrin, disliked spreading rumors.

Peeking out from the drapes, she gasped in surprise. There were so many customers that an actual queue had formed at the counter. She took one last sip of the tea then carried out a tray full of herbal drinks.

Dabak sighed and stepped away from the counter. His smile faded. "Ten pots, nine pans," he said under his breath.

Ling repeated the fortuitous idiom. One more pot than pan meant demand outpaced supply. But she thought that this count was exactly where they wanted to be. Every customer secured a little more of their future.

"How may I help you?" Ling replaced her uncle at the counter who headed to the back to fill the more complicated orders. She listened as customers shared their tales of headaches, back aches, coughs, and many other symptoms. In the moments between, people asked questions about her:

How was her final year of study?

Did the university admit local girls?

Had Ling's mother asked for blessings from the oracle?

Ling was blunter than her uncle. "We don't trust her," Ling replied, handing an auntie dressed in a loose cheongsam a packet of pills. The closest oracle lived inside the Walled City and was referred to as "Wupo." On the other side, on Hong Kong island, seers were labeled as prophets. Oracles were always an older lady, who passed down her practice to an apprentice.

Ling's family had reason to dislike the oracle. Ahma blamed her father's disappearance on Wupo's advice, which had encouraged him to join the crew of the *K. Hooper* at any cost. The old decrepit woman was the reason her father hadn't heeded Ling's dreams.

A person behind the auntie cleared her throat, a woman with streaks of white in her hair. Ling expected a forthcoming tongue-lashing, but instead, the woman said, "You're better for it. Wupo has been rash and unpredictable recently."

Other people nodded along, then turned to their neighbors and chatted.

"I heard her apprentice Mei died last spring."

"Wupo has been asking for a new student."

"It's a shame she's so inaccurate. We'll have to ferry ourselves to the island..."

A woman with silvery hair approached Ling, laughing. "Miss, wearing such worry on your face will give you wrinkles early." Deep grooves around her mouth showed she liked to smile.

Ling softened her face. "Ahyi, how may I help you?"

"What do you have for a sore throat?"

"Do you have a fever?" Ling pulled up her sleeve to touch the patient's forehead with the back of her hand.

The woman smiled. "No, only my throat hurts."

"Show me your tongue." Ling inspected the thickening film on her tongue and the red tip. Both indicated stagnation of her *qi*. A person's energy could be blocked by strain, stress, and any number of other environmental factors. She wouldn't be able to narrow down the causes in such a quick visit. "How's your sleep?"

"Horrible." The woman crossed her arms, pouting. Ling narrowed her gaze. The woman wanted help but apparently wasn't prepared to divulge details. Ling would have to interpret the symptoms without more explicit context. The pain in her throat and insomnia pointed to irregular circulation. Did the ailment originate from the heart, liver, or spleen? There was no way to tell. Regardless, she had enough information to suggest a tonic of sour jujube seeds, mushrooms, and licorice roots.

"If you can return in an hour, we'll have the tonic prepared as well as ingredients to take home." Ling watched the patient nod, the frustration evaporating from her expression. With more information, Ling would be able to streamline her prescriptions.

After ducking into the back to hand the script to Dabak, Ling returned to find the queue vanished. More than ten waiting customers had left. Was it something she had said? She sighed, stepping out into the sun to see where they had gone. Then she turned and gasped.

Enlai stood in front of her, in clean slacks and rolled-up sleeves. He beamed with a shaven face. A black bandana was tied around his head.

She couldn't contain her dismay. As she tried to escape back behind the counter, he grabbed her hand. "Let go," she mumbled, trying not to make a scene. She glanced at the tail of the snake illustrated on his arm.

"Is all well?" Dabak called from the back.

Another man, wearing the same cloth around his head, slid in front of the stall. He was even taller than Enlai, with broader shoulders and a crooked smile.

Blood drained from her face. "Can I help you?" She spoke the words from practice as she trembled inside.

"I sure hope you can." He studied her from head to toe, taking unsavory pauses at her hips and her chin. Under his gaze, she started to question her own dress. A sly smirk slowly formed on his face. What was he starting at?

Enlai bumped his companion with an elbow. He let go of Ling, allowing her to duck behind her uncle.

"What do you want?" Dabak jumped out from the back. To Ling's amazement, Dabak did not seem surprised at the visit. "We cannot talk here," he said. He waved the unsavory man from the shop toward the docks. As the man followed the doctor, the stranger turned and winked at Ling. Her stomach turned. Men from all walks of life visited the shop, but most didn't make her feel so loathsome.

Enlai leaned over the counter. "Sorry about Brother Tam." He looked down at his hands while apologizing to her. Looking back up again, he asked, "Did I see you last night?"

She swallowed. "Why would you?"

"I swear, you were at the West gate of the Walled City."

She stared with a desire to admit anything. But if she lied, then what made her better than him?

"Or did I dream you up?" He flashed her his teeth, slightly yellowed by his new smoking habit.

She shrugged, deciding to withhold as much information as she could.

"Are you going to the celebration in two days?" Enlai asked, as if nothing had changed between them in two years. As if they both hadn't grown up in different parts of Kowloon and taken different paths. "These people are doing something special for Ghost Month."

She didn't know how to respond to such an innocent question. It seemed like a trap, opening her up to more probing questions. "Why are you harassing us?" she blurted out.

Enlai looked down at the ground. "Brother Tam wanted to pay a visit to the shops, so I came to protect you." Enlai leaned forward.

"I don't believe for—" she started to say.

Enlai narrowed his eyes. "There are people way worse than me out there. It's better that I am here, trust me."

Her lips quivered. She knew far more than she wanted about human nature, especially since last night. She thought about telling him about the creature and Lady Tun. He would understand, because when she had told him about her dreams with the faces of the dead, Enlai had not judged her or made her feel weird for straddling the world of the living and the deceased. And after his experiences with the Red Society, his advice about murder could be enlightening.

But she had long since severed their friendship.

"Ling, we haven't spoken in a while. I know you're still upset..."

She didn't want to look Enlai in the eyes for even a

second. Otherwise, the truth would spill out of her. Had her uncle finished his private conversation? She glanced over at Dabak, catching Brother Tam's gaze. The thick scar down his right cheek wrinkled as he smirked in her direction. She turned away, crouching behind some shelves.

Enlai reached over the counter, grazing the top of her head. "If you need anything, ask for me here." A business card landed at her feet. In red letters, it read "Café de Sourire," alongside a logo of a smile. Then she heard his footsteps crunch over the gravel and vanish behind the stores.

Dabak returned with his brow furrowed.

"What did they want?" Ling asked. The visit wasn't about medicine, not with them arriving and leaving in such a huff.

"The society has increased their protection fees." He sighed. "Brother Tam said the strike is putting stress on their men. The Brothers used to be about a noble cause. Thuggery has no logic. An equilibrium has been disturbed. Someone has to pay for it."

"Dabak," Ling said with a stern expression, ready to talk. "Things are really bad."

"It's not ideal...but we will still make a profit..."

"No, not that. I mean... I delivered...Lady...the patient," Ling stuttered. "...is dead." She bit her lip, feeling the achy return of the strange voice. "I...I...I. She...there was..."

Images of the evening felt disorganized. She had seen too much. The blood spilling from Lady Tun's eyes, the reptilian flesh, and the terrible smell all hit her like a sack of stones. Her thoughts seemed muddled like the waters of the marsh.

"Niece. Take a breath." Dabak looked like he wanted to believe her. He patted her on the shoulder. "Whatever befuddles you is no longer here. Speak."

She inhaled the salty air, but the heaviness felt trapped in her lungs. Words tumbled out with her next exhale. "Lady Tun. I wanted to help the store..."

His eyes grew wide as she confessed her midnight delivery.

"She was alive when I brought the package. A creature took her eyes. Carved them out, cut her open, stuffed your herbs in her mouth, and then jumped into the water." When she finished explaining, she felt an openness in her chest. Sharing her burdens eased the tension in her jaw.

Her uncle pursed his lips. "Oh dear." He covered his forehead with one hand. His eyes bulged from behind his glasses. "The herbs will lead the authorities to traditional doctors immediately. I didn't know..."

She had no idea what to do next. Could he tell her what he did know? Dabak's uncertainty unsettled her. He seemed less concerned with the patient. But this made sense. Lady Tun was already dead, and he was right to be vexed instead about his reputation.

"Could they trace her back to us?" Ling asked.

Dabak pulled her behind the tarp. "Did she recognize you?" he asked in an exhale.

Ling shook her head. "I checked her pulse."

"You touched her?" Dabak's eyes grew wild. "I should have properly warned you about her. What about the creature? The shadowy figure that enacted the violence."

"It sensed me, but I never revealed myself to it." Ling thought of the hour crouched in the dark. Her legs ached at the memory.

"Sensed?" Dabak repeated. "You're brave, Ling. Let that guide you through life."

He frowned, placing his hands on her shoulders. "Don't speak of this to anyone. Things need to play out." His voice was grave. "Even your mother cannot know."

"Am I in trouble?" Ling whispered, concerned by the rising urgency in his voice.

"It's not your fault." Dabak stood. Sweat collected along his hairline. "Lady Tun wasn't a good person. Our land is haunted by more than the ghosts. We have been beaten. We have been poisoned. Yet, a rebellious spirit remains. This action was needed for the strike."

His passion surprised her. The meanings of his words were evasive. She couldn't believe he was mentioning the strike outloud. His change in demeanor spiked her curiosity. "What were the blue flowers for?"

"A disastrous affliction, one I hope you will never have to treat." He put his index finger to his lips.

"Should I worry about the creature?" Ling pressed. Why did she need to wait for knowledge? Surely, witnessing Lady Tun's brutal end meant she was ready for anything.

Her uncle opened his mouth, his eyes earnest. Ling couldn't believe it; she was finally going to get answers. She could hardly breathe.

"*Jiou san.*" The greeting cut into the intense moment. Ling peered over Dabak's shoulder. A man in a bowtie stood a few feet away. Headmaster Lee from Ling's school. Ling and Dabak both stared at the arriving customer like a stunned deer.

"A windy day needs healing tea," Headmaster Lee said. He adjusted the lapel on his jacket. Tension lingered in the air. Ling tried to read his expression. Had he overheard Dabak's monologue? Headmaster Lee tilted his head. "Is this a bad time?"

"No. Sorry to keep you waiting," Her uncle's face remolded into a smile, reaching across the counter for tea. "*Tai dou sap hei.* Humidity is heavy on the spleen."

Ling detected a quiver in Dabak's voice. He sounded

more frightened of insulting the headmaster than the back-lash from Lady Tun's death.

Headmaster Lee patted the perspiration from his mustache with a handkerchief. "Miss Shaw. You're so diligent, working for your family and attending classes. Did you tell the doctor about your progress?"

Her uncle seemed lost in thought.

Headmaster Lee continued. "She received the highest marks in literature in her class. Her poetry is lovely." He beamed. "The late start in her education had not distilled her talent."

Ling busied her hands, cleaning the empty containers and dusting the cabinet. If not, Headmaster Lee would've seen her blush. His kind words made her uncomfortable.

Dabak touched his chin. "She didn't mention it. But I am not surprised. My younger brother was also very studious. He memorized constellations and sailing routes. A true man of the sea. One of the best navigators of the South Pacific. I told Ling she should go to medical school."

"Ah, I see. Academics runs in the family. A few women are in fact registered at the university. Perhaps I can make an introduction on your behalf?" Headmaster Lee extended his hand with payment.

"No fuss." Dabak waved off the money. "I hope Ling will continue to improve and honor the time she spends with her teachers. Please have tea any time, on us."

The headmaster nodded, looking satisfied. "Young lady, shall we head to school? Classes start in fifteen minutes."

Ling wanted to decline, to stay back and ask more questions. She was frustrated to have this moment of candor with Dabak snatched away. Murders were not commonplace. Dabak had never before advised keeping information from Ahma. She was more confused now than she had been earlier in the morning.

Her uncle shot her a firm look, reading her hesitation. "She'll be ready in a minute."

Ling hung her head. She switched to her uniform jacket in the back. Wiping her sweaty palms on her apron, she walked out.

"Your priority is to protect the family," Dabak whispered, slipping a note into her hands.

"From what?" she asked. But there wasn't time for more details. Her uncle didn't often speak of dangers. It wasn't usually necessary. The hazards in Kowloon, so close to the Walled City, were apparent.

The wrinkles on Dabak's face deepened. "We'll discuss the plan later. Now go and secure your future."

Ling forced herself to nod then tore herself away from the moment. Lady Tun was no longer here to answer questions. She was dead at the hand of a mysterious creature. Her mouth filled with petals that could draw the authorities to her uncle and other local healers. She hoped Dabak could handle the repercussions. Ling didn't feel entirely free, a nagging still remained. As she tried to conjured a smile for the headmaster, she saw a darkness in his eyes.

EIGHT

Ling fanned her face with a sketch pad. Even with the all the windows opened, the second-floor classroom trapped the summer heat. She loved botany class, but her mind drifted to terrible things. She had to do something to keep from falling into the abyss. As other students slumped over their desks she submerged herself in her father's journal, combing through entries about sirens, octopi, and fish with spiked teeth. He had been the first to introduce her to unexplainable creatures. Today, she was looking for references to part-human creatures with reptilian skin.

Her father's notes highlighted his love of the sea. Despite the danger of adventure, the waters gave him motivation to live. How did her father reconcile leaving the sea for his family? Could one be jealous of another's adventures? After Ling's birth, he had inscribed a telling verse:

To the desires that trebled life in me,
The dreams that seemed the future to foretell,
The hopes that mounted herward like the sea,
To all the sweet things sent on happy souls,
I cannot choose but bid a muted farewell

To the best of her knowledge, the sea was where life started and ended for her father. Her birth had made him question his ways. The years he had docked himself to the land had shriveled his spirit.

As she drifted, a deep tenor called to her from the pages. *Do you see?*

Was this the voice from last night? How had it followed her? It was still nipping the same question at her ear.

Miss James laughed, drawing Ling back to the stifling classroom. The teacher instructed two men in the doorway to push a cart full of plants to the front of the room. Her heels clicked over the hardwood floor. At the chalkboard, she wrote the Latin names for the bush varieties being wheeled forward—*Laurus nobilis, Syzygium polyanthum, and Persea borbonia.*

Ling rubbed her temples, remembering the note from her uncle. Conversations with the headmaster and then her classmates had distracted her from reading the scrap of paper. She spread out the crumpled paper on her lap. The message was unfortunately smeared. She could only make out a few words.

...Lan.....help...

Was *Lan* a patient, a friend, or another doctor? Ling jiggled her leg. What needed help? The dried flowers? Her sanity? She hadn't mentioned the orphaned eyes. She felt stupid for carrying them around. Even just thinking of them made her instantly nervous. What if a nun inspected her bag?

A loud squeaking from the cart up front interrupted Ling's thoughts, as a neatly folded, pink piece of paper landed on Ling's desk. She pulled the square onto her lap. A backwards E inscribed in the corner told her who it was from. Ling unfolded the missive from Emma: *Soda and ice cream after class? My cousin's working.*

Ling perked up. She couldn't decline an offer of sweets. When Joseph managed the soda shop, he treated the girls to their favorite candies and drinks, a luxury Ling could no longer otherwise afford. She loved spending time with her carefree friends. This invitation was a gift, a chance to pretend life was still grand.

Miss James cleared her throat, her rose-colored dress looking pale and washed-out. "Class, I present three beautiful laurels: Mediterranean, Indian, and Indonesian." Her thin long arms gestured to the potted plants. "These are examples are on loan from the garden of Sir Robert Ho Tung." She walked over to the specimens in heeled leathered shoes like a gazelle. With her hair pulled back, the light brown freckles dotting the back of her neck matched the color of her hair. She glided her fingers gently over the thin branches before adding Tang characters under the Latin.

Ling recognized the laurels as bay leaves from her herbal studies. They were mentioned in other texts, but she couldn't recall the exact reference. This bothered her. Her razor-sharp memory had always placed her ahead of other students. What irked her even more was not being able to identify the flowers on a spectrum of blues from last night. This wouldn't do. She must be exceptional. If she aspired to practice Western medicine, she must be the best.

Miss James glowed. "Don't let these plants' similarities fool you. Only one is the original, carrying well-known nutrients for foods and medicines. But which is it?"

Ling pulled out the petals from last night, comparing them to the much bigger bay leaf at the front of the room. She ran her fingers down the jagged pattern on the petals, hardier than she would have expected. The petals matched the thickness of the bay leaf. The hue still held fast. In fact, this flower was more similar to a bush than any flower she knew of. What kind of flower was both beautiful and sturdy?

Ling wiped her forehead with a handkerchief. Dabak said there was a plan. Until they spoke after school, she would have to concentrate on something else. Trying to discern the identity of the petals was a game she could pursue.

The teacher plucked leaves from different branches, marking each one with a number. "Pass these down and make your guesses."

She handed the leaves to a student in the front row.

"Inspect these specimens and choose the preferred leaf for cooking. Use what you have learned from your texts to identify the Mediterranean Bay Laurel's scent, taste, and appearance." Then Miss James put a leaf in her mouth and bit down. Ling detected the slightest wince.

The girls flashed confused, worried looks at each other. Ling scoffed. Had her classmates even boiled an egg before? As far as she knew, Ling was the only girl interested in plant science. She had a copy of the *Foundation of Botany* by Joseph Young Bergen in her desk. It was the only book her uncle mentioned alongside the *Bencao Gangmu*, or the Great Pharmacopoeia, which had been compiled by the last rulers of Han descent in the 16th century Ming Dynasty. Not readily taught, the eccentric remedies inside had once saved Ling's life.

Miss James must have noticed the desperate looks around the room, because her mouth tightened.

"Can anyone share some insights from last week's readings?" When no one took up this offered escape route, she added, "must be the heat disintegrating your senses."

A few coughs echoed in response. Ling slumped in her seat as the teacher threw a glance in her direction. Everyone knew her uncle was a traditional doctor and that she could be counted on to understand herbal remedies. But she was busy thinking. She remembered now the other place she'd read about bay leaves—in her father's journal. Her father had written about a woman boarding his ship with a satchel of these hearty leaves.

"Miss Yi." The teacher had called on the girl wearing diamond stud earrings, whose father was a land baron.

Virginia Yi mumbled something inaudible. Her chin touched her chest. Miss James walked closer to her desk and leaned over her. As the class waited on the conversation, Ling flipped through her father's journal, tipping the book to view the bottom half of the pages.

"Excellent. The leaves can be steeped in hot water to use as a digestive aid. The infusion is also helpful with soothing respiratory problems. But no, your answer is not precise. Now, Miss Pei?"

"The leaves enhance flavor," Frances Pei offered, her answer more confident than Virginia's.

"Very good." Miss James wiped the sweat from her brow with a cloth. Frances's response wasn't correct either.

Ling's attention returned to the journal page, which had a drawing of a woman with braids. The characters *jut gui yip* were inked several times over. Nightshade leaves. The pen had dug grooves into the paper here, invoking a special significance to the nocturnal plant. She lifted the pages closer to her face, smelling the sweet ink and coming closer to the lady's hollow glare.

With blank pupils, the woman appeared to transcend time. Ling didn't blink, and the background faded away.

The notebook slipped out of her hand. When it slammed onto the floor, the entire class snickered. Ling hastily snatched up the journal as faces scowled. Virginia flipped her hair in irritation.

"Miss Ling. Did you hear the question?" Her teacher crossed her arms. "Heat getting to you too?"

Pity stained her classmates' stares. They all viewed Ling through the lens of charity. After all, she had arrived at their school through a scholarship.

"It's nothing." Ling lifted her chin. "We...we are missing protection. Bay leaves repel unwanted energies." As she was answering, the silhouette of figure at the shack materialized in her mind. She decided the creature wasn't good, even if Dabak doubted Lady Tun's character. Ling had evaded capture, and the night's dark whispers. However, the incident made her want greater security.

Ling willed the image away, forcing her thoughts back to class. "The Mediterranean Bay leaf has an earthy taste, not a cinnamon flavor like its Indian counterpart. And it is dark green, not reddish like its Indonesian cousin." She picked up the samples that had landed on her desk. After rubbing them between her fingers and nibbling on each, she announced: "In response to your initial question, leaf number two is the answer."

Miss James nodded with satisfaction and wrote out an assignment on the board. Ling wanted to smile, but Virginia mouthed "show-off" and scrunched her nose. Ling sunk into the chair, sweeping the leaves into the pages of the journal. She didn't want to see them right now. She looked down at her lap, grazing her fingers over the witch's stare in the book. If only she possessed the power to disarm others with a single glance. When would life become easy?

———

After class, Ling cleaned the blackboard for Miss James, wanting to apologize for returning a book late. Emma waited for Ling, swinging her legs atop the teacher's desk. As she wiped off the chalk with an alcohol-soaked rag, Ling ran through potential flora in her mind: Bluebell or *Hyacinthoides non-scripta*, Forget-Me-Not or *Myosis*, Gentian or the alpine flower. She could go on forever.

"Didn't sleep well last night?" Emma asked.

"Not very much," Ling admitted, turning around to look at her friend. She had been reciting the plant names aloud without noticing. The prospect of sleep felt like an impossible luxury. "I cannot get sodas with you today."

"What? Root beer floats are your favorite!" Emma jumped off the desk and placed her hands on her hips. "Come on. It won't take more than thirty minutes."

Ling chuckled. She loved her friend's inability to take no for an answer and was happy to be bullied into the detour. "How do you do it?"

"What?" Emma flashed her a band of white teeth.

"Change people's minds. Get people to open up to you. Command them to do things." Ling could think of countless times others went out of their way to help Emma: they would share their homework with her, allow her to leave class early, excuse her from a test with a feigned cough.

"Because I know what's good for them." Emma spun in a circle and curtsied. "Also, my dad is a lawyer."

"If you know what's good for me, then you can help me finish cleaning the chalkboard." Ling dangled an extra cleaning cloth.

Emma grabbed it from Ling's hand. "See, you're good at persuasion too. I only do this for you, no one else." Emma wiped away the chalk in heart-shaped patterns.

"Who are you so lovey dovey on recently?" Ling could tell when Emma had a new crush. From fellow parishioners at church to young associates at her father's firm, Emma had her choice of a good life.

"No one." Emma batted her eyes.

Ling curled her lips and furiously scrubbed another section.

Emma bit her lip. "Fine. I'll show you a trick. If you want to know something, ask a seemingly unrelated and open question. And act curious when you do. Directness will not get you anywhere in the ways of the heart. Remember, even when they are being secretive, people hope to share their deepest desires. They merely require space and interest."

Ling nodded. Her mother and Dabak always barraged her with questions. It had never occurred to her to redirect their requests toward a more advantageous position. "Is that why you asked me about my sleeping habits?"

"Maybe. So why are you reciting flower names?" Emma stared out the windows.

"I encountered something new. Do you want to see?"

Emma clapped her hands. From her pocket, Ling unwrapped the petals from the cloth. Despite the circumstances, she was excited to share the discovery. Emma was usually the one who showed Ling new things.

"I want these for my wedding." Emma's eyes sparkled.

"Wedding?" Ling tilted her head.

Emma looked away. "Father says at eighteen...." She paused.

Ling knew the expectations for Emma were different than hers. Even though there was a year and a half between them, Ling was never in the marriage market. "Well then, we'll have to figure out what they are first." Ling needed an ally. Maybe that was what the note from Dabak meant. Find friends.

As the young ladies marveled at the color and fragrance of the petals, they didn't hear Miss James creep up behind them.

"What's this?" Miss James peeped over their shoulders

with curiosity. She plucked a magnifying glass from her desk and hovered it over the samples. Freckles were sprinkled across Miss James's cheeks like umber stars. "An amazing find."

"Have you seen this before?" Ling wrung her hand. "It's a medicine. But I don't know the name."

"Not sure. The shape is very unique." Miss James pointed out the peculiar antennae sticking out from the middle. "Why don't you ladies check the library in the morning? I heard a mention of sweets after school. If you ladies are done with the board, you should get going. After all, ice cream awaits."

Both Emma and Ling curtsied. As Emma left the room, Miss James called for Ling to stay back a moment. Ling gestured to Emma with a finger. She would follow her friend soon.

"One more thing, Ling. During class today, I was surprised you went with the supernatural explanation," Miss James said as Ling approached her desk.

"You don't believe in the unexplained?" Ling asked.

"I didn't say... I teach in a certain way. Plants do have magical qualities." She flashed a mischievous smile, wearing a response in her expression. "It's fine for students to express themselves. However, the school pays my wages and houses me, so I am limited by their views."

Ling touched the petals again. Miss James was the only other person in the world Ling could ask about plants. "Can you keep this between us? I don't know if Dr. Shaw would approve of me sharing his medicines."

The young teacher nodded solemnly, a hint of agreement curving the corner of her mouth.

NINE

At the soda shop, Ling ordered her favorite dessert from Emma's cousin. Joseph was considered handsome by most. He had long lashes and olive skin. His smile supposedly melted most ladies' hearts, but not Ling's. She had no interest in him, aside from the free soda and delight he gave Emma.

"Why don't you practice on my cousin?" Emma leaned toward Ling. Her breath was sugared with vanilla, her pink fingernails tapping on the marble counter.

Ling tilted her head. "Practice what?"

"The art of asking questions. Like if you wanted to know if he was single then..."

"But I don't want to know." Ling couldn't care less who Joseph courted. She was more concerned about Emma's betrothal choices. Who Emma married would determine the future of their friendship.

Emma rolled her eyes. "That was an example, silly goose. But it would be fun, if you became family. Joseph is uncommitted at the moment."

Ling shrugged. Emma often teased her about small things.

"Should we meet at the library tomorrow morning?" Emma twirled on the stool.

"Yes. I'll tell my uncle that I need to study." The prospect of spending time with her friend made her giddy. Ling could also use the time to find leads to the mysterious petals and wanted to avoid another visit from the Red Society.

"What's wrong?" Emma studied Ling's face. "You got very quiet all of a sudden."

"Nothing, er..." Ling fidgeted with her hands. She couldn't possibly tell her prim and proper friend about a bloody murder.

"You're terrible at hiding things," Emma kicked the side of the counter. "Is it about school?"

Ling shook her head. She didn't want to burden their friendship with the dark details of her life. Time with Emma was a rare bright spot.

"It's something with Enlai, isn't it?" Emma persisted, coaxing Ling to divulge more information.

Ling nodded hesitantly. Emma had made a lucky guess. It wasn't the entire truth, but he had indeed been part of last night. If he hadn't been loitering in the corridor then perhaps, she would've arrived at the peninsula sooner and not seen everything that had transpired. "He came to the shop this morning," Ling said.

"How did he look?" Emma continued with the wrong line of questions. It was a relief.

"Taller, and he has a snake tattooed on his arm." How else could she describe him? Without fear or surprise, the face of a man cropped up in her thoughts. His childish face had morphed into that of a handsome young man. He had cut the Manchu queue, which was still required by the Imperial government. Rebelliousness suited him.

"Will you see him again?" Emma glanced over at Joseph.

The question stirred discomfort in Ling. If Dabak couldn't answer her questions about Lady Tun, then she might have no choice but to consult Enlai. No matter her distaste, his knowledge on the darker side of life could help them avoid trouble. The Walled City hosted priestesses that spoke with the dead, sold hallucinogenic experiences, and promised good fortune by divination. Did the Red Society also handle problems with mysterious creatures?

"My cousin is coming." Emma lifted her eyebrows.

Joseph brought their orders. Setting out a sundae and a float, Emma nudged her friend's leg. Ling cleared her throat. "Oh, Joseph. Um. How's school?" Out of the corner of her eye, Emma starting to giggle.

"I graduated last year. Just helping my parents until they accept the fact that I am not studying law or become a policeman like my dad. Emma told me you're going to medical school."

Ling's heart warmed at Emma's family taking an interest in her studies. "I am applying to Hong Kong University. If you will not become a lawyer, then what else would you be?" Ling took a sip of the dessert. When the creamy liquid touched her lips, a thrill rushed into her limbs. Her worries evaporated. She was more convinced than ever that the events from last night shouldn't concern Emma. This moment was the closest to happiness she had experienced in the last few months. Nothing should jeopardize this.

"I don't know. A sailor?"

Ling nearly choked.

"Not a good idea?" Joseph flashed his dimpled smile.

"It's too dangerous." Ling coughed, also thinking of the many threats in Kowloon. "Do you..."

Emma jumped in. "She should know. Her father was a... I mean is...a ship's captain."

Ling shifted her eyes to the tiny beads of water sliding down the frosted glass. She wished Emma hadn't brought up such a sore point. "It's taking quite a bit longer for my father to return from his last journey. I was saying...do you prefer adventure?"

"Joseph would not survive," Emma said confidently as she spooned ice cream into her mouth. She plucked a few taffies from a jar on the table.

"You're one to talk. Emma can barely ever be without bruises." Joseph squinted.

"I'm clumsy," Emma said in a unusual tone. Ling didn't believe this statement. Emma had excellent balance in dance class.

Then bells on the front door sounded, and Joseph could not have looked more relieved. "Be right back, ladies."

"I bungled that up," Emma said once Joseph started chatting with two other customers. She handed Ling the candies. "I apologize if I upset you."

"I've got everything I need right here." She drank from her glass, pocketing the soft sweets. Her brothers would love to have a taste, and if she could give them these taffies, maybe then they would not be enticed by the promises from a stranger. The cold drink slipped down her throat. How wonderful. Medicines were never this pleasant going down.

Emma's eyes softened. "What did you *really* want to know? My aunt and uncle must be so mad at him."

Ling smiled. "His greatest dream. I think I got pretty close."

Emma put her hand over Ling's. The warmth between them felt reassuring. Ling needed to stay the course of medical school. Their friendship was the source of the strength. She couldn't possibly drag her friend into the mess.

"What's your dream?" Emma asked her.

Without a pause, Ling gave her standard answer. "Medical school and to live in a beautiful house on the island." Getting the proper profession and house seemed the best thing she could do for her family. She didn't have the means or gender to embark on frivolous journeys. Ling's choices had impact on generations ahead. "You?"

Emma sank into herself. Her perfect posture crumpled from her midsection. "To go far away..." She stared out of the window. "On top of some mountain in a jungle."

Ling squeezed her friend's hand. She so rarely spoke this way. The unknown stoked something dark inside of both of them. It seemed perhaps secrets troubled them both. Ling hoped that Emma's weren't as dark as her own.

TEN

As Ling headed toward the medicine stand, the horrible sights from last night flooded unwanted into her mind. Her muscles tensed, and the back of her head throbbed. She had allowed herself a small reprieve with Emma, one taste of the sweet life. Now, it was time to confront the consequences of disobeying her uncle. She didn't understand the situation completely. It was strange for Dabak to have made her wait. Lady Tun was dead, and her body was decaying out in the sun. He wasn't telling her everything, which was odd.

From the tree line, she noticed two men in uniforms standing side by side at the herbal stand. They were speaking with Dabak. Her uncle was scowling, locked in an intense discussion.

Ling surveyed the options. She wasn't naive. Something was wrong; they didn't often get official visits from the police. She prayed they weren't asking about Lady Tun. The police worked slowly, often dragging out local cases for months. They rarely found missing children. Had they even spent any time looking for Cili?

Ling lowered her head, blending in with the bustle of the travelers. She ducked into Kai's fruit stand, and he turned up the volume on his radio. The announcer listed the times for the upcoming horse races at the track, interrupting the other conversation.

"The two ghosts have been talking to your uncle for a good while." Kai searched her face. "What I heard sounded serious. One of them asked him for an alibi. I mean, I saw your uncle board the ship home, but I didn't interject." Fear permeated his gaze. She wasn't sure if his testimony would help or hurt them. As Dabak had told her, it was better to stay neutral or quiet.

Kai tapped a pencil against the horse betting pages. "Maybe the cobbler heard more than I did." The shoe repair stall was closer, directly behind their medicine stand.

Ling stared at the wall, not sure how to proceed.

"Go around back. Find out if we are in any danger." He untied the flap to the alleyway that ran between each stall. This was a private space along the busy pier, a narrow gap about the width of her shoulders. She sometimes did her homework or read a book there when she didn't want to be bothered. She ducked behind Kai's store, squeezing around bags of potatoes and cases of beer.

The sound of men's voices grew louder. The cobbler had closed shop earlier. When she reached the familiar containers of pickled eggs and aged black vinegar, she put her ear against the heavy tarp. The conversation was sharp.

"If you cannot tell us where you were last night, then we'll have to take you to the station." The man's voice sounded scratchy. "Then who will manage your shop?"

Ling imagined her uncle's stern look. Wasn't it easier to tell the police he had gone home to his sick wife?

"Chinamen should speak English. Don't you agree, Officer Robert?" Ling's hair bristled at the officer's condescending tone. It was like he was spitting into her uncle's tea. Dabak had attended school in London on a scholarship from the church. He was capable of anything.

Her uncle cleared his throat.

Officer Robert enunciated his words. "If you don't know anything, then explain the snake oil found covered with blood."

Ling gulped. The officers were here because of her delivery. The package had been torn open. Herbs had been scattered to the wind. Guilt tugged at Ling's heart. If only she hadn't defied the warning. Lady Tun had been mutilated by a monster, not her uncle. Ling had witnessed the brutality. But the police wouldn't listen to her statement.

"Why are you shaking your head? Explain... You're the only suspect, the only person with the arrogance to kill a genteel woman. Was this a ploy to steal her fortune? We heard she hoarded some shiny things down by the water."

Dabak wasn't arrogant. His intuition was unique, and people depended on him. Many ghosts, including Lady Tun, sought her uncle's advice. Why wouldn't he say so?

"Let's take a trip. The council will have their questions answered by any means necessary," Officer Roberts said, annoyed. "We'll find out what you're hiding."

Running out and incriminating herself would make things worse. She had stupidly carried the eyes with her. A basic search would uncover the evidence she carried in her bag. Mud from the swamps still caked the bottom of her boots, sitting by the front door at home. The police would arrest them both. She couldn't risk herself. The customers and this stand were her family's livelihoods.

Ling crawled from the alleyway into the backroom of the medicine stall. The curtains were drawn, hiding her movements. She peered out of a small hole. The police smashed their batons on the tables, sending teas and tonics flying through the air. The taller policeman bashed his baton against the shelves as observers gathered nearby, gaping at the gratuitous destruction. The crowd cursed at the policemen.

"All right, gentlemen," her uncle shouted, lifting his hands. He calmly walked over the broken objects. A piece of paper fluttered to the floor. The taller officer, who Ling could now see had a scar across his forehead, pulled Dabak forward by the scruff of his neck. Her uncle turned around and winked in Ling's direction.

She was startled by this gesture. How did her uncle know she was here? Why did he act so nonchalantly? Was this part of a larger plan somehow? The police didn't notice. The shorter man cuffed Dabak and pulled him toward a police car.

Ling took deep breaths. As soon as the police were out of sight, she emerged from her hiding place. She was shaking, unable to speak, until Kai raised his hands to the high heavens.

"Ming is a good man. There is no reason for these accusations. He returned to his sick wife on the island. Every single night, he does this." Kai was panting, nostrils flaring.

"*Ai yaaaaiii*. Steady, Kai, you'll give yourself a heart attack," an older lady scolded him. "Do you want to be arrested too?"

Kai huffed, grabbing a broom. "*Sik sei mau.*" It was a colloquial saying. The police were forcing Dabak to be the scapegoat, to eat a dead cat.

Ling fumed as she began picking up pieces of glass and fishing out salvageable herbs from the wreckage. Destroying their shop was a warning. They could do much worse to Dabak and her family. But first, they had to pin the murder on her uncle. Ling picked up the paper Dabak had dropped. She prayed it would tell her what to do.

Eleven

April 1923
The Guianas

Xie clutched the menthol tin. Only a little bit of salve was left. His last bit of home. Every night before he slept, he said his full name, whispered goodnight to his family members, and recited the coordinates to sail home. Grueling fieldwork withered men's souls, and keeping even a spark of hope alive took diligence.

On nights with a full moon, he was especially apprehensive of sleeping in a hut with no door. This was a time when he regretted not heeding the symbols from his daughter's dreams. Even with five capable men, no one kept watch. They were exhausted.

Every month, laborers fell ill with a blood disease near the full moon. Xie couldn't help but blame the lack of a damn door. The symptoms started with a sharp pain, which was followed by pale skin, sensitivity to light, and loss of appetite. The decline was rapid. After a few short days, guards carried the desiccated bodies of the sick out to burn.

The dwindling number of laborers hadn't concerned the land baron. He had been purchasing machines to replace manual laborers for seeding, sowing, watering, and harvesting.

In the hut, he felt exposed. He kept his sanity by remembering the good times—navigating his ship and cooking food for his pregnant wife and daughter. They would be proud of his resilience and impressed with the strength collected from his years of fieldwork.

Stones and logs had been put up as inadequate barricades in the open doorway. Workers didn't only give their lives in the fields; they were also forced to give up their flesh. Families in the big house hung straw men and charms to ward away the night demons. But trinkets didn't keep away the hungriest creatures. Doors did.

Xie twisted open the metal lid, inhaling the menthol. His brother, the budding doctor, had mixed camphor, eucalyptus, mint, and bay leaves for protection and healing. The bay leaves had been his own idea.

His hutmates stirred on their piles of dried grass. They laid only inches apart.

Once, a woman wearing heavy braided pigtails had chartered his ship to explore the Pearl River Delta. They had developed a good rapport, and after the five-day guided tour, she had paid him in silver and a basket of leaves.

"Where I come from, these plants are more valuable than gold." The chunky rings that pierced the woman's nose, lips, and earlobes glowed. She had worn flowing skirts covered in a net of silver. "That is, if honor is what you seek."

From that day, he had carried a little bit of her magic, although he had still ended up on a cursed island. What god in a past life had he insulted to deserve this fate?

The island was haunted. He used a tiny bit of salve, just

enough to ward off the shadows roaming the dark. How else could he have survived for so long? He'd managed to avoid the virus which had befallen so many before him for nine years. Pulling the round tin close to his heart, he closed his eyes as the crickets sung him to sleep.

———

Xie felt a prick. Fire spread from his neck to chest. A weight pressed into his lungs as he fought to breathe. He opened his eyes. Dark figures curled over the other men in the hut. Knotted fingers went to his mouth as Xie screamed. His eyelids fluttered. All of his strength drained from his body.

"Shaw Chi Xie." Its voice dug into him like barbs. He imagined his wife's face, and energy flooded into his arm. He threw a punch with all his strength. A loud crack erupted as his tin crushed into bone. The gnarled figure collapsed. Its scaly skin splintered, and its needle-like teeth were drenched with blood.

Xie caught his breath. White salve was smeared down his right hand. He laid as still as he could as warm blood dripped from his wound.

Four more intruders hunched over his hutmates, pressing their faces into the necks of the sleeping laborers, draining their lives drop by drop.

Xie tensed. He broke away from the center of the pack and crept around the edges of the hut. Just when the doorway was within reach, the hunters reared their heads.

A shadow sprang toward him. Xie grabbed a stick and knocked the thing to the ground. In the light of dawn, he could see the creatures' sagging skin, bristled tufts of hair, and abnormally shaped heads. Whatever they were, they weren't human.

Another lunged at Xie, pinning him to the wall and

staring with hungry black eyes. Rotted flesh melted from its bones. The creature bared its long teeth and pointed them at Xie's eyes. The tin lid was still stuck to his hand, so Xie shoved the lid into his assailant's neck. The monster let out a high-pitched screech as the medicine burned into its flesh. Xie gripped the edges of its skull and jabbed the stick into its head.

Power surged through Xie. He wanted to rid the world of these vile things. They had taken the lives of his hutmates and likely more on the island. This was a cruel injustice. He had less than a year left of servitude and still this island wouldn't let him go. Rage sent his hands deeper into the beast's head. Putrid sludge oozed from the obliterated skull. Crimson streamed from the punctures in his own chest.

The other shadows slithered closer, howling as Xie held chunks of gray matter in his palms. The creatures rotated their arched spines and bobbed their heads like they were crying. Only hatred stoked in his heart.

Xie bolted to the forest. The trees and the creek would hide him. Howls of grief sounded from the hut as he fled. Yet, no one followed.

Sprinting to the stream, Xie felt stronger than he ever had. The sun had already begun to rise. No one was trailing him. He could rest before the dogs came. Or maybe the owners would assume he was amongst the corpses and leave him alone.

He washed the wounds on his chest, his head aching as he remembered the horrific scene. The water from the stream couldn't satisfy his thirst. The sun beamed, and he was suddenly very tired. He curled into the bank of the river, cradled by the roots of a tree. The names of his children brought him comfort as he surrendered to his dire situation.

———

The initial glow of freedom faded as a fever ravaged Xie's mind. He chewed on ginger roots and lemongrass to temper his unease. No one ever chased him down. The dogs never came. He was forced to straddle life and death. Even with herbs, the two holes over his heart festered, turning a grotesque purple and swelling with oozing pus. A colorful warning of death.

In his daze, he imagined bringing home toys from around the world. His daughter hugged a velvet teddy bear. His son squealed with delight at a set of model trains. These were his dreams of an imaginary freedom.

Xie slept when the sun rose and explored the creek at night, scavenging food scraps that floated down the river from the villa and foraging wild plants. He memorized the location of fauna and flora along the water.

During a full moon, he stumbled upon eclectic flowers, hundreds of them along the banks of the river. The wind encouraged him to dip his swollen feet into the cool waters. The trees and grass were a lush green, not burned by summer's heat.

He scooped water over his ankles and toes. The night was quiet. He marveled at the brilliant blues budding from the soil. Was this a trick of the light? He had never seen this specimen before. They smelled of sugared lavender. His stomach grumbled, so he pinched the leaves from the stems and imagined them stewed in broth or baked into bread. He felt peace.

With nothing to lose, he popped a handful of petals into his mouth. A sour taste hit his tongue, turning sweet when he chewed. He grabbed a handful from the field and filled his mouth with more than a dozen. His mind felt cleansed and body less rickety. The flowers no longer appeared blurry in his field of vision. These were real.

The petals had a subtle medicinal taste with the nuttiness of *wai san*, slices of dried yams. Even his chest hurt less, and the flow of pus from the wound ceased. Slowly, the flowers began to heal his flesh.

Over the next few days, he carefully collected and separated their stems, leaves, and ovules. The future still wasn't clear, but at least he knew he had one. These ephemeral plants had saved him.

He curled himself into a hollow trunk, suddenly unable to recall his birthplace. Was he from this island? What was the name of the far away land with lush rolling hills and banyan trees? His name came to him slowly. Every gift had a price.

Twelve

On the note, Dabak had written two characters: *Zek Ngan*. The phrase meant *these eyes*, reminding her of the pair she carried in her bag. The rest of the proverb, *Zek Ngan hoi, Zek Ngan bai*, meant "eyes wide open, eyes wide closed." This was the point—her uncle literally told her to turn a blind eye, taking in and letting go. She didn't know how her uncle knew, but it was clear that the eyes had to be disposed of before anyone else found them. She had to burn, bury, or bludgeon the purple eyes. Their existence was too damning.

The crowd helped her clean the broken glass. Even Headmaster Lee stopped to offer his support. She closed the shop, feeling reassured by the community's strength. With Dabak's arrest, she had to tell her mother.

On the way home, Ling dumped the eyes into the harbor. Dropping her burdens into the waves felt freeing. Yet, an unexpected grief trembled in her soul.

At the kitchen table, Ling mulled over money and pages of her uncle's ledger while waiting for her family to return. If Dabak had been so specific in the second message than there must be something to glean directly from the first. The spelling of "Lan" could be the romanticization of a Chinese name or the start of a foreign one. Either way, she had to try.

She flipped through the pages, scanning each line. *Lanhua* meant orchid. *Lanmei* meant blueberry. *Toulan* meant laziness. Not all the papers were here. Medical records were stored in a safe inside his flat. She could go there tomorrow or the day after to continue sleuthing for clues. She hoped her uncle's innocence didn't rely upon two incomplete notes. His arrest would soon turn out to be a misunderstanding.

A part of her regretted throwing away the eyes. They had magic embedded beneath their skin, a different flavor than the *wu* advertised by Wupo. She was afraid of the secret being revealed to her. The authorities promised ruthlessness, and Ling believed they would deliver.

When the front door jingled, Ling squinted.

Ahma stood in the doorway. Her chest was heaving. "I am going to see your uncle."

Ling hid her face. "Headmaster Lee said he would phone the police chief and put in a good word for him." She attempted to convey hope, but her words only created frustration on her mother's face.

Ahma turned up a lip. "You told him?"

"Dabak's arrest is not a secret. The headmaster saw the shattered glass. Other vendors helped us clean up, too." Saving face wasn't possible. There was nowhere to hide. "Headmaster Lee wanted to do his utmost to make the process fair."

"Fair?" Ahma scoffed. "He's loyal to the crown through and through, although I do not know why. He was born in these mountains, unlike your lineage."

"Loyal to the King of England?" Ling asked.

"Not the man alone. He's committed to their culture, principals, and...." Ahma's expression grew dark. "And their rituals."

Ahma plucked three incense sticks from a shelf and lit them to Guan Gong. His fierce face pointed fearlessly into the street. "Did you see it happen?"

Ling nodded. She divulged the facts, except for Dabak's note and the eyes. This was out of respect for her mother. The anomalies were more than even Ling could handle. Her mother would lose her wits if Ling started to reference vampires, moving body parts, and a bloody murder. Safety was more important today than honesty.

"You did the right thing." Ahma hung her head. "Your uncle will be proud..." She lowered her gaze.

Ling pressed her lips together, worrying about Dabak's health. She hadn't told her mother the whole truth, and her world hadn't imploded. The truth may not need to be spoken.

"The twins are next door...I didn't want them to see me upset." She wiped her tears with her sleeve. Her eyes grew dark as she mumbled, "That bastard, getting us into this mess."

Ling stepped back against the wall. It wasn't Dabak's fault. He knew this and had still made her promise to not tell her mother. The truth wouldn't help now. "How will your visit help him?"

Ahma ignored her question. "Your brothers don't know much yet. They'll hear about it soon, so prepare them...."

"I should go to the police station with you," Ling said, interrupting her mother. Ahma wasn't connected or well-versed in the art of conversation. She would flounder by herself.

"My brother-in-law Ming isn't at the Kowloon holding cells. The police sent him to the armory on the hill, which isn't a place for children. I don't...." Ahma stumbled with her reasoning.

The armory stirred Ling's curiosity and alarm. Why was he sent there? What information did they need from her uncle? These weren't questions for her nervous mother. To protect the family, Ling must see her uncle too. The twins would be safe with the neighbors.

"If I am to keep the shop open, I need the safe's combination for patient notes and herbs. We cannot continue without those," Ling reasoned with confidence. She surprised herself with her own opinions. Dabak hadn't told her to say these things.

Ahma frowned. "Fine. I'll inform Wong Popo the boys are staying for a couple of hours longer. You"—she leaned close to Ling— "hide the earnings."

"Give Kit his slingshot. That trinket makes him feel strong. These toffees might quell their complaints, at least for the night." Ling sympathized with the twin's feelings of being left out. She wished it was her comforting them and answering their questions. Under stress, Ahma wasn't a gentle mother.

Ling divided the paper and coins. Wrapping a large batch in gauze, she buried this portion in the jar with the carcass of a pregnant rat. Most thieves weren't interested in stealing folk medicines. She pulled out her father's journal from her bag. As she slipped it back on the shelf, the bay leaves from botany class fell out. She picked them off the floor, pocketing them. A tingling in her ear said she would need the more protection.

When Ahma came back, Ling met her at the door. Her mother frowned. "We are not going to an ordinary prison. This is not a place where they bring silly drunks and pickpockets." With deep wrinkles on her forehead, she placed a hand on Ling's shoulder. "Do not say or do anything without my permission. These men will not treat us like ladies."

————

The station holding Dabak was more than an hours walk from their home. It wasn't reasonable to make the trek so late. Ling had seen an illustration of the structure once in a history book. It was perched on the side of Kowloon Peak, the namesake of the area. It was a place where mythical stories grew.

Constructed during the Song Dynasty between 900 and 1200 A.D, the structure was older than the surviving stones around the Walled City. It had existed before pursuits by the British crown, back when a primordial mother had blessed the lands and people communicated with animals. Its original purpose was unknown. Now, it was under the ghosts' regime.

In the short distance it took to hail a rickshaw, her mother grilled Ling on the arrest. Ahma must have thought she could ferret out missing pieces in the narrative. She rubbed her knuckles from one end to another. Ling's stomach tensed each time her mother's fingers restarted at her index finger. The truth was weirder than anyone could imagine. By the time an available driver appeared, Ahma's hands were chafed raw.

They sat shoulder-to-shoulder in the cushioned seat while the driver pulled them up the steep slope. Her mother's closeness made Ling smile. Ahma smelled of sweat, sawdust, and grains of rice.

"Remember, I'll give you cues. Otherwise, remain silent. Neither of us need to draw attention to ourselves. I am glad you changed into trousers. These men—even your uncle— don't want what's best for us." Ahma rarely spoke ill of

Dabak. "In this world, men can save a girl or cause her immeasurable suffering. They usually choose the latter."

"Are you speaking about Ba too?" She refused to consider the possibility that her father wasn't decent. Her mother shouldn't speak of him this way. He wasn't there to defend himself.

Ahma's expression dropped. "You would ask such...." She paused, eyeing the back of the driver's head. "I married your father thinking that I had won a prize. He didn't drink, smoke, or gamble. He had a sturdy ship and worked hard. We were set. But something in him turned. He brooded. Talked of grand plans. Sometimes it is not worth it to fantasize about an impossible future. You can dream when you're dead."

"His whereabouts are still unknown," Ling said.

"Yes, your father could come back." Ahma's voice was flat.

The last report had said the ship he'd boarded had sailed out of rough waters, losing a handful of men to sudden storms. But the ship's notes didn't list the names of the missing. This was the reason his wage couldn't be collected.

A bump in the road hurled Ling forward and then back. Her head smacked against the back of the carriage.

"Apologies," the driver said, wiping the top of his head. "Pothole."

"A warning next time." Ahma placed one hand on her chest and patted Ling's knee with the other.

Ling rubbed her sore head. The landscape swiftly changed from ramshackle homes to farmland. The urban clutter melted away. She glanced into the few simple houses along the road. Families were gathered for dinner. She had once done the same with her mother and father. Wafts of garlic spurred her appetite. She pulled out the tin of her uncle's salve and rubbed menthol into the special points.

Good smells could be shielded as much as the rotten ones. The idea of defense sprang to her mind. She pulled a bay leaf from her pocket.

"Ahma, do you want a leaf?"

"What for?" Ahma shot her a suspicious glance.

"Safeguarding," Ling recoiled.

"Where do you get such ideas?" Ahma snatched the waxy leaf from Ling's finger.

She'd thought about suggesting that Ahma rub ointment into phantom points, but her mother's reaction persuaded her to keep the rest of her suggestions quiet. Ling didn't dare mention her father's journal.

Ahma hissed. "Did your uncle have protection when visiting the Lady?"

"Well, he wasn't the...." Ling almost admitted the truth. Her heart skipped. It was better not to speak. Secrets had a habit of slipping from her grasp. "He wasn't about to share that information with me."

"Superstitious nonsense has never worked," Ahma snorted.

As the sky blackened, Ling began to see the top of the armory. The massive structure gazed down upon them with a slight golden glow. Ahma stiffened at the sight of massive stone and wood walls jutting from the earth. An eeriness emanated from the windowless facade.

Ling's skull tingled as the rickshaw slowed to a halt.

"Ready?" Ahma squeezed Ling's hand. "Remember: no extra attention. Make yourself as small as possible."

Ling slid out of the carriage, feeling the foundation tremble under her.

Thirteen

A ringing started in Ling's ear. Like a mosquito, it buzzed around her head. A grating trill of insects and creatures radiated from the dense surrounding jungle. The air was thick.

Ahma paid the driver to remain close by for the return trip. He grunted, keeping his head down, and wheeled the cart to a nearby tree.

She heard voices whispering from the vegetation. As they walked toward the building, Ling applied more salve on her temples.

Ahma threw a suspicious look at the entrance. Rotting wooden boards exposed a layer of stone in the curved entryway. They paused under it. A gas lamp flickered next to the slightly ajar door.

"Dash it, I forgot my scarf," Ahma said, running back to the driver.

Ling tilted her head back, her eyes adjusting to the light. Sand rained down from above. Ling licked her lips, tasting the salty particles. Dust clung thick and heavy on her tongue. She shuddered as her nostrils filled with grime. The scent was faintly reminiscent of the Walled City.

Symbols carved in stone littered the entryway. As she explored the etchings over her head, she was reminded of ancient carvings.

Textbooks had documented the evolution of her language. Tangwa had evolved from unrestricted lines into a strict, yet magical writing form. Her vocabulary had been built one picture at a time.

She traced a bronze script for eye (眼):

"Eye" in ancient bone script.

This picture, paired with a "person," had informed the earliest depiction of "oracle," a being with skills of divination.

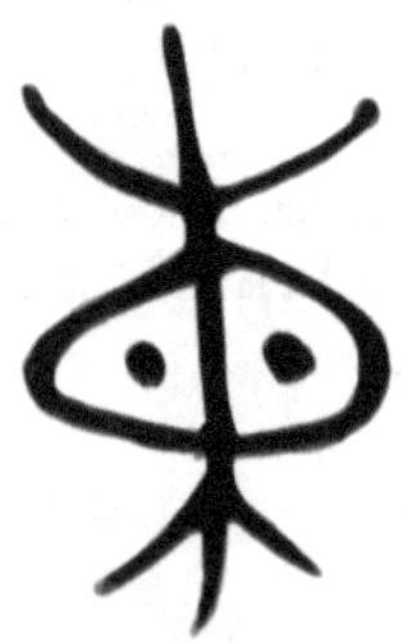

"Oracle" in ancient bone script.

Ling lifted onto her tiptoes. The style of the strokes mirrored the words inked onto her arm. As she brushed her fingers against grooves in the rock face, the images spoke to her.

Thou shalt see.

Ahma hurried back. "Sorry I left you here." Her mother apologized frequently for small things that didn't matter. She passed Ling a reluctant glance before leading her into the building.

The inside was dimly lit by flames. A man in a dark uniform sat behind an elevated desk. He didn't look up.

Ahma craned her neck. "I am here for Dr. Shaw Chi Ming."

Ling stared into the nostrils of the grim-faced man. He scratched a protruding mustache. "And who are you?"

Her mother didn't flinch. "A relative."

"Sit down." He motioned to the bench at the other end of the room. Light from a desk lamp cast shadows on the officer's face, darkening the area under his eyes.

The man jotted something down while rubbing the ends of his thick facial hair. His wrinkles creased deeper. He picked up the receiver and dialed.

"Evening... yes, we loaded the most recent shipment." His eye twitched. "Someone here for Ming."

Ahma perked up, leaning toward the phone.

"A doctor? Uh-huh... it's only one to see him." The light flickered, extenuating his cheekbones, jawline, and whites of his eyes. Ahma didn't react. Had the officer not seen Ling? Testing a theory, she raised her hand and waved. The officer turned his lip but stayed silent. Was it possible that something was obscuring her presence?

Ling was feeling brave, and stepped away from the safety of the bench. Her breath quickened, but she decided to push the limits on an outlandish speculation. She skipped.

Her heels landing on the hard concrete echoed. The officer didn't so much as budge.

Ahma gritted her teeth. "Stop," she gurgled from her throat.

Ling held up a finger, preparing for a grander gesture.

Ahma eyes widened as Ling waved her hands overhead. "Excuse…" Ahma started to scold, but the man at the desk squinted at the bench. Ling rested her hands back at her sides.

For a few minutes, the officer kept staring. Then he yawned, losing interest in the quiet. "Please keep to yourself."

Her mother put her hand to her mouth. The officer had not noticed Ling standing in front of his desk. Silence stirred her insides. She was invisible. For the first time, she enjoyed being unseen. The possibilities were limitless.

However, the danger inside the outpost didn't dissipate. Her senses were put on alert.

She snuck to the side of the podium and caught a glimpse of the officer's shoes. The lamp angled to show off the shiny leather. He reached down to scratch his ankle, exposing a tattooed mark. A set of interlocking eights was inked into his skin. This tattoo gave her pause. It seemed like something she had seen in a book. When he sat up again, she scanned the desk, spotting a pile of letters and envelopes.

The officer still cradled the receiver in his hand. "Unfortunately… the headmaster called earlier…." In response to the person on the other line, he made a ticking sound. "Fine. I counted everything we received, twice. Something smells off." He sniffed the air, turning his nose downward.

This sudden movement raised hairs on Ling's neck. She retreated, not pushing her luck further.

"Lady, you'll see him," he said to Ahma, returning the phone back to the cradle.

As steady as possible, Ling walked to the middle of the corridor. No one stopped her. It felt incredible and utterly impossible. Perhaps there was value to being ignored.

She slowed as she approached a hole in the wall. From the waiting area, her mother frowned after her. Ling decided to keep investigating. From the opening the width of her fist, a light shone out. Her curiosity compelled her to look inside.

She brought her face close to the rock, smelling the corrupted scent of almonds and bananas. What was this scent? Peering in, she identified the outlines of shipping containers. The entire space was filled, but not likely with rotting fruit. The light inside the room was electric. A shadow moved between the boxes, and Ling crouched down. Her body trembled as if she was in front of Lady Tun's shack.

She made herself small. Being discovered seemed more likely than her newfound invisibility. What if the officer was just near-sighted? On the ground, an item shimmered out of the corner of her eye. Ling reached over and picked it up. The item was oblong with a flat bottom. Without enough light, she couldn't identify it. She stashed the thing in her pocket to inspect later.

She got up and ventured further. Around a corner, the corridor sloped downward. The floor turned from concrete to sand. A door at the end of the hallway appeared to lead outside. Two heavy metal rods barred intruders from coming in. This was as far as she could go.

Returning to Ahma's side, she waited with the little patience that remained in her. She maintained a stillness only by reciting poetry about the sea. Then, she counted the wrinkles on her hand. Once, on Ba's ship, a client with many piercings on her ears and face had read the lines on her palm. Hoops on the seer's nose had jiggled when she laughed. The reading predicted that her father would live forever, and then she tattooed identical symbols into father's and daughter's skin. They were bonds that was supposed to last their lifetimes.

"This is a shield," the tattooist had said with intense brown eyes.

Ling often glanced at the circle enclosed by a star on the underside of her arm. What had it protected her from? A triangular mound was drawn on the inside of the curve. When she had first gotten the tattoo, there had been three lines. However, two of the lines had long since faded. She was unsure what the marks meant, but their existence reminded her of her father's expected return. He had to be scheming somewhere, loading his found treasure and almost ready to return home.

After far too long, the doors at the end of the corridor swung open.

"Mrs. Shaw," called a man waving from the area where Ling had snooped. He wore a brown uniform, similar to those of the arresting officers. Ling pinched her mother's arm.

A wind blew through the hall, whistling through the crevices as they walked. Ahma narrowed as the wall sconces flickered. Ling marched behind her mother, examining the rows of symbols along the passageway. The writings were similar to the cave-like drawings over the entryway. White flecks had flaked off the walls, showing a poor attempt to cover up the marks with paint. But the coats couldn't cover what cried from the stones, what pressed out through the many layers of paint.

A stout officer grunted at her mother and led them to a small room. Dabak sat behind a table in middle. Blood stained his collar. His glasses balanced on the bridge of his nose, though they were cracked and crooked now. His legs and arms were shackled by chains.

Not looking up, he said, "You shouldn't have come. Nothing. Do you hear me? Nothing in this material world will help." He turned an inch toward Ling. "I already told you what to do."

Ling's mouth went dry. Ahma didn't know Dabak had left her with two notes.

"Let us maintain civility," said another officer in a raspy voice. Ling recognized this one from the docks. Her face grew hot. This was the man who had thrown disrespectful comments at her uncle.

Ahma thrust herself into the empty seat across from Dabak. She cupped her hands around Dabak's fingers. Ling stood behind her mother.

"Headmaster Lee was adamant that you get to see him, so here you are. Pray, say what you must, for it may be the last time." The officer directed his statements past Ling to Ahma, who held her stoic silence. She didn't even blink.

"Ahhh, another mute," the officer said, before slamming the door.

No one moved, each studying the other's shock. Then Dabak let out an audible sigh. Ling wanted to leap up and hug him. But when she opened her mouth, her mother jabbed an elbow into her side.

"Ohmph," Ling swallowed at the unexpected thrust.

"How are they treating you?" Her mother laid her hands on the table. Dabak did the same.

"As good as any man with false charges." His eyes dulled.

Ling bit her lip.

"The business," Ahma said in the tongue of the ghosts. She glanced sideways at Ling. English wasn't their preferred language. "We hope you are healthy and safe." She elongated the last word. It was an odd way of speaking.

Dabak held out three fingers on one hand.

"I will do my utmost to take care of your customers," Ahma said.

He nodded. "Yes, the fifteen will keep you busy." This was an out-of-place thing to say. There were much more than fifteen customers on any given day. His list of private patients included more than fifty.

Then it dawned on Ling. They were speaking in code.

Ahma and Dabak were playing a clever ruse. She hadn't thought her mother to be so calculating. But she was coming to realize that their whole lives, her family had been hiding things.

Ling stored the numbers in her mind.

3-15

Dabak tapped the table. "It's like what they say about the tea pots. We must have enough lids."

"Always about teas and flowers," Mother smiled, an unexpected display of humor. It was quickly retracted.

Dabak switched to their familiar tongue. "I will be out by the next moon." He used *yut,* the formal verbiage for the moon, as if quoting a Tang poem; this was a longing word. It was also thirty-one days long. "If we're lucky, less than two days."

Ahma lifted her eyebrows. Ling noted the days of this month minus two.

3-15-29

"You can put my house in order." Dabak squeezed Ahma's hand. His face held a scowl, but something sparkled in his eye. Then he lowered his head and whispered words she could barely make out. "We'll be the walking dead... warn others... efforts by the Queen to move against the strike."

Mother's mouth quivered. "How do we know?"

"Everything is here." Dabak shot Ling a knowing look. "*Se galoth nauth.*"

With a sinking feeling, Ling recalled these words. The language from the seaside shack had followed her home. After Lady Tun's death, these guttural phrases were whispered to her. They stuck fast in her mind. How did her uncle know this tongue?

Ahma's eyes grew wide.

"This is how you save us...." Dabak lowered his head to the table. "The rites, *Dho-ur...*" As his mouth twisted, calling syllables from outer worlds, two policemen burst into the room. Ahma backed up against the wall as the smaller officer grimaced.

"No more nonsense." His thin voice frayed at the edges. He was nose-to-nose with Ahma. The officer raised his hand, about to strike. Then his arm shook, suspended, preventing him from bringing down his hand. It was like something held him back. No one moved. The officers both scowled.

"What are you all doing?" The other man in uniform grabbed Dabak. "All right. Let's see how long he lasts."

Dabak screamed. "I am a doctor. Not a scribe."

The officers gnashed their teeth, pushing her uncle out of the room. Ahma and Ling followed them. In the corridor, more officers rushed out from unknown directions.

A random voice shouted at her mother, "If you bring back the Lady's fortunes, then maybe he'll get to leave." In a quick instance, they evicted Ahma out the front door, leaving Ling alone in the hall, apparently still unseen. From what her uncle said, there were still things left for her to find.

Ling watched Dabak disappear down a corridor. The commotion dissipated as others returned to their rooms. Every door was locked. As she passed the empty front desk on her way out, Ling heard Dabak's words again: "Walking dead, efforts against the strike." She eased herself around the counter, examining papers the desk officer had been concentrating on. She rifled through the stack, passing over what looked like shady notes and illegal receipts. She stopped at a cargo boat's manifest, dated a week ago. The name "Jose Da Silvia" and the number "7-1" were scrawled at the top. Ling's stomach dropped. The contents of the delivery turned on a light in her head. Her uncle's message became clear. From foreign lands, weapons had been delivered to Kowloon. Hundreds of sacks of gun powder, rifles, and grenades. Her fingers went to the object in her pocket, which under the lamp was clearly a bullet. After pocketing the manifest, Ling exited the outpost.

Outside, in the dark, Ling put her hand over her heart. Violence had skipped over them. Whether it was the bay leaves or a special force inside the outpost, she understood that she had been aided by something unseen. She held the words Dabak passed on. His hints would save lives, prevent their community from being destroyed. There must be a plan to fight back. The people had to be told about the weapons. Someone had to stop the casualties.

The driver carried a lighted torch. Ahma sniffled as Ling approached. Ahma hugged her hard and then motioned to leave.

They rode home in silence. The movement of the cart brought them a temporary reprieve. Lost in her own thoughts, Ling sunk into her seat. Ahma didn't prod her to speak. There was so much to consider. Ling's mind didn't have enough space to take in the enormity of the next steps. In order for their lives to continue, they couldn't allow the Queen's force to crush the strikers.

Back at home, Ahma and Ling transferred the sleeping twins back to their own beds.

Ahma's face was riddled with worry. There was desperation in her voice. "Ming cannot stay in that awful place. They'll drain him. Those ghosts will have their way."

Her uncle was in a precarious state. Why did the police keep him alive?

"The labor strike is in danger too," Ling said as Ahma closed the bedroom door.

"We can discuss it tomorrow," Ahma said.

Many people would die without action. Their business would evaporate. Their family would lose everything that they worked for. Something had to be done, but it was clear Ahma wouldn't handle the situation.

In the moment, Ling decided she would've to be the one to help. She would hatch a way to free her uncle and prevent a battle that could destroy Kowloon.

FOURTEEN

In the safety of her room, Ling curled up with her father's journal. How could her uncle be freed? She had no clue about the whereabouts of Lady Tun's treasure. Could someone sneak or force themselves into the outpost? The locals couldn't possibly stand up to an armory full of weapons. Questions circled her mind relentlessly:

What would her father do?

That night, she traversed Ba's journal entries. Instead of sleeping, she explored his longings for elsewhere in lines of poetry.

I must go down to the seas again, to the lonely sea and the sky,

And all I ask is a tall ship and a star to steer her by;

And quiet sleep and a sweet dream when the long trick's over.

Having a father was part of a demented dream. Losing a father was common. But she couldn't accept the simple answers. Not every parent was noble. Not every gentleman adhered to a code of morals. What if he had simply chosen not to come back? Was it too hard for him to be responsible for three children? What if she ran to the sea? Sailed her way through life? Maybe she could go with Joseph, like Emma had suggested.

As her body relaxed, something brushed against her ear. She turned to one side, ignoring the crawling sensation down her neck. She grumbled, touching a damp spot on her sheets. Had Gou been in her room? Then she felt cool water dripping onto her shoulders. Dread wormed its way into her stomach. A sliminess slithered down her arm. She opened her eyes slowly, afraid of what she might see.

Dangling from the window was a single eye. She squealed, swatting it to the floor.

From the ground, the purple eyeball gawked at her. Its tentacles were clumped together like roots. It beckoned her closer. It was grotesque, but somehow so... human.

Guilt overwhelmed her. They weren't weird anomalies. The eyes had been a person, part of a whole being.

"Sorry, I panicked," Ling whispered. Would the eyes forgive her for throwing them into the water? Somehow, they would understand.

As soon as she touched the eye, a tingling started at the top of her head. Images came through as droplets, invoking a familiar feeling. She was seeing a vision, except she wasn't sleeping. She was dreaming while awake.

The vision showed her that the eyes had crawled out of the bay, hitched a ride under a cow, and snuck into her room. She was impressed by their fortitude. Why were they so determined to be with her? Why had these eyes picked her? She heard a tapping above. Lifting her chin, she saw the other eye holding a pebble with its veiny tentacles.

"Why did you come back?"

Jak ngan. Her interpretation of her uncle's note shifted. Blindness, not seeing, was the problem and not the solution. Could the eyes help get her uncle out of jail?

She brought them back together and rinsed them in the basin. The eyes didn't shine. Nothing improved when she placed them into the saline. Their color was less vibrant.

Had the polluted bay waters caused their dull state? The eyes sank to the bottom of the jar as Ling formed ideas. The orbs weren't just part of a whole; the pair held complete consciousness by themselves. They seemed to absorb their environment. She hurried to the pantry and searched for ingredients.

When customers complained about lethargy, Dabak checked their retinas. The eyes and tongue were windows into the health of the internal body. Imbalances surfaced as striations on the tongue and stains in the whites of the eyes. When the liver failed to cleanse the body of toxins, the eyes turned yellow. Patients usually took remedies by mouth, inhaled incense smoke, or received needle pricks. Could submerging the eyes in an herbal concoction induce healing? She gathered sun-dried goji berries and chrysanthemum flowers. A tightness converged in her chest.

Depositing the white petals and red berries into the water with the eyes, she watched with urgency. The ingredients floated and then like snowfall dropped to the bottom. The color of the eyes began to brighten.

When she leaned closer, little tentacles shot out from the water. Ling met them with her fingertips. A current of electricity loosened her taut muscles.

She left her physical body. Ling's spirit drifted elsewhere. She was on a rock, with waves lapping at her feet. Lady Tun's shack loomed nearby. A fire raged inside the massive stove. The grasses in the marsh swayed, but Ling felt no breeze on her skin. This was a vision. A much stronger version than before.

When Ling opened her eyes again, she was on the floor in her room. The side of her head throbbed. Rubbing a tender area on her hip, she wobbled back to her feet. She must have blacked out. Where had seen been? Her shoes were drenched. She squinted at the eyes, which had sent her a message. "You want me to go back to the shack?"

The eyes bobbed up and down, churning in the medicinal soak. If eyes could be elated, this was it. The irises flashed a brilliant purple.

After changing into dry socks, she packed the eyes in her bag. She also gathered a candle, matches, a knife, bay leaves, and Dabak's protective salve. Flipping out of the window like a fish gasping on the deck of a boat, she took note of the time. An hour past midnight. Another sleepless night. Distracted, she failed to pay attention to the uneven pavement. When she landed, her ankle rolled. She winced, muffling a cry. Inconvenient at best. Discomfort couldn't stop her from following through.

The possibility of losing her uncle made her feel like there were tiny fish bones trapped in her windpipe. Life without Dabak would be bleak. She had worked at the store for years. Customers might not return at all without the doctor on call. There was only so much Ling could do before medical school. Could their family support her while she pursued higher education? Did the officers really believe her uncle killed Lady Tun? She knew she couldn't confess the details about the murderer. With the ghosts, truth and justice were blurred. She had to prioritize her freedom over any superficial idea of fairness. After all, life was inherently unjust for the people in Kowloon.

She clawed at irritation in her throat, walking under a streetlight on the main road.

"Why must we keep meeting in the most awkward ways?" The familiarity of the voice distressed her.

When Ling looked up, Enlai stood under the glow. She slouched. There was no escaping him now.

"Perhaps we should not ever be meeting."

"Better to be with me than Brother Tam." He turned his lips into a frown. The top buttons of his shirt were undone, exposing a gold chain.

She recoiled. Unfortunately, this time she wasn't invisible.

Enlai pushed his hair to one side. "He took a liking to you, but I told him we are together. I am a better choice. Unless...." His dark eyes pierced hers.

She stared back.

Enlai obliged her to him. Even love for her wasn't a choice. How had Brother Tam garnered power in her life? She backed up. "If it is decided, then I'll be on my way." She moved sideways, gripping the bag.

Enlai expanded his chest. He towered two heads over her, no longer the skinny boy who she had once battled with marbles. "In the middle of the night? Only certain types of ladies roam the streets at this hour. It will be safer if I go with you."

"No, absolutely not," Ling said, preferring not to explain her movements to a thief. "I do not need help."

His face fell. His voice lowered. "Everyone needs help. You helped me."

She tried to keep her voice even. "If you want to assist, then move out of my way."

"I just want to be friends again." Enlai opened his arms and motioned for an embrace. "I am in a better position, do you not see?"

"Then return my father's compass." Ling backed away, holding her hands out in a preemptive block.

Enlai's mouth twisted. "Was it not enough that I thanked you? Your father doesn't need it, and eventually, I'll get it back. It was an initiation present for my *Luo Ban*. But one day."

The idea of him using her father's Royal Navy compass as a gift to the Red Society's leader infuriated her. Ling fumed at the insult. "You benefit at my expense." Tears welled in her eyes.

She could see Enlai thinking about saying those hurtful words.

"Do not say it," she warned him.

"Why must you deny it? He's dead." The statement came so casually.

Red flashed across her vision. Certainly, she had considered her father's death somewhere on the Pacific Ocean. But this wasn't for Enlai to dictate. She insisted on controlling her own thoughts. She rushed up to him, then stomped on his foot and elbowed him in the gut, knocking the wind out of him. Then, she ran.

But he was fast. He grabbed her wrist before she went far. "Caught me off guard."

"You have new friends. Leave me alone." She struggled against his hold. Her bag bumped against his stomach.

He chuckled. "With your dad and uncle out of commission, I can be your guide. Like Confucius says.... Trust your husband, father, brother, and then son. You need a man."

Ling clenched her fists. Her father's disappearance and Dabak's detention made her sick. She was losing the people she loved most. People who believed in her autonomy. "I'll get my uncle out."

"I can do a lot for you. Trust me." His smile didn't match the desperation in his eyes. Curiosity crossed his face as he pried the bag from her hands. "What is this?"

"Stop stealing from me." Her fingers held on as tight as she could.

"Relax." He yanked the sack from her shoulder and rummaged in the pockets.

"Hands off." Ling felt helpless. "You've always been

greedy, ever since we were kids," she said, trembling with rage. Back then, when he had coveted her shiny marbles, she'd let him have them. Back in the day, she hadn't understood character. "Why bother me? I do not have anything."

"Trust me," he whispered, untucking the towel around the container.

"Do not look," she softened her tone. This secret was one she couldn't share.

Under the light, his expression froze. "What are these?"

His eyes filled with terror. The sight of the jar conveyed what Ling's words and blows could not. Enlai threw the jar into the air and ran in the opposite direction.

Ling dove for the eyes, crashing into a bag of garbage. By some miracle, the jar hadn't cracked. Limping into the shadows, Ling picked food scraps off of her coat and steadied her nerves. Why had Enlai acted so punishing towards her? The eyes glowed. Why did she endanger her life for random body parts? Her first priority needed to be protecting her family, not exploring strange visions.

She unscrewed the lid and asked, "Why am I going back?"

Instead of a vision this time, the eyes transferred words. The other worldly phrase spoken by Dabak at the outpost. *Dho-ur* conjured dark images. Venomous plants and rotting innards, parts of plants, and animals that couldn't heal. The words Dabak had spoken earlier were the title of a text. It didn't seem like the sort of book she wanted to read.

"Where would I get such a thing?" she asked.

The eyes didn't respond.

Could it be in Lady Tun's library? The small chance that she might unearth this volume was enough to continue on. Dabak wouldn't lead her in the wrong direction. Would he?

Fifteen

Ling fumbled her way from the marsh to the shack. The murder had altered the seaside. Two nights after the full moon, shadows loomed longer and thinner over the way back. A blanket of fog entombed the heaviness in the bay, blocking the breeze. Muddled noises and smells floated down from the Walled City. An eerie quiet had settled over the peninsula, as if everything was dead.

A dark circle marked where Lady Tun had fallen. The congealed blood appeared like a hole to an unknown netherland. If Ling stumbled, then she would fall into an abyss and never find her way back out.

The door was ajar. The one-room house had been ransacked—shelves toppled, chairs overturned, and floors dug up. In the ruins, the ghost of a presence loomed. A black metal door stood next to a fireplace. There were no more treats to be found here. The stale stench of loss spiced the air.

Why did the eyes beckon Ling to return? There was no treasure. This hermit woman had no treasures in her shack. Ling questioned what she remembered from the night before. Lady Tun had lived before her mother was born. Yet, the ghost had appeared young, not like the frail old lady she ought to be. Had the moonlight played tricks on Ling?

She located an unbroken lamp and lit it with one of her matches. A glow spread into the cluttered space, illuminating ripped curtains, holes bashed into the walls, and a pile of books. Lady Tun's mattress was torn and stained. Next to a cold fireplace, a large steel door was shut tight. She scanned the jumbled texts, attempting to locate out-of-place letters and words. An eeriness emitted from a flipped over wooden chair in front of the charred fireplace. The blood coated legs echoed the violence of the past. Had the figure killed someone else too? Fear spiked in her stomach. She desperately wanted to sprint home but waited for the feeling to pass.

Her bag wiggled. *Splat.* A curious squishing sound rebounded against the walls as if someone was walking in wet shoes. The eyes had escaped from the jar. Saline liquid spilled down her pant leg. Ling frowned. Had she not tightened the lid?

Crouching, Ling cursed at herself for heeding the eyes. Alone in the middle of the dark room, she wondered what she was doing here. A metallic clanking sounded, from the door, drawing her attention. What could be inside?

She had a knot in her throat, but she still walked closer. Soot and grime caked the door. The door handle felt warm under her fingers. She hesitated at looking inside. Hadn't she seen enough horrible acts in this lifetime? But when she looked down, something sparked her interest. A small bow laid at the threshold of the oven. The accessory must have belonged to a little girl. Could someone be inside? She placed her hand on the door handle. She knew this wasn't a good idea. But she pulled down against her better judgement. The hinges creaked.

"Hello?" Her quavering greeting echoed dully into an iron-walled space. Did the owner of the purple eyes sit behind the door? A rancid smell assaulted her senses. It was a mixture of ash and burnt flesh. Ling plugged her nose, wishing she hadn't chased her curiosity. Some animal had indeed been cooked in here.

Escaping outside from the horrible stench, she realized that the eyes had wandered off. Wet lines marked their path, showing that the eyes had slithered toward the cliff. Leaning over the rocks, she searched the descent. The water had receded, exposing the boulders below. Ling lowered herself to the sandy bottom, trying to ignore the soreness of her injured foot.

She found the eyes perched on a rock covered in algae, beckoning Ling with their tentacles. When the tip of her finger touched the veins waving in the air, a message appeared in her mind: *Move down the path*. Ling cradled the eyes in a fold of her skirt while walking down the wet sand. Turning a corner, she found the mouth of a cave. She stopped and asked the eyes another question: "Why am I here?"

Suddenly, she was somewhere else. Her vision dangled, swaying back and forth. Shadows formed at edges of her vision, and she was looking into a dark room with different eyes. The glow from a hearth highlighted an empty chair, a dirt floor covered in fresh straw, and a table piled with cut onions and carrots. A long mirror hung over the fireplace, coated in ash and yellowed at the edges. Questions rang loud inside her mind.

It was obvious Ling wasn't herself. She attempted to move a limb, but nothing shifted. A gust of wind swayed her back and forth like a swing. She saw trinkets hung around the front doorframe: straw figures, dried herbs, and forbidden symbols. On the next push, her form was launched high. She glimpsed a fisherman's knot that attached her to a ceiling beam. A willowy woman entered, carrying a silver bowl filled with water. The hem of a velvet dress dragged behind.

From Ling's point of view, hanging from above, she could only see the woman's dark hair. A crown of mud and branches rested on top of her head. Brown sludge dripped from her face down her sharp nose. She moved with grand gestures, preparing the small space. Placing the bowl by the chair, she lit dried herbs and draped the seat with the white smoke. Ling had seen this ritual. It was for blessing a living creature before its sacrifice. Haze filled the room while the woman struggled with something large at the edge of Ling's vision. A pig or a baby cow? The space was too cramped for anything full-grown.

Ling tried to move, but she had no limbs, body, or mouth. She could only watch as the scene unfolded beneath.

The woman lumbered back into view, dragging the body of a human. As the white cloud dissipated, the body's head rolled from side to side, revealing the features of a girl with the symbol for "oracle" branded on her forehead. This must be an apprentice. No young person bore this mark without initiation. It wasn't a symbol to trifle with. The girl's eyes fluttered as the older woman hoisted her flaccid body into the chair and secured her with a rope.

The jagged reflection of the woman's blackened smile made Ling think of Lady Tun. With an eyeless face under the moonlight, choking on a mouthful of petals. Was this the living version of Lady Tun?

With one knobby-fingered hand, the woman pulled back the girl's head. She read from an illustrated book. Red symbols on its cover showed a set of interlocking eights. It was the sigil tattooed on the outpost officer's leg.

Wake up, Ling wanted to scream at the girl. Spots

dotted her vision. She wanted nothing more than to fall from the beam and disrupt what was going on below.

The woman inched a blade toward the unconscious girl's eye, piercing the soft flesh like gelatin. The cuts were precise. Blood spilled down the young girl's cheek, gathering in pools on the hay-covered floor.

The splotches obstructing Ling's view expanded. The world shook. Her vision went black.

Ling put her hand to her chest. She was back, whole again. The girl in the vision had a soft face and seemed close in age to Kit and Gou. This communication from the eyes puzzled her. Did they know the dead girl? The eyes weighed heavier in her skirt.

She walked under the rocky roof and examined the salt-eaten walls. Was she looking for something specific, a path or a rope? Wind and water from the tunnel began to churn more loudly. Ling panicked. Did she have enough time before the tide rolled in? She stared into the horizon. The water had risen since her arrival, but luckily, low tide should last for a few more hours.

She surveyed the entrance. The darkness went deeper than the light extended. The tunnel narrowed quickly to a hole no bigger than her body. She crouched. A draft blew from the entrance, telling her the other side was close. What could be hidden down the way? The eyes shone brightly, cheering her onwards.

Limping a short distance before getting down on her knees, she secured the eyes in her bag. Soon, the narrowing walls forced her to start crawling on her forearms. She pulled herself over the barnacled rocks. Her front was soaked. Sharp edges nipped at her skin. Ling ignored the burning in her wounds from the salted water. Small critters brushed against her face. She endured them as best she could until a spider skittered across her forehead. She screamed at the unwanted sensation.

About ten body-lengths later, nearly a lifetime, the lantern went out. A final glow flashed, like the fire was taking one last breath. She struggled to dig through her bag and pulled out the eyes again. Their glow wasn't enough. Tears gathered in her eyes. She had a choice: move forward or go back. Hesitation would be fatal, with the rising tide.

Going backward would take longer. She pushed up hard. Exhaustion overwhelmed her. Never in her life had she felt so beaten. The eyes pushed against her, coaxing Ling to continue on.

Finally, a breeze hit her face. Her eyes sprang open. A strong scent of grass lured her forward. Moonlight spurred her forward to the edge of the passageway. Here in the middle of the cave, the moonlight pooled on the floor. Water trickled from above. It was a relief.

Tucking her legs, Ling swung around to stand. She sighed. A buoyancy circulated the cave, like she was submerged in a thick liquid. Wooden crates were stacked around the edges of the room. Nothing was marked; there were no drawings or writings to indicate any information about her find. Her thoughts turned to Lady Tun's treasure.

Each box was nailed firmly shut. The blade of her pocketknife wasn't strong enough to pry open the tops. She concluded that she needed a crowbar, and another person to move the assumed valuables inside. Emma would've never made it through the tunnel. Enlai would agree. But could she trust him around these found fortunes?

She scrutinized the walls and found a boarded up doorframe hidden behind the heavy containers. The ground sloped downward with the edges rising up high, keeping most of the crates out of the water. On another wall, some stone had been chipped away. She pressed into the attached boards. The nails had rusted, and the wood bent easily under her fingers. She punched into the waterlogged panels. As the planks crumbled, multicolored lights seeped out from the fractures. Ling grinned. With a few more blows, a shelf of miraculous items emerged.

The sight struck her dumb. It was a whole collection of eyes. There were eight or so pairs, floating in decorated jars. She inspected a red set, running her fingers over stone vines wrapping around the thick glass. Ling's heart sank. Most of the eyes were even smaller than the ones that followed her. Every colored iris represented a family that had lost the whereabouts of a loved one.

"Who are your friends?" Ling's question echoed as she exchanged the fiery eyes for a saffron pair. None of the eyes responded to her proximity except for a pair of jade ones. She picked up the jar and inspected the bottom, finding the initials WML underneath.

"Where is the vessel for you?" Ling searched the cave for the purple eyes. She spotted them on a nearby ledge. Also on the shelf, she noticed a bundle of letters wrapped in water-proof oilcloth. She pulled the package out from behind the jars. Water was rising steadily at the lowest point of the cave. She realized that she had to make a quick choice: leave at once or stay here for the rest of the morning.

"I'll be back," she promised the suspended orbs. Relighting the flame in the lantern, she started the journey back to the other side, the package tucked in her tunic. There was much more work to decipher clues from the eyes and their vision. The letters from the cave could be the key to unlocking the details of Lady Tun's murder.

Sixteen

L ing knocked on her own front door. She was wet and cold. Her hands were cut from climbing back up the jagged rocks. Thinking about morning congee, she rapped again. No one answered. There was also no smell of tea or rice. That was odd.

She tried the door. It was open. Ahma had already removed the padlocks and left with her brothers, leaving a message for Ling:

Please see Aunt Marcella. She needs her medicine. I went to seek advice.

Wish me luck,

Your mother.

Help in Kowloon came in two ways: the temple Hau Wang Miu or an oracle. Ling had a sick feeling about the choice her mother would've made. Ahma didn't believe in prayer. She described fortune tellers as sneaky salesmen. Monsters were fantasy. Requests to the walled-city oracle required great sacrifices. She hoped her mother wouldn't do anything rash.

Aunt Marcella had been alone since Dabak's arrest. She

had assumed Dabak and her aunt had hired help for their extra needs. Marcella was, after all, related to the family's long-time friend, Lord Charles Langley.

Ling scribbled a reply. *I'll be back by eight.*

While packing books and herbs for the trip across the bay, she belatedly remembered her promise to meet Emma in the school library. If she hurried, she could stop by the library and still make the morning ferry to the island.

———

The third-floor library had a side entrance into the school. It had been converted from the personal chambers of Father Superior to the only English dedicated library in Kowloon. Ling slipped through the unassuming door. Luckily, Sister Winters was not in the rocking chair. However, a tea pot was steeping near her desk, so she could not be far.

Inside, two stories were encircled by a high ceiling rotunda. It was a grand room that Ling couldn't imagine had once been the personal space for a priest. A winding staircase cut into the ceiling of the languages classroom below, so naturally, students came and went before and after Sister Maggie's discussion on the portrayal of morality and British society in modern writings. Dickens, Hardy, and Stevenson books populated the large table on the bottom floor. It was empty now, before the first school bells rang.

Ling found Emma huddled in the row next to the rare books section. A "No Admittance" sign hung across two rows. Looking over the balcony, Ling had a clear vantage point of the empty rocking chair. Even though the sister could see everything, she couldn't monitor everything all at once. When she was distracted by other students, one could rearrange the books or hide away a dirty comic for others to find without her noticing.

Emma leapt to her feet. "I thought you were indisposed!"

Ling didn't admit to nearly forgetting their meeting. "I'm visiting the island after this. My aunt is ill."

"I pray she gets well soon." The side of Emma's face sloped downward. "Can I go with you?"

"Not this time. She's been sick and is getting worse." Ling touched the spines of the biology and botany texts in the aisle.

Emma knit her brow. "Then why do you have to go during school? Cannot a servant visit her?"

"Helpers might not understand how to prepare the medicine she needs. Normally, my...." Ling stopped herself, hoping Emma wouldn't ask about the arrest.

"What is it?" Emma always caught Ling's hesitations.

Ling looked down at the door, confirming Sister Winters hadn't returned, then whispered, "My uncle was arrested last night."

Emma sucked in a breath. "What for?" Her brow wrinkled with concern.

Ling licked her lips. How did she want to describe what had happened? Murder was a harsh term reserved for criminals and thugs. "A misunderstanding."

Emma tilted her head. "Come on now. If your uncle is innocent, then why did they arrest him? The police would not arrest a gentleman over a misunderstanding."

Ling knew that they certainly would, which was the main difference between her life and that of her best friend. In Emma's world, everything happened for a reason, for a benefit, while inexplicable tragedy had set Ling back over and over again. The world had tested Ling's resolve and ability to turn sour hawthorns into medicines. Ling didn't want to explain the tense relationship between the Royal

Police and local residents. Emma must not know about the strikes either.

"The authorities said he murdered someone. But he did not." She was far more guilty than her uncle, but that wasn't an idea to share. Anyone could overhear and go to the teachers.

Emma's posture shot up. "What? Who?"

"He did not do it." Ling bit her lip.

Her friend's eye grew wide. "How do you know?"

"I... cannot say." Her confession dangled from the tip of her tongue.

Emma leaned closer. "Miss Ling Tang. You must."

Ling sank into the wooden floor. "I have not told anyone."

"I am not anyone." Emma touched Ling's wrist.

"Fine. I witnessed Lady Tun's... death by...."

Emma blinked. "Who's Lady Tun?"

"I do not know her real name. She lived on the peninsula." Ling looked down at her hands, afraid of what truths Emma might glean from her expression.

"When did you go all the way out there?" Emma lived up in a gorgeous house with a view of the ocean, from which she wasn't allowed to venture far. Kowloon was too wild for a genteel woman.

"On the full moon. Two nights ago," Ling continued.

"Why? Never mind. Annie is related to her. The girl in the other class with the Portuguese accent. Lady Tun, as you call her, is in fact a Lady from England. I think she said the relationship was estranged." Emma's voice perked up.

Ling was startled. Where on Earth did Emma hear such things? She seemed to gather up details in every conversation. She had insight into different sides of arguments. Ling didn't want to be another piece for her friend to collect. "I will not say more. I don't want people to know about my family problems."

This wasn't a problem to be solved. Did Ling really want to know Lady Tun's real identity? Would it stoke more chaos?

"They will not hear it from me." Arrogance seeped into Emma's voice.

"This is not a game. There are consequences to taking the wrong steps." She hated to be reprimanding Emma. Ling clenched her jaw.

Emma noticed Ling's concern. "I am so sorry. I will not do anything unless you want me to." She hung her head.

"I am not frustrated at you. I visited my uncle at the police outpost. The police are up to something. My uncle made it clear something bad is going to happen to those involved in the labor strikes."

"You went to the police station?" Emma asked.

"Not the one in town. He's being held at the outpost up the mountain." Ling was reluctant to share more. Emma already knew too much.

"Do not worry. My father is a lawyer..." Emma put a finger to her mouth. "Wait, then who killed Lady Tun?"

The mysterious figure flashed in Ling's mind. How could she accurately describe its ashen face and bald head. "It wore a jacket. Kind of like...." She scratched her chin, struggling with how to describe it.

"Draw it." Emma pulled her notebook out of her bag and flipped open to a blank page. "Here."

Ling sketched a form in long coat with golden studs. She took a deep breath. Sharing her secret felt better. Saying the words out loud relieved a heaviness in her chest. The situation seemed less hopeless somehow. Enlai was right; everyone needed assistance from time to time. She kept moving the pencil, trying to match the images inside her head to the page.

"I have seen that somewhere... keep drawing." Emma scooted out of the row and turned left in the direction of the rare books. Returning as quickly as she had left, she bumped a manuscript against Ling's arm. The text had a fine leather cover decorated with floral gilt. "This is an instruction manual from the Order of Leopold, a remote monastery in Romania."

Ling touched the grooves in the leather. Her eyebrows knotted in confusion. "Where did you get this?"

Emma smirked. "Out of bounds, in the no admittance section. But I swear the sisters set this whole thing up to entice students to read otherwise uninteresting books. I study them more than I should."

"This whole school is a kind of mad experiment."

Emma exploded in laughter before catching herself. "Oh, sorry. Sister Winters probably heard that."

Ling flipped through the handwritten words on pages of linen. She stopped at a picture.

"This coat"—Emma pointed to the opened page— "is similar to your drawing. It's a uniform for the hunters of the undead."

"A priest's uniform?" Ling hadn't seen one single holy man at mass wear anything militant. In Latin, the book described the long coat as a special type of armor. The leather was stretched and made with dyes blessed by the Pope. Each of the studs were copper, deadly for monsters listed on the following page: demons, werewolves, necromancers. Other peculiarities of the attire were encoded in mystery.

"No, a monster hunter. The book orients newcomers to the monastery, which has a mandate to eliminate supernatural beings."

According to this book, monsters did exist. This meant Ling's sanity was still intact.

"Who is up there?" Sister Winters had somehow climbed up from the classroom without the girls hearing. With one hand on her desk and the other gripping the cross on her necklace, she wheezed after her rapid ascent. "The hour for lessons is fast approaching."

Emma tapped the book. "Take it with you," she said in a sneaky undertone. "The school will not notice someone borrowed it. The books in the restricted section are gathering dust. I can distract the Sister, and you sneak out the side door at my signal." She pecked Ling on the cheek. "Listen for the word countryside.'" Emma hurried away before the nun could notice Ling.

Ling's face warmed as she squeezed the delicate cover. The information it held seemed enormously important, but she couldn't bear to remove it without permission. The book didn't belong to her, so she wasn't entitled to its contents.

"It is I, Emma. Good morning, Sister."

Sister Winters didn't look up, pouring tea into a mug.

Leaning over the wrought-iron railing, Emma asked in her loudest voice, "Sister, where can I find *Lives of the Saints*?"

She referenced a compendium of stories meant to inspire a pure and moral life.

Sister Winters nodded as Ling crouched down, waiting for the right words.

"Emma, I did not know it was you," Sister Winters replied. "The volumes are over here. I cannot tell you what a joy it is to hear you asking for it. You are the exact student I knew would enjoy those stories. Now, which one?"

Emma smiled up at Ling and disappeared under the stairs. "Which one do you recommend? I quite enjoyed your reading about the Bulgarian Empire. I love the *countryside* references." Emma proclaimed the last words in a loud, clear voice.

Ling hustled down the stairs and out the side door, taking a quick glance at Sister Winters and Emma. Her friend, ever so slightly, winked. Emma could fend for herself well in a conversation about martyrs and the path to sainthood.

A trip to Hong Kong was exactly what Ling needed to clear her mind. She hadn't seen her aunt in a very long time. Boarding the 9:30 a.m. British Canton commuter line, she pondered the idea of monster hunters. How could she contact them for help? The ship would traverse the bay in less than hour, stopping at several locations before arriving at her destination, Connaught Road. She had a lot to read, and this would be ample time to gather her thoughts.

As the boat pulled away from the docks, her long skirt swayed. The air weighed heavy. She could see the shops from the boat, and she half-expected her uncle to open the tarp to the store and smile at her. Ling waved anyway to the thought of him.

Sitting down, Ling shuffled through the papers from the cave. Their wrappings hadn't protected them well. Moisture had destroyed most of the correspondence, which was between Lady Tun and someone named Lord Eggers. Out of nearly thirty letters, Ling could only read three. She tried hard to decipher the smeared and faded words, squinting and angling the paper in the light. It gave her a headache.

Lord Eggers had attempted to persuade Lady Tun to return to England. He didn't understand her obsession with the small island colony, writing in a reply: *How do barbaric lands provide for you? Our estate is ten-fold.* Their conversation went back and forth. Responses filled the margins.

Stepson,

I am happy with my improvements. Englishmen speak of burning witches. There is no such crusade here to purify women. Colonies are plentiful in their land—and people.

Knowing Lady Tun's demands to Dr. Shaw, this made Ling's stomach churn. Was her collection of children's eyes for pleasure or health? What medicinal value did eyes carry? Ingesting the eyes of steamed fish were common for supplementing vision. Yet, the shop didn't carry eyes from any animal as a remedy. She wondered if she was missing knowledge that might be found in the annals of the *Bencao Gangmu*.

Ling chided herself. *Don't be judgmental.* When she was ten years old, a *mantou* dipped in human blood had cured her of consumption. The creepy melody of the twins' song about the blind mice slid into her thoughts. Its eerie rhyme spoke another truth, where "they have no eyes" replaced "see how they run." She couldn't ignore the difference, but didn't know what the change meant.

Halfway between Kowloon and the island, the boat jostled. The letters tumbled from Ling's lap, scattering onto the floor of the cabin.

"Hold onto the rails!" the captain called into the hull. She crouched, thrashing against the seats and ground. Battling with her balance and the rocking motion of the vessel, she scrambled to collect the papers one by one. The other passengers shouted at her all the while.

"Come on, girl!"

"Stop messing around!"

"Are you mad?"

When she had salvaged each note, she apologized for the commotion. The crinkled letters must've looked like rubbish to everyone else. As she reorganized the stack, she caught a name at the bottom of a nearly illegible letter.

Lady Winnifred Eggers.

Lady Tun had signed her real name. She couldn't wait to tell Emma.

For the remainder of the voyage, Ling rested. The wooden seats were hard, but she was too exhausted to care. Seagulls cawed and fish splashed along the hull as she recited her father's favorite poems:

The tide rises, the tide falls
The twilight darkness, the curlew calls.
Along the sea-sands damp and brown
The traveler hastens toward town,
And the tide rises, the tide falls

The waves soothed her. Despite her actions, worries, and neglects, the tides rose and fell. Regardless of the doings of others, the world always carried on. But that didn't mean life had to remain in a status quo.

Ideas could change.

Vileness could be exposed.

Justice could be served.

SEVENTEEN

April 1923
The Guianas

As the nights grew longer on the island, Xie grew bolder. The sun now burned his skin. Existing alone had diminished him, torn out his ambitions and mauled his spirit. He wasn't even sure who or what he was anymore. His nocturnal existence made him feel between worlds.

Once, he was in the light. The lines on his hands and cuts on his legs proved he had toiled. The tattoo under his arm meant protection. He often touched the runes before he could fall asleep.

During an unbearable night, he dreamed of a woman with braided hair and caramel skin. They were on a ship, holding hands. She stroked his cheeks as winds whipped the sails and dark waters flooded the deck.

Over the roar of the waves, he cried, "I don't know where I am. Who are you? Please." He tightened his grip. Monstrous waves lifted the boat. His consciousness wavered.

You will find the way, she said in a glance. Her weight pulled him forward. His nails dug into the back of her hands. Her reassurance tightened the knot in his stomach. His shoulders knocked against the rails so hard he let go. He held fast onto his companion. Gritting his teeth, the ocean disintegrated his resolve. No matter his determination, the woman slipped away.

Carry the moonlit flowers back home. She smiled as she slipped away.

He scrambled and grasped at nothing. "Come back!"

She had disappeared into the sea. In truth, he wanted to be the one called into the ways. To let go of his forgotten life and go after his lost friend would be a blessing. As the rain beat against his body, the boat creaked and groaned. He tried in vain to remember the woman's name. In the turmoil of the storm, the memory did not return.

"Release me! Why did you not kill me?" he screamed with all his might.

From his home to the island to scavenging for plants, he had many chances to die. Why this punishment? Life was suffering. Only the immenseness of the sea stared back.

When he awoke, Xie was on dry land. The nightmare had jolted his memory. The braided woman had once told him: *Xie, you will never die.*

In the quiet night, whispers replaced the past. But the eerie divination stirred inside his heart. Even while strange voices called him by new names, he held on fast. Huddled along the riverbanks, he rejected their desires. He demanded that the shadows leave him alone, but they laughed.

You are one of us. Nobody else can help you.

Xie covered his ears. This wasn't the woman. In his broken heart, he knew there was something sweeter than this. He was more than this land surrounded by water. More than what the shadows told him he was. He wasn't a monster. Although, he did feel like one, because his teeth didn't quite fit into his mouth.

While the scars on his arms had healed, his nose felt bulbous and out of place. A cut over his heart was a reminder of his curse. Would the creatures return to finish the task?

While roaming, he learned the lands. He picked flowers in meadows, cooled off in the streams, and napped under the trees. He discovered more plants to cure his stomach ills, warm his chills, and sooth his dried skin. Leaves scented in peppermint with a licorice taste brought back a spattering of memories. At night, he cultivated the moonflowers. Their iridescent petals were his only pleasure. According to his dream, they would help take him off this island.

One day, he heard the braided woman's voice again, carried upon a noreasterly wind. Wrapping him in a sheath of warmth, it whispered a message about his previous life.

"Do you remember me?" Xie spoke toward the dimming sky.

You were once at the helm of a ship. A master of the stars. A husband and father.

Xie smiled. The flesh under his eyes thawed. He wanted to believe the beautiful ideas.

You can have it again.

The words sparked a flame inside his heart.

Steal onto a ship. Convince the owners in the big house that you're a medicine man. Cure the blood disease on the island with the flowers. Stop the ones feasting on human flesh.

"Are these the creatures who did this to me?" He touched the darkened scar across his chest.

They turned you into one of their kind. But have not enticed you to accept the change. You have the courage to remain yourself.

The wind lessened, and the song faded.

"How will I stop them?" Xie's breath quickened. He ran in every direction, grasping at the elusive visitor.

You will know, medicine man.

Your little one will show you.

Eighteen

She was the only passenger to disembark for Connaught Road at the Eastern Street Pier. Having her feet on dry land steadied her again. Only then did she appreciate the warmth of the sun on her skin.

Dabak's residence was up the road past the Western markets. The streets were sparsely populated here, without vendors hawking savory congee, sugar-covered fruit, and molasses crackers. They too had fled North, in solidarity with the workers' strike.

As she huffed up the steep hill, Ling repeated the code she'd heard at the police station to herself. At the halfway point while crossing Taiping Shan Street, she spotted the terrace of her uncle's apartment, which overlooked Blake Gardens. The lush expanse of greenery had been built over razed slums, where many had died of the last ghost plague.

Arriving at her former abode, Ling rang the third-floor bell. She hadn't been worried until she reached the apartment door. What was the state of her aunt? After the sixth ring, sweat from the humidity drenched her blouse and her heart was racing. She ran to the other side of the road, which was elevated and could see into the first floor. Maybe she could get someone else's attention.

"Mrs. Brown, over here!" she shouted at the terraces, hoping one of the residents would hear her. Otherwise, she might have to wait until someone arrived home or even attempt a dangerous climb up the wrought-iron rails.

A few minutes later, a white-haired woman poked her head over the first-floor balcony. "Are you the niece?"

Ling nodded. "My aunt is ill."

The lady coughed and held up her hand, then disappeared inside.

Ling twisted her ponytail.

After a short delay, the gate unlocked. "Here you go, Miss," said a boy wearing suspenders. He propped open the entrance while he stared at her with his deep jade-colored eyes. As she walked toward the door, he started to sing:

Three blind mice.

They have no eyes.

Ling's ears perked up. The lyrics were the same as twins' nursery rhyme. She stopped short of the steps, watching the boy's face grow duller with each verse.

They ran away from the soldier's wife.

Who gouged their eyes with a carving knife.

Her mind tingled. When Ling took a step forward, the boy stopped.

"Wait, can I...."

Before she could finish her question, he ran up the stairs. She caught the door before it closed, watching the boy's golden hair bouncing on top of his head. The sight of him drew her mind back to the eyes inside the cave.

Inside, her footsteps echoed as she walked. She gripped the cold, iron banister. The marble walls cooled the building by at least ten degrees. At her uncle's apartment, she turned the knob instead of knocking. The door opened to an unlit entryway.

"Aunt Marcella, are you here?" Her voice reverberated through the empty hallway.

Ling had expected the smell of roses, lavender, or fresh-baked cookies. Instead, an ominously stale scent had settled over the apartment. Her eyes narrowed. She flung open the curtains in the sitting room and swung open the windows. Her ragged breaths slowed as sun flooded into the sitting room. The light pushed out the dampness and terrible smells. Goosebumps riddled her arms as she proceeded to the next space, continuing to bring in fresh air. When she didn't see Aunt Marcella in the bedroom, possibilities raced through Ling's mind. Had she gone somewhere else? Had she been rushed to the hospital?

Returning to the sitting room, Ling searched for clues of her aunt's whereabouts with increasing alarm. Dirty clothes and papers were scattered about the ground. Books lay open. Ashes were heaped in the fireplace. Winter coats rested crumpled on the floor like slumbering animals. It was clear little cleaning had been done since the last cold spell more than four months ago. Dabak was Aunt Marcella's primary caretaker, and it appeared he needed assistance. Ling searched for the telephone wire, hoping to find the receiver to call for assistance.

As she tugged on the thick insulated wire, a groan shook from underneath a quilt. Ling jumped back, dropping the cord. Aunt Marcella peered from a pile of linens. Normally a head taller than Dabak, she seemed impossibly shrunken behind the paisley squares. Hair was matted onto her face. From under the blanket, a blackened finger stuck out.

Ling didn't move. She didn't understand the illness. What if it was contagious? "It's your niece. Are you well?" She didn't intend to embarrass her further.

A gurgle escaped her aunt's mouth. "Closer?" She shifted under the sheets, exposing more charred appendages. "I am under the weather."

A fetid stench of spoiled rice and dead fish, smells which blew in at low tide, assaulted Ling. Part of her mind tried to diagnose the odor, to align it with a condition she could understand.

Ling pinched her nose. "Can I help?" She was confused by her aunt's aged look. Had illness morphed Aunt Marcella, a healthy twenty-nine-year-old, into this feeble patient?

"Medicine. I need..." Aunt Marcella wheezed. She squinted from behind her stringy hair. Ling could have sworn that her aunt's eyes were black, hollowed of all emotion. "Everything hurts. The light burns."

A ringing started in Ling's ear, so she backed away. Her aunt was in pain. Dabak treated ailments with needles and plants. "I'll start brewing right away." She curtsied and scrambled to the kitchen, feeling like she was escaping something terrible.

"Hurry," Aunt Marcella screeched after her.

In the kitchen, Ling latched the door, fear spiking in her stomach. Packets of medicine lined the shelves next to gold-rimmed fine dining dishes and bowls. Ling searched for instructions.

Luckily, Dabak had prepared the medicines in advance. Ling could recognize the clean, rigid strokes of her uncle's penmanship anywhere. Each of his words took up only the necessary amount of space. He listed precise measurements for each ingredient, which had to be washed and boiled for at least six hours. In contrast, her father's letters in his journal stretched out descenders, curved loops, and expanded across lines. Her father expressed himself outside the confines of convention. At least, Ling liked to think so.

She unwrapped the inner wax paper with nuts, dried roots, desiccated leaves, and... something unexpected. The same petals that had been stuffed into Lady Tun's dead mouth. Holding her breath, she inspected the flower.

"We meet again," she said to the toothed petals.

She rotated the yellowish stem between her fingers. What did Lady Tun and Aunt Marcella have in common that they both needed this flower?

She dropped the ingredients into a clay pot filled with water. Her aunt's condition meant administering the first dose in an hour. It would contain only ten percent of the medicine's potency, but hopefully it would begin to ease her aunt's pains. As the ingredients cooked, she scanned the view of the manicured gardens below. None of the flowers hinted of blue.

The gentle rumble of the pot lid lulled Ling into a state of ease. Steam from the medicine snaked from the stove to the open window. Spreading out Lady Tun's letters on the counter, she scanned them again. Had she missed something? The reason for stocking eyes seemed to be hidden in these messages. Could the references to Lady Tun's health point to the reason for her cruelty?

The stillness eased her muscles, and the lack of sleep caught up to her. One moment of rest would recharge her. She laid her head down. But as she drifted off, a force reached out from the dark. A whisper beckoned her forth. Ling refused to go at first. Her body wouldn't settle. Her mind showed images of twisted limbs and dead faces inside the medicine jars. She was horrified at the sight. Teetering between the realm of the sleeping and the waking, she plunged into bedlam. Tingling fingers numbed her hands.

Ling materialized in the marsh amongst buzzing insects and waves crashing into the rocks. The mist was even thicker in her dreams. A fog rolled around her ankles, shackling her in place.

Whispers tickled her ears. *Listen. Heed.*

A breeze cleared away the haze. Ling gazed upon a woman in a white dress. She radiated compassion like the marble statues of the Gwun Yin. Dark hair flowed down her long neck and wrapped around her translucent arms. Her milky white fingers reached up to the star-dotted sky.

Behind Ling, a snake-like creature quivered. Its breath shifted the fog. The white clouds tumbled into a gray color. It slithered across the ground, lurching over the stones. Reaching Ling first, its human eyes glowed red under its bulging forehead. The thing traversed up Ling's leg and swirled around her neck. Once there, it squeezed.

You're not quite ripe. It retreated from her neck, descending toward the stargazing figure.

Ling opened her mouth, but no sound came out.

"Be careful!" she wanted to cry. She was frozen as the half-serpent and half-human figure flung itself into the fog. It left behind a trail of black sludge.

When the magnificent figure noticed the animal at her feet, she smiled. The snake lifted its head and hissed.

Without hesitation, the goddess bent down. "What did you say, little one?"

The creature lunged forward, splaying open its jaws, which proved to be massive. Its tongue grabbed the woman and took her into its mouth. From head to toe, the lady sank into the belly of the snake. The movement of the mist swirled, changing direction.

Each bite broke through skin, cartilage, and bone. The victim didn't utter a sound. Pieces of the woman's billowing dress spilled from the creature's lips. A dark liquid stained the serpent's teeth. Ling trembled. She had watched several people die now, but still the cruelty didn't escape her. This death was horrible beyond imagining.

The fog dimmed to gray as the creature sprouted legs and its skin shed its scales, morphing into a half-woman, half-snake hybrid. It sprouted hair, its lips reddened, and its new skin beamed iridescent. She glowed without benevolence. When the figure turned to Ling, the new form of the creature was devoid of eyes.

At the sight, Ling's legs gave out. She woke up as she toppled from the three-legged stool. Hitting her shoulder against the table, she landed on the tiled floor. She groaned on her side as the clay pot lid clattered. Water rumbled and spilled over the sides. The charcoal hissed. Dazed, she strained to stand up. Without thinking, she reached over the flames and pulled off the lid. The steam burned her hand as the contents simmered, and Ling hissed in dismay.

She rubbed her sore fingers. Finding the minty salve in her sack, she slathered the salve onto her pulsing skin and into the aches in her muscles. As she put away the tin, her fingers grazed the bullet from the outpost. Closing it into a small pocket, she prepared to serve her aunt the boiled herbs.

On a tray, Ling carried out a bowl of the pink tea. The mixture would continue to transform in the process. In five hours, the instructions said the medicine would turn the pigment of soil.

Aunt Marcella covered her face with a sleeve. Veins protruded through the pale skin on her forehead like tributaries of the Pearl River Delta.

"Set it down." Her aunt twitched and then cradled the hot liquid in one hand. Blowing away the steam, Aunt Marcella took an urgent gulp. Her face relaxed.

Ling remained puzzled. Her aunt's behavior wasn't like

anything in textbooks. If only Dabak had been there to instruct her.

"Call out if you need me." Ling excused herself to the bathroom to wash her hands. She rubbed the citrus suds into her skin, but a filthiness remained stuck under her skin. In the medicine cabinet, Ling checked the skincare products and makeup lining the two shelves. A Three Flowers Special Cleansing Cream promised to clear the muck and mire of the day. Ling unscrewed the cap. The scent of roses opened up her senses as she scrubbed her forehead and cheeks. She wished she could wash her face every day with such fineries. As the fragrance faded, Ling was left staring in the mirror, looking pale. She knew that her eyes lacked the luster that shone inside her classmates' eyes, especially Emma's. Thinking of her friend, she selected a rouge lipstick and swiped the color across her lips and cheeks. The little bit of stain perked up her face and added years to her age. *Could she pass for a Lady?*

This question felt silly given the gravity of the situation. Her aunt was battling a debilitating disease. Dabak was in jail. Monsters roamed her homelands. Something troubling was happening everywhere all at once—in this house, inside her mind, and around the bay. These sour feelings nestled into her bones.

Nineteen

Not hearing any complaints from the sitting room, Ling headed to Dabak's study. His collection of books and the safe ought to hold answers for her. She pushed open the door, pulling the string on a tall lamp. The bulb flickered to life, mercifully banishing the shadows to the corners. In here, a heaviness enveloped her, draping her in the mysteries of the island.

She turned to something familiar. The herbal medicine cabinet against the front wall was meticulously labeled. Remedies for pains and ailments brimmed from a hundred small cupboards.

Each drawer displayed the name of the herbs in Tang characters, and relevant symptoms for treatment. In addition to memorizing applications for the stem, seed, flower, and leaf, Ling was required to know the most potent method to prescribe. Depending on whether it was dried, steamed, or roasted, the preparation changed an ingredient's energy and how it healed a body.

Living in this house had supplied her with resources to learn. Unlike in the restricted space in Kowloon, where she felt small and less worthy. She used to spend countless hours in this study reading texts in Tangwa and French. She felt a calling back to the island.

While she examined the familiar bookcases, she noticed two shelves of newly acquired texts. She had never seen these books before. Some bindings exposed the center folds of pages, a sign the texts were hand-bound and one-of-a-kind. Others had gold-embossed spines.

She was drawn to one with an ornate floral pattern. It looked like the design that Emma had shown her from the school's library. She pulled out the ruby-stained leather cover. With astonishment, she realized that it was a hand-book from the vampire hunter's order. Why was this here?

She flipped to the picture of the sacred uniform. The studded leather jacket worn by knights of the special order was there, similar to the copy from this morning. Written at the top of the page: *Blessed are the pure in heart for they shall see.* She was quietly pleased that her decision not to take the book from the library had not cost her the knowledge within.

Reading more, she discovered facts about strange crea-tures much more complicated than the church's demon and devils referenced at mass. The text whispered of the ways monsters could be killed and subdued. It also told her of corruptions that could afflict humans—by bite, rite, or death. It warned of the promise of freedom from those who themselves were enslaved to depravity.

Ling shut the book when a faint ringing started in her right ear. She breathed in the strange smell of the binding and focused again on her present worries. Knowledge was strength. Understanding the murderer would get Dabak out of jail. Fate wanted her to know about the knights. Studying the origins of ancient creatures would take her a step closer to unearthing the truth.

To free her uncle, she needed more recent documents. She rolled up the wooden panel over the desk. Her uncle's silver fountain pen lay next to shop ledgers and a black book. She thumbed through the numbers, many of which had been entered by her. The black book, a collection of stories written by H.P. Lovecraft, stirred her interest. Based on the author's name, she assumed it was a romance.

Tucking the ruby handbook and the romance collection under her arm, she unlatched the closet, pushing aside shirts, ties, and slacks hanging on wooden dowels. Reaching into the back corner, she found a steel box that had been bolted to the floor. A whisper tickled her ear. She turned to find no one.

Ling shook off the feeling of being watched. She bent down and twirled the combination lock. Resetting the wheel several times, she stopped at the first number. Before Ling could turn to the second digit, Aunt Marcella called out her name. Ling cringed. She threw a jacket over the safe and closed the closet door.

Bracing herself as she entered the sitting room, Ling was relieved to see a rosy glow on her aunt's face again. Her irises had deepened to dark hazel. The quilt she had been buried under was now neatly folded on a chair. Even the bad smell had dissipated.

"How is Ming?" Aunt Marcella looked up with puffy red eyes. "Why has he not returned?"

Ling explained the situation including the arrest and visiting him at the police station. "Uncle Ming is fine. We are trying our best to help him."

Ling patted her aunt's bony shoulder. She was thinner than last time she had seen her.

Aunt Marcella dotted her forehead with a silk handkerchief. She reached for a personal notebook. "It sounds like there is more to this than meets the eye."

Ling had expected her to react with emotion. But Aunt Marcella seemed to know already that an underlying strangeness existed in their world.

Flipping through the pages of her notebook, Aunt Marcella scanned names and phone numbers. "If only Uncle Charles were in town, he would know the people to call. There would be no trouble."

Aunt Marcella's lips looked purple. "You need food to maintain your health." Ling stroked her chin. "I saw an open produce stand on King Street, close to the apartment."

"Lovely. Food will help us think." Aunt Marcella smiled, though it seemed forced.

After refilling the cup with more medicine, Ling rushed down the stairs to the closest produce shop, which offered fresh haw berries, mangos, and lychees. Her stomach rumbled. She hadn't eaten since last evening.

"I picked these off the trees in the morning." A vendor pointed to the oranges gathered in a crate.

"I'll take six. Why didn't you leave with the strike?" Ling asked the skinny old man packing up the fruit.

"I am not well. Cannot travel far, might as well die in a place I know." He held out her bags, his hands shaking.

She nodded. Death was closer than she liked. But this old man didn't show fear in facing the end. His expression was relaxed as he packed up the items.

"And after all, if I left, then we would not have met."

After buying fruit, Ling purchased garlic rice and white cut chicken. Her empty stomach begged for a warm meal. She also paid a nearby restaurant to deliver congee and steamed vegetables to Aunt Marcella in the morning. Food and medicine would see her aunt through for another day until Ling worked out how to get her uncle out of jail. Another stall close by sold frivolous items rather than food. She picked a hair clip for mother and a set of marbles and jacks for her brothers. She secretly missed their annoying morning wake-up call.

Ling had a key to enter the apartment this time. Aunt Marcella was now perched over the railing with wet hair that had been tied up with floral ribbons. She had changed into a youthful pastel dress embellished with French lace. The wizened, blackened figure beneath the blanket had disappeared into thin air.

Ling lined up the oranges on the table and peeled the skin from one, releasing its appetizing scent. The fetid reek from earlier had faded into a memory.

"My favorite." Aunt Marcella picked up a piece and chewed the slice.

Ling couldn't resist digging right into the chicken and rice. The fragrant flavors made her heart sing.

She turned to her aunt. "You should eat more." Ling sounded like Ahma.

"I am quite all right with this," she said, still slowly enjoying the orange. Aunt Marcella hugged her arms, wincing in pain. While her aunt appeared young again, worry weighed on her. "I love the red lipstick on you."

Her aunt smiled and gazed into Blake Gardens in full bloom.

Ling curled her lips together as she took in the colors. White, red, and pink roses. Sunflowers presented their yellow petals to the sky. Purple lilacs dotted bushes along the walkways. She could smell the face wash again. From the porch, she could also see the bustle of Queen's Pier, a thirty-minute walk down the hill. Ships of all sizes moved in and out of the port, carrying passengers and cargo to faraway places. Tourists waited for a tram to Victoria peak. Taxis queued for passengers around a rotunda. The commotion was exciting. It seemed like an entirely different world from hers.

"Don't you love the tropics? Plants remain in bloom for much longer than in northern climates." Aunt Marcella sounded distant as she pulled a blanket across her chest. "But the summer heat is oppressive."

The contrast between her aunt's words and actions was puzzling. She missed Dabak's wild stories of living in London, the odd creatures in the Thames River, and foraging for mushrooms in the Black Forest.

After the oranges were finished, her aunt reached into the pocket of her dress and pulled out a thin cigarette. Tiny creases formed around her lips as she struck a match. She sucked on the tobacco until a cloud rested over their heads. She seemed weary. "All right. I am ready to tell you the truth."

Twenty

"The alps by train were stunning. A perfect start to our honeymoon." Aunt Marcella paused, inhaling her cigarette. The earthy smoke twisted toward the late afternoon. Her hand shook as a strand of hair unraveled from her bun. Aunt Marcella's eyes sparkled. Right now, she was herself again. The person Ling had first met. She even wore a string of obsidian gemstones across her neck.

Ling recalled the excitement of the couple leaving for the whirlwind trip.

"My mother is from Switzerland." Her aunt's eyes turned glassy. "On the train, I met a mother and daughter. They seemed nice... a part of me was charmed by the idea of having children. We still might, I mean, when I get better." Her aunt's voice shook a little.

"What were their names?" Ling asked. She doubted she would know them, but the more information the better.

Her aunt's right hand squeezed the bridge of her nose, easing herself into a chair. "Dear, I should... the medicine stunts my memory." She stopped for a minute. "Countess

Breza and her daughter, Catherine. From a hamlet in England, one that I had never heard of."

She shook her head. "I should have trusted my gut."

Ling listened in rapt attention, nibbling on pieces of chicken. Could Countess Breza have known Lady Eggers or vice versa? They both hailed from the European countryside.

"I told Catherine where we were headed, and quite coincidentally, they were going there too." Aunt Marcella took another drag on her cigarette. She leaned forward with a regretful expression. "I should have known... I was naive."

She hadn't ever thought of her aunt as anything but educated and worldly. Had they hurt her? Ling reached for her aunt's hand.

Aunt Marcella bit her lip. "Little birds shouldn't trust strangers. Things will turn out badly. At first, it was fun to have Catherine around. Ming was able to attend business meetings while I hiked and enjoyed afternoon tea with the ladies. But one night, I woke up hysterical." Aunt Marcella's face turned pale. "I was screaming as Ming ran into the room." She unbuttoned the top of her blouse, displaying two punctures in her chest. "Blood dripped from my neck."

Ling squinted at the wounds. The two holes were about the circumference of sharpened pencil tips. An eeriness rose up from her stomach. She had read about this.

"I could swear that I saw Catherine in my room. It wasn't the first time. She had appeared in my dreams... nightmares." Aunt Marcella covered her ears with her hands, as if to block out the sound of her own story.

"Do you need more herbs?" Ling stood up, not wanting to hear more.

"No, let me finish." Her aunt fidgeted with her necklace. "Catherine had consumed me. Ming believed my story but what could he do? It was too late." She sighed. "My injuries still have not fully healed, as you can see."

Ling's heart lurched forward. The situation was worse than she thought. The details she imagined were closer to *Camilla* than she expected. Monsters didn't scare her. It was what happened to the victims that turned her insides. Was Aunt Marcella on her death bed? When Ling had arrived, things seemed dire. After the medicine and the oranges, the illness seemed to have faded. But it was still there, like a shadow in the corner.

"The rest of the honeymoon, I was ill. Ming spent his time and energy searching for advice. We should have told Uncle Charles sooner."

She labored through the many strange cures Ming had tried, struggling to remember every one. Her breath shortened with each reveal.

"Finally, when nothing else had worked, Charles told us about a rumor, a cure for a blood infection. One with similar symptoms as mine."

Ling met her aunt's hungry gaze with wide eyes as she understood. "The blue flowers come from Guiana. From a man...um.... But I am afraid they only keep the symptoms at bay. I have to continually ingest the medicine, or I will get worse and eventually...."

Wrinkles marked her aunt's anguish. Between her eyes, on her neck, and around her mouth, the folds deepened. Should Ling be more skeptical? Is this how a frenzied woman appeared? Did she blur reality?

But Ling believed this story. She had almost seen the evil materialize. Before her aunt had taken the medicine, she had been engulfed in a strange aura. She had cowered from the light. Her skin had been as pale as a turnip.

"How did Charles know how to help? Did he have special medical education?"

"Treating my type of infection was part of some training he had when he became a monk." Aunt Marcella's eyes drooped. "He gave me his old books. I did not want them, but he insisted. Maybe they would interest you. They are in the library." She placed her fist under her chin and extinguished the cigarette in her dish of untouched food. "I am so awfully tired. When do you have to go?"

"The medicine needs to boil for two more hours. I'll leave a large bowl out before I leave. Either my mother or I will return."

"You can stay, if you wish." Aunt Marcella blinked, gesturing toward the rooms. "Plenty of rooms to...." Her head bobbed, interrupting her sentence.

"I told mother I would return this evening," Ling said, biting back her guilt. She preferred not to spend the night with her unpredictable aunt.

"Search the names in my personal address book. Someone in there can surely help Ming." She opened a notebook to a list of people with addresses and phone numbers. "What about his customers? Does he keep a list?" Aunt Marcella spoke quickly, running out of energy by the end of her questions.

Ling looked down at her lap. Dabak only kept his ghost patient's names inside his head. A swell of emotion overwhelmed her thoughts. Could she help them as much as her uncle? In a few years, she would be able to do more. It wasn't time for her to take such responsibility for patients. But under the circumstances, she would try her best.

She skimmed the names in the address book in a blur. Who did her aunt and uncle know best? Any councilmen or high positioned socialite? Did they, perhaps, know Lady Eggers? When Ling lifted her head again, Aunt Marcella had gently collapsed into the arms of the rattan chair. A peacefulness draped her face.

———

Ling went back to the safe. Her uncle had said he kept special dried herbs inside. She hoped for more than that. Blood throbbed into her ears as she turned the dial three times to match translated from her uncle. She held her breath when the door clicked open.

She was greeted by a startlingly large collection of bills and gold bars. Inspecting each stack in disbelief, she flipped through the faces of King George V, Tang palaces, and battle ships. With this, Dabak could buy a large house and set up a permanent store on the Queen's pier. Ling slipped two local bills into her pocket, promising to pay him back.

Next, Ling found manila folders filled with correspondences. The top letter had been sent from Guiana, likely from the person Aunt Marcella had referenced in her tale. The paper was silken and finer than anything Ling had ever touched. She read a letter addressed to Lord Charles Langley from a man named Wai:

I appreciate meeting the acquaintance of a man of your stature. A solution for the rare blood disease will be difficult to transport across the ocean. I am compassionate to your struggles, for I too had a family once. Your niece is an innocent victim of longtime feuds. I believe the necessary plant would thrive in your colony's tropical climate. If you are amenable to commissioning the voyage, I have enclosed the specifications for the ship. I am willing to make the attempt.

Ensuring the plants arrive flowering will be a challenge, but your city, I admit, has arisen in my dreams. I had put aside the place as a fantasy until the letters came in from Doctor Shaw. Besides my own trivialities, I pledge to ease the symptoms of your niece's disease to the best of my abilities. She may never be fully cured, but like me, I believe she can live a long and mostly satisfying life.

Something inexplicably familiar emanated from the words. She traced the signature of Wai of the Guianas. The lines in the lettering flowed with elongated descenders, reminiscent of her father's cursive.

Blueprints for a boat were included with the letter. There were notes on the ideal environment for transporting live plants, and instructions for the required water and soil during the three-month journey. The custom structures included a greenhouse on the deck and a lightproof container in the barracks. Darkness nourished the seedlings, while moonlight coaxed the flowers to bloom. A peculiar plant.

The other papers were invoices for herbs purchased from across the Pacific Ocean, receipts for the twin's tuition, and a copy of Ling's medical school application.

She opened another folder and covered her mouth.

Dabak kept patient charts. She had never known; he hadn't shared this part of his practice with her. These notes had been under lock and key.

This folder bore the name *Tun*. The file listed complaints about insomnia and loss of taste and smell. The patient had a propensity for blood remedies. Her uncle had prescribed congealed blood of snake. But it hadn't been enough. He had applied herbs to expel toxicity in the blood: stone silkworm grass, *Victoria polita*, and yellow ginseng. The treatments had escalated, calling for exotic animals, human hair and nails, and more discarded waste. Disgust rose in Ling's throat. Lady Tun engaged with immoral approaches to her health, which was mentioned in her correspondence with Lord Eggers. Had she made Dabak guilty in her depravity?

The blue flower, however, seemed to cleanse the blood. It was the difference between using herbs for the living or the dead. The priest swung frankincense smoke down the pews during Sunday mass. Sandalwood incense burned at the temples. Mugwort protected the living at the yearly festival of the spirits, when the specters visited from the lower realms. Herbs offered the deceased honor and dignity, as well as cursing and banishing malevolent souls.

Ling inspected the contents of five more patient folders: two housewives, an assistant to a city official, and the police captain, Stewart. Could she use what was written inside to help Dabak? This question went against the doctor's ethical codes. But, in the literal sense, she hadn't taken an oath. And justice stood on the same plane as ethnical goodness, did it not? It would be worse to allow one moral principle to block another from thriving.

She dove into these notes. Dabak had detailed several issues – physical pains in Captain Stewart's body as well as specific mental derangements. She shuddered, because she learned that he sought out children too. The details were hard to read. It wasn't a coincidence that the authorities generally failed to pursue missing children. Her heart ached. She copied the captain's phone number and address into her father's journal. Dabak's stringent rules about sharing patient details made more sense now. He was protecting his loved ones. Medical details were burdens to be borne by the few. These secrets were worth more than gold.

Before she closed the safe, she spotted a black and white photo. Three men were huddled together close. Two local boys, with a ghost in a captain's hat. A younger Dabak, and another man who shared her eyes and nose. She had never seen this picture before. Her heart beat faster. This had to be him. Her father. The boys would be so excited.

On the way out, she called Captain Stewart's home. She left an urgent message with his staff.

"Please tell the captain I am calling on behalf of Doctor

Ming Shaw. In my uncle's absence, I can provide the *same* services for his ailments. I insist we speak over the phone."

She didn't know when he would call back. But if he feared what she implied, then the captain would find her and surely, he would release his trusted doctor.

TWENTY-ONE

Behind Lion Mountain, a haze crept in from the south. Ling pursed her lips. A fog could spill into the bay and prevent her from traveling home. Yet, the ship captain hadn't cancelled the trip. To distract herself from the ship's possible delay, Ling read the first story in the black book. It was immediately apparent that Lovecraft didn't pen romance, but much darker, stranger tales. A lighthouse keeper's longing for adventures in "The White Ship" drew her in completely.

A boarding call whistled. She followed along as passengers hustled onboard, prodding the crewmen to depart in haste. Middle-aged men and women carried armfuls of packages and gunny sacks. A few children followed close behind.

Ling headed toward the upper decks through the passenger bay, an area enclosed by steel walls and circular windows. A woman with silver hair smiled in her direction as if they were old friends. However, Ling didn't smile back. The visit to Aunt Marcella's had infected her with melancholy. Life could be abrupt, wringing even the happiest moments into long-lasting pain. Ling climbed up the ladder to a spot where most passengers wouldn't go.

The boat sail flapped over her head. Ling tucked herself in a corner, pulling out the H.P. Lovecraft book again. Despite some turbulence from the ship, she kept reading about the dreaming lighthouse keeper who sailed away in an inter-realm vessel. His story slid her from a dim mood into a more contemplative dream state.

As the boat's motor cranked hard, Ling shifted her attention to the mountainous terrain across the bay. The rolling hills were raw and not yet corrupted by the colony. She rarely saw Kowloon from this side. Water sloshed against the hull as the motor's roar pushed the boat from the dock. Gripping a metal rail, Ling steadied her bag, which was now filled with books, papers, and presents.

Further into the bay, the thickening fog broke over the mountains, tumbling toward the water. Vapors rose to the lower deck. The engine slowed, narrowly missing a collision with a metal buoy. Crewmen bellowed. Ling closed her eyes, imagining the terraces of unknown cities appearing inside the mist. She conjured lily and crystal-lined shores. Bells and horns quaked in every direction. The Land of Sona-Nyl and Cathuria in Lovecraft's story, at the moment, seemed as real to her as New York City and Paris. Gray obscured both shores.

The blanket of milky white drifted up to her level. Cold draped over her shoulders and seeped under her skin. The masts glowed fluorescent. The sails rippled. Wind swirled and beckoned lores to come in from faraway places.

She was in another place. A different person. In a different time.

Floating in between lands, the lighthouse keeper's thoughts gnawed at her: *The oceans are more ancient than the mountains; their wisdom will carry you homeward.*

Despite the beauty of the sentence, gloom nipped at her spirit. She didn't have a real home. Ling had been born at sea and had grown up on the family boat. She had been able to rig the sails on her own from the age of six. When her father left, he had abandoned them on land. It wasn't fair, because she and Ahma were just as devoted to the sea.

The memories stirred a longing. She called out to her visions, summoning dreams of corpses or anything else needed for understanding the future. She wasn't frightened any longer. She stood up and outstretched her arms into the mist. Her fingertips seemed to disappear into the fog. Drops of moisture tickled her palms. Without reason, she began spinning.

The caress of the wind felt like flying. She twirled until her head vibrated with glee. If this was madness, she welcomed it. Laughing out loud, she didn't care if she attracted attention. Exhilaration burned her lungs, and it was marvelous. This was freedom.

Ling stumbled, catching herself on a railing as she almost fell down the stairs. She took a step backward and leaned against a cold wall, grounding herself for a moment. She should be careful not to fall overboard. Her neck would break from bouncing off the steel.

When the mist thinned, she descended the stairs, back into a more solid reality. The passenger bay had a wall and roof. It was more than half-full, shielding people from rain and lessening the wind. The mountain ridges came into view as the boat started again.

Then, a ringing started in her ear again. It vibrated at the same frequency as it had at the police outpost. A silhouette stepped out of the haze. The shadow approached her, clad in the hunter's ankle-length jacket. Copper studs dully reflected light from outside. Ling slipped into another aisle, trying to find a hiding spot. From the other row, she observed its gnarled hands stretched out from the sleeves like knotted tree branches. Dark welts and scabs ate away its leathery skin. She knew it was searching for someone. Most likely her.

She exited the area under the cover of some other passengers. Pressing her back against the steel wall, she wondered if she could evade this creature. Unlike the handsome illustration in the book, this soldier's cheeks were collapsed inward. Nothing holy existed in its expressions or movements. Every hint of humanity had faded except for a slight hint of pink on its lips.

I am here.

The voice from the seaside shack returned.

What did it want? Ling panicked. The bay became quiet. A darkness inched closer to her. She edged to the circular window that looked into the passenger bay. Flashes of light showed her the position of the figure. This must be the creature from the peninsula. The voice and the figure were one and the same. She dropped to the ground when it was less than three rows away.

Taps on the glass, *plink plink*, cracked her wavering resolve. The sound made her want to scream. A sour feeling tickled the lobe of her ear. She was trapped.

Your heart is pure.

Ling shook her head, afraid to speak.

Where is my William?

What was this name? She wanted nothing to do with this creature or its William. It was the cause of her torment. It had killed Lady Tun and got her uncle thrown in prison.

"I don't have anything left," she replied, hardening her thoughts against the monster.

I seek to free him. It hovered above her now. *It seems you may also require liberation.*

"Why are you torturing me?" Ling groaned.

Y'gnaiih. Freedom exists in one form.

"I only need to release my uncle." Ling felt its cold breath on her cheek. "Why did you kill Lady Tun?"

Mgepogor lloigazath.

Ling trembled with the weight of the revelation. The vibrations alone conveyed anger and disappointment. "What did she do?"

"*Ny'ghft Zhro'khal.* Summoned the abyssal one to feed the compulsions of her human desire."

Nausea swirled into her stomach. Did all this amount to punishment? A moralistic lesson? She covered her ears. Should she listen to the words of a monster?

Please help me. William.

The request was rooted in feelings. It was a plea from someone caring. A person desperate for answers.

"Are others in danger?" She thought of the twins.

She looked into its hollow eyes. A fire danced in them. The image of Lady Tun with flowers bulging in her mouth sliced into her vision. For a second, it felt like she was back there. This wasn't exactly the answer she sought. How could Lady Tun still be a menace? She was dead.

Before Ling could ask more questions, hands pulled her backward. The touch was warm. Ling shrieked. Burning herbs stung her eyes. The decrepit monster retreated. The strange noises subsided. Ling turned to see an old woman who had pulled her to safety.

"*Jow gway. Koi gway.*" Her scratchy voice commanded evil spirits to leave, expelling negative energy with grand swipes of burning herbs clutched in one hand.

"*Lang mew,*" the woman with hanging eyelids addressed her. Silver hair peeked out from her kerchief. "Girl, I saw you stumbling about. You could have fallen overboard."

"Popo, I thought...." She realized that this grandmother

had saved her life. "A man came out from the fog...." She trailed off, hesitant to tell her more.

With pinched eyebrows, the lady stared. A line of smoke rose up from behind her back. "Man?" The old woman paced the area in front of her.

Ling didn't have a choice but to ask, "Did you see the monster?"

"Why do you think I am burning protective herbs on a damn ship? If the captain curses me out, then you will help me explain." She scrunched her face, waving the burning bundle in a figure eight. The white smoke formed a wall around them. Her thin lips muttered the healing chant of Gwun Yin before she threw the remainder of the bundle overboard to disappear into the spray and the gray mist.

"What did you see?" Ling asked again.

The old lady tightened her scarf. "This land is old. Other creatures lived here first." She waggled a finger. "I feel an imbalance. More darkness has landed since the full moon. I saw something, but I do not call it a man. People are not always as they seem. Forms shift like the winds."

Ling squinted. Since the full moon her life had been turned around. Could Lady Tun's murder have had an impact on the world's equilibrium? "What can be done?"

The woman spoke in a comforting voice. "Nature knows how to reset. But sometimes, it requires darkness, a lot of it."

Ling fidgeted with her hands, knowing what the woman alluded to. The missing children, Lady Tun's death, and the agitation of the strikers, when mixed together, produced enough negativity for many lifetimes. Yet, Lo Popo's words made these events sound inevitable. As if there was nothing at all she could do. "Then there is no one to blame for anything that has happened?"

"Ah, I see that are you acquainted with life's sufferings."

The old lady's face drew in. "Blame is a long chain of links. One person might appear to be the cause only because you're concentrated on one moment in time."

Ling bit her lip. "Then why do you burn herbs. What do you call that?"

"Clearing out the unnecessary." The old lady slapped an unused herb bundle into Ling's hand. "Something tells me you'll need this."

Ling took them gratefully. There was a ribbon wrapped around the dried leaves, with a word painted on either side. "Why is oracle written here?" She pointed to the red words.

"Wupo passed along several batches of these before she disappeared." The woman turned her face to the waves. "Mei was a lovely girl with white skin and a talent for divination. She was taken from us."

"The assistant?" Ling had overheard a customer mention yet another tragedy, but had not made the connection that this was the girl in question. "So little has been done to locate her."

The Popo peered through her lashes. "We suspect foul play. Wupo changed. The last time I sought her out, she sold me herbs spun around a rotting rat tail. It sounds crazy. I think... I'd swear the ghosts had taken possession of her, too."

Ling no longer thought this was crazy at all.

Twenty-Two

About a dozen people disembarked from the boat at Woyi Tsun Pier. Ling thanked the older woman and watched her blend back into the crowd.

At the stand, Ahma was speaking with a young lady about Ling's age. The conversation looked serious. Papers covered the counter in front of them.

"I am so sorry. These are the records my fiancé found. You'll have to clarify with your brother-in-law." The young lady wore a flowing sun dress. Her soft and round face were a stark contrast to Ling's squared jaw and cutting gaze.

"Thank you so much for going out of your way," her mother said to the visitor, and then Ahma spotted Ling. "Please meet my daughter, Ling. This is Beatrix." Her mother's cheery tone sounded forced.

"Pleased to meet you. My mother mentioned your engagement to the barrister." Ling glanced at the sapphire on Beatrix's ring finger. "Will you become a lawyer too?"

Beatrix laughed. Pink rose to her cheeks, brightening her rouge. "Your daughter is sweet. I should be going. See you both next week at the banquet?" She grazed a gloved hand over the official seals on the documents.

Ahma fawned over the wedding news again. Beatrix popped open a lace parasol and strolled off to meet another friend. Ling took note of the young lady's confident strides.

Alone with Ahma, Ling picked up one of the letters, which was from the offices of Thomas Dunlop & Sons and the Business Bureau, the island's government department that handled contract disputes. It was the company that had commissioned her father's voyage.

Ahma's grin faded quickly. "This is a mess. Dabak is indebted to you...." Her face turned a bright red, watching Ling read. "Men are good for nothing. Do you hear me?"

Ling wrinkled her brow. Sneaking a glance at her father's photo, she quickly put it away. She had been so excited to share it with Ahma. Not any longer.

"What is that?" Ahma pointed to Ling's pocket. Ling hadn't been quick or stealthy enough to hide the picture unobtrusively.

Ling debated showing her. Ba had flaws, but still he was her father. Making a quick decision, she unveiled the black and white photo. Her mother couldn't be mad at an image.

Ahma squinted at it. "Chi." Her voice went up an octave. The man next to her uncle was a young man with ear-length curly hair. "The other person is Charles Langley, Marcella's uncle."

"Lord Langley is Aunt Marcella's uncle?"

Ahma nodded. "He also taught your father sailing and financed his boat. He is the maker of our lives. Past and present." Mother turned away from her. "He stopped speaking to us after his son.... well, we don't need to discuss those things now. Your brothers will be excited to see the photo."

"A son? I have a cousin?" Even though the cousin was a

distant relation by marriage, the prospect of more family excited her.

"At the end, your father left. Your uncle is a liar. The twins. Oh, your poor brothers."

Ling was dumbfounded, uncertain if she had heard correctly. A liar? Her mother never spoke ill of Dabak. He had been reliable and had passed down knowledge to her that most women didn't have the chance to study.

"It's right here." Ahma handed Ling a receipt stamped with last year's date, handling it gingerly as if it were a thorned stem. "Your uncle redeemed the money from your father's labor contract." Her mother threw a light shawl over her face. Under the cloth, she sobbed. "He took it from us."

The receipt was indisputable. Ling had no explanation. It would explain the large sum of money sitting in the apartment safe. Still, she refused to jump to conclusions, even as her heart tensed. Dabak was hiding something, but was it greed? "We must inquire. Dabak deserves at least that."

Ling thumbed through the stack of papers. Was Beatrix telling the truth? Maybe her mother hadn't asked the right questions. She spotted the name of an estate in the Guianas. Her father had signed a contract to teach sailing in the West. She frowned. Wasn't the Guianas near the Caribbean? Did the place have anything to do with the man who had brought over the cure for Aunt Marcella? Of course, this didn't excuse the theft.

Ahma swallowed hard. "I am concerned for our future, which is why I sought Wupo." She smoothed out the front of her dress.

"For what?" Ling's attention stayed on the forms. There was still more potential information about her father. She didn't see the sailing manifest or logs here. There was no death certificate for Shiu Chi Xie among the papers. She was relieved.

Ahma sighed. "Mei, her apprentice is gone. Missing or ran away, no one is sure. Supposedly, Mei was a jittery thing. Always spilling herbs and confusing prescriptions. Misfortunes can be opportunities too."

Ling looked up at her mother with her mouth agape. There was something wrong about Ahma's desperation. "But you never believed in mystics." Once, a soothsayer aboard her father's ship had predicted that he would have a long life. Yet where was he now? Ling didn't believe in prophecies from people for hire either.

Ahma bowed her head slightly. "While medicine is your path, Wupo's work is very lucrative. She actually wants you as an apprentice. With your father gone and Dabak incapacitated, I have begun to reconsider a new offer from Wupo."

Ling couldn't decide if Ahma was being open-minded or opportunistic. What had happened to Mei? Why would she evaporate without a trace? The girl had been with Wupo at least fifteen years. "Ahma, possibilities are well and good. But I...."

"This is too big for you." Ahma scrunched her face. "The point is, you have an unnurtured gift. When you were young... you had dreams. They were so vivid. You always knew the tides and weather. Do you know, if it hadn't been for you, we would've perished in the Indian Ocean." She choked up.

"You're rejecting what you have not even heard? An idle woman cannot do anything for us." Ling crossed her arms.

"You should be grateful. Wupo said my children have great destinies."

"Dreams do not save people," Ling mumbled under her breath.

"Do not think for one second you could have stopped

your father," Ahma said severely. "Your father was your biggest advocate, but he was overtaken by hubris when he boarded the last voyage. He would not even stay for the birth of the twins." Ahma started to walk away.

Ling pursed her lips, watching her mother recede in the distance. She hadn't heard that story, where her dreams had saved the ship from disaster. Doubt was the only thing people had ever shown her. After deciding not to transport teas to the colonies, her father had written about growing despondent. Why hadn't Ahma shared these events with her before? It would've saved her a lot of heartache.

Thinking about Wupo caused an ache to throb in her stomach. She had a vague recollection of meeting the old woman with her father. There had been an argument, and Ling never saw the oracle again. Well, even if her mother didn't trust her, Ling's plan to free Dabak didn't involve groveling or begging. She had other ideas.

Twenty-Three

January 1924
The Guianas

Xie snuck aboard a clipper ship, slipping through the commotion of people loading and unloading cargo. The vessel's shape was strangely familiar. He somehow knew the location of all the doors, even the hidden ones.

He crept into the accommodations of the first mate, who would be busy directing the loads of sugar and tea. Inside the cabin, he wiped the dirt from his face, cleaned under his nails, and brushed the yellow from his teeth. Then he donned a fresh set of western clothes: slacks and a starched shirt.

Back ashore again, he waited for more ships to flow through the docks before introducing himself as a healer from an unknown land.

"Where are your papers?" a hotel clerk curled his upper lip.

Xie had collected a variety of bills, treasures, and weapons. One document called him Wai. The name was unimportant; all that mattered was that the identification said he was a free man. The manager brushed back his long hair and sniffed at Xie. Three days ago, the manager might have kicked him out for smelling wild, but Xie had cleaned up enough, and had spritzed a gentleman's musky cologne.

"Do not get many free Chinamen. What is your business?" The manager extended a smug smirk. It wasn't enough that Xie was free; he also had to matter.

"I practice traditional medicine. I've arrived to cure the malady plaguing your island." Xie spoke with confidence bestowed by a wind spirit. The divine had spoken to him.

The whites of the manager's eyes widened. "You do not say...." He waved over a boy from the back. "Please help this guest to the room with the view. I will phone Señor Da Silva. He will be interested in what you're selling." Turning back to Xie, the hotel manager smiled pleasantly, no trace of the smirk left. "Señor Da Silva is the man you want to meet."

Xie had seen the Da Silva name stamped on boxes leaving the island. On a contract on the ship, Frederick Da Silva had been named the recipient of thirty laborers who had disembarked the clipper ship.

———

Xie waited for days at the hotel. Da Silva wanted to meet with him after the Feast of the Presentation of the Lord, a holiday which celebrated Mary and Joseph presenting the infant Jesus to the church. During these days, Xie slept in a soft bed and walked among the alleyways in the evenings. He bought new clothes and browsed the toys available for sale. He knew he had children, but could not remember them. How old were they? What toys would they like? In his mind, he picked out a doll, a wooden horse, and illustrated story books.

Strange voices followed him. In the town, they called him to feast.

Human flesh will make you stronger. They are not unclean. Untainted blood will nourish you.

He continued to refuse the call, finding sufficient comfort with cow's blood and replenishing his energy with handpicked herbs. With his new, distinguished demeanor, he asked questions. Answers always came. When he inquired about the health of the island, some shopkeepers lied while others overflowed with strange hypotheses. An elderly woman who he met in a tavern told him an old tale.

"This island used to be a haven. Far enough from land to evade greed for hundreds of years. But then the master's wealth expanded, acquiring ships to collect more gold and souls. This humble island does not provide treasures. The sun is bountiful. Medicine man, you should know what I have heard. The wind says you will shepherd us from suffering." She poured him a clear liquid from the pitcher at the table.

"What did nature reveal to you?" The earthy smell of the liquor knocked him back.

"I know the spirit from the lands. It is unhappy with the situation. We did not grow sugar cane before the masters arrived, you know. They changed the terrain and chained hands to work on foreign crops.

"How do I assist?" He tasted the potent drink and cringed inwardly.

"What do you do with vermin?" The woman swallowed the remainder of her own cloudy beverage. Her face puckered. "Mercy to rats means allowing disease. Mercy to corrupted minds dooms future generations. Mercy is for people with no miseries."

It was cloudy on the day when Xie was invited to the big house. A carriage drove him straight to the iron gates. The house was windowless on the lower floors. Only a thick wooden door reinforced with metal allowed entry to the home. This was not the home of a master who trusted in the affections of his people.

A darker-skinned man with a shaved head greeted Xie. His linen shirt draped off his broad shoulders. In precarious silence, he guided Xie through a dim hallway to a library that opened up to cavernously high ceilings. Skylights filled the space with light. Jewels and minerals lined the inlaid shelves filled with leatherbound books and atlases.

"Master Da Silva will be with you soon. Please feel free to browse."

On a table in the center of the room, miniature ships marked locations on a map overlaid with the constellations. Xie smiled faintly. The stars were his friends. They had brought him comfort as he slept outside. Xie oriented himself to his exact location on the Atlantic Ocean. He remembered other points, moving his finger to a location called Hong Kong with latitude 22 degrees north and longitude 114 degrees east.

Detached thoughts lurked at the fringes of his consciousness. A tangle of names seeded his mind. But before he was able to investigate them, footsteps echoed in the hall.

"Como estas? Navega?" An unfamiliar accent flooded the room.

Xie wanted to answer yes. "I don't sail. I am a medicine man."

At the edge of the map, he noticed a nautical compass pointed in the wrong direction. He struggled to control himself, keep his hands away from the table. Yet, a jolt ran through his veins. He reached out and turned it to face north. A symbol made of repeated numbers was etched into the device's side.

Da Silva raised an eyebrow. "I am Manuel Da Silva. I own the farms on this island and my laborers are getting sick. I lose hundreds every year. But you know that somehow."

Xie did know about the deaths in the harvesting fields. He remembered mothers grieving their children. Husbands mourning their wives. He shook off images of the hellish landscape, responding with a smile. "The innkeeper must have told you about me. I am here to help."

"Who says I need an outsider?" Da Silva studied Xie from the opposite side of the table, as if sizing up an opponent. He stroked one side of his thin mustache.

Xie glanced at the compass again. The symbol jumped out at him. He couldn't remember his birthplace, or the name given to him by his parents. Yet, he recognized the intertwined figure eights. The symbol had been on the ship that had brought him here. Clear as a bell the name came to him. "Captain Wright."

Da Silva narrowed his gaze. "Curious. Let me check something...." He mumbled in another language and left the room, leaving Xie waiting to guess Da Silva's next move.

Xie's attention shifted to a nearby woven basket. The container was filled with green stones. Most of them were smooth with a hole at the center. He flipped the polished circles in his hand. These stones were meant to hang on chains. Each one embodied *qi*, a life force. Bringing the article to his heart, his mind drifted to happier places. Had he previously owned a similar pendant?

"Please have one." Da Silva had snuck back into the

room. "I have no use for them. They belonged to those who have perished."

"You do not send them home?" Xie asked without thinking. That would be the correct thing, the respectful course of action.

"Most of the men did not have families." Da Silva brushed dust from his sleeve. His expression was uninterested.

Xie knew this was a lie. The women and men who died on this island were burned with the rubbish. It was then that a surge of anger forced a memory back into his mind. Of the voyage here. He had wanted to reach the new world. "How many ships get detoured to this little island?"

Da Silva's eyebrow twitched. "What are you insinuating?"

"The laborers do not leave," Xie said. On the voyage here, Captain Wright had blamed the weather for veering off course. But all along Wright and Da Silva had planned to route thirty men here to work the sugar cane fields. Free and unencumbered labor. Xie had fought when he became aware of the detour and had almost been thrown overboard for mutiny.

"Sir, I hate to repeat myself." Da Silver frowned. "A sickness takes the laborers before contracts are fulfilled. Really so sad and terrible. I am of course happy to pay for services rendered."

"Their last service to you is their blood." Xie circled around the table, maintaining his distance from Da Silva. "It is quite smart. You never have to pay out."

Da Silva stopped and leaned over the table. "Who is your informant?"

Xie stepped toward the door. "The wind."

"Regardless," Da Silva's hands disappeared under the table. He flashed a pair of sharp teeth. "What happens here remains here. How do you know about my island? There is no way. Unless you are from here. So, from which swamp did you crawl out?"

Shoosh. The table shook. Xie jumped left.

As he launched himself, heat sliced into his leg. He glanced over his shoulder at the arrow stuck in the wall. Blood dripped down his calf as Da Silva pounced from the table with a knife lifted over his head.

Da Silvia landed on top of Xie, stabbing at his chest and face.

Xie pushed up against his wrists. He shoved his knee into Da Silva's breast bone, eliciting a grunt. They bounced across the tiles. Then Xie punched Da Silva in the nose. There was a satisfying crack before Da Silva fell to his side, holding his face.

Grabbing the heavy compass and a model ship, Xie charged at his opponent. Their bodies collided. Xie swung and crushed the paper weight into Da Silva's temple. His other hand speared a mast of a tiny ship into Da Silva's neck. The host went limp, his face vacant. Leaning over an unmoving body, Xie picked up the knife and made sure the monster would never divert another ship to this island again.

Twenty-Four

Ling slipped into her morning class, avoiding the glances of the girls with perfect hair in the front row. She licked her chapped lips and tried not to scratch her scalp. Finally, she'd had a night of sleep, albeit one full of visions. At least, she'd woken up rested and was better able to mull over Dabak's arrest. She tried to focus on the assignments piled high on her chair instead of what she would say when Captain Steward called.

Flipping through yesterday's missed lessons in math, several unread chapters of a Dickens novel, and some Bible verses, anxiety hit her. A surge of exhaustion threatened to fog her mind again. Then a note from Miss James broke through the pessimism. On the botany syllabus, her teacher had scribbled: *Classroom 204 in the morning?*

Ling's heart fluttered. Had Miss James discovered information about the petals? Or was this about an assignment? She had already theorized the petals' medical efficacy as an ingredient to extract toxicity. Based on the color that the blue flora stained the soup, first pink and then a red deeper than dates or jujubes, she had concluded that they helped the blood.

Someone tapped her on the shoulder. Ling flinched.

"I was waving at you, but your mind is elsewhere." Emma stood in front of her and held out a strawberry candy. "Is your aunt well?"

Ling gratefully plucked the sweet from Emma's palm. "Just fine." So much had happened since they'd last spoken, Ling didn't know where to begin. Discussing her uncle at school would only stir unflattering speculations. "What did I miss in botany?"

"Shrubs are on this week's curriculum. I thought they would be boring, but Miss James started lecturing on the flowering varieties. Roses and lilacs. They smelled so lovely. I never thought of roses as shrubs, did you?"

The twinkle in Emma's eyes showed that she shared Ling's excitement for plants. Multicolored roses were in bloom at the Blake Gardens. Her passion wasn't only a novelty. She understood the abilities of flora to strengthen and heal the human condition. Plant medicine could even distract from the condition of womanhood. It was an outrageous idea that she kept to herself. But if nourishing yin energy made women more feminine, then an herb must exist to achieve the alternative.

"So, I heard you had a gentleman caller." Emma leaned toward Ling. She breathed the sugared question, tapping shiny pink fingernails on the wooden desk.

"What?" Ling's response was sharp.

Emma shifted her attention back to the assignments. "Is it true?"

Ling curled her lips. "Do not believe everything you hear."

"I take it that is a no. The boy who used to come around...what was his name?"

Ling's ears got hot. She knew Emma meant Enlai. "Who else has heard this? The label is only for convenience."

Emma didn't know Enlai had stolen from Ling. Her father's compass was a precious treasure she would never get back.

"My mistake. Someone mentioned the Red Society men, so I remembered him. They have an honorable cause."

"But one that does not fit into the church's agenda." Ling's mood was darkening. She was filled with fury at a boy who wasn't even here. Even the sweet candy didn't soothe the discomfort crawling under Ling's skin. Was Enlai trying to ruin her life? No. Enlai was just sending a message. It wasn't Emma's fault; her friend was attempting kindness. Ling managed to crack a half-smile, trying to salvage the moment.

"I apologize if I upset you," Emma said. Her eyebrows knit together. "I think he really likes you, but of course he made some bad choices." She picked up an assignment list. "I can give you my notes on the reading if you wish. Dickens is horribly bland."

Ling relaxed. "It is all right. I'd much rather hear it from you. Enlai was never..." He was a lost cause. They could never be together, but she admitted that perhaps his position in the underground society could be useful. "You have to promise me. Do not trust him."

Emma nodded slowly as she remembered something important. "Yesterday, I asked other students some questions pretending that I was working on a heritage project. I gathered facts about their extended families in this region. This is it." Emma turned to a list in her notebook. Down the page were the names of students and surnames, some that weren't their own. "Most people are no more than twice-removed from aristocratic lineages. I mean even you're related to a Lord."

Ling scanned the page, comparing the list of names to Aunt Marcella's list. "What did you ask the other students?"

"Lineage, last names. It was no trouble at all." Emma examined her nails. "Everyone has a story. A platform and an eager ear are all that they needed."

"You would be a great journalist," Ling admitted. Her eyes stopped at Annie's name.

"You think?" Emma looked elated and crossed her arms on top of the desk. Lying her head on her forearms, she let her face relax. "If only women could have careers. Which names interest you?"

Ling understood Emma meant proper ladies when she said "women." Plenty of women had jobs of course, but not those of Emma's class. Those with status and wealth couldn't and didn't work. They did not have passions like the low born.

"Is this correct?" Ling stared at the description of Annie's relations.

"As certain as I could extract." Emma straightened her back.

Annie's last name was Sousa. But Emma's notes also showed a relationship to the Eggers family.

"She hesitated when she gave me the second name. Perhaps the family is not on good terms. Her ties with Portugal and then Macau are obvious...I talked with her a little longer than the others." Emma reached out and touched Ling's shoulders gently. "Is something wrong? You are tensed all the way up to your ears."

Ling's tone turned serious. "Did Annie have anything to say about an estranged relative who lives on the peninsula?" Even with Lady Tun deceased, her confessions in the letters reverberated now in Ling's mind. Had Lord Eggers been privy to Lady Tun's corruption of children?

"Only that Annie wasn't allowed to see her." Emma

shrugged. "Lady Tun apparently didn't do well with children."

"I think... I think I found a way to ask the Chief of Police to help," Ling said. "Let's not draw attention." Ling peered at the other students, who were beginning to turn their heads towards their conversation.

"What do you have?" Emma touched a finger to her cheek. Strands of purple radiated in her hazel eyes.

Ling shifted her lips from side to side, overwhelmed. What had transpired since they had last spoken was too much. Her aunt's condition seemed hopeless. The fact that her mother had suggested an apprenticeship with Wupo annoyed her.

Emma continued. "Be careful, okay? Ling, you're the smartest person I know, but in negotiation, it is the most patient and quiet person who usually wins." Emma put her hand over Ling's. The warmth felt reassuring.

Ling looked earnestly into Emma's eyes. "I should get going. Can you cover for me if I'm late? I have to go see Miss James."

Emma smiled. "I always do."

TWENTY-FIVE

With Miss James's note in her pocket, Ling hurried down the hallway. Without students congregating along the edges, the corridor seemed cold and stoic. Conversations echoed faintly from the teachers' office. Wheels squeaked behind her. Helpers were transporting hedges cut into different shapes toward the classrooms. Ling stopped to peek at the tea stations, expecting Miss James to be chatting with the nuns. However, her teacher wasn't with the others. Ling was uncertain what to do. If she asked anyone where Miss James was, she might be reproached.

Catching up to the men wheeling the plants, she cleared her throat. "Excuse me."

The cart squealed to a halt. Their heads turned. A pale man gazed at her with cloudy eyes. His pupils blended in with his irises. Ling held her breath, noticing for the first time that odd scars ran across his chalky face. The puckered indentations in his skin could've been the aftermath of a rake being dragged across his face. A shiver trickled down Ling's back. Why hadn't she noticed before? They were so prominent.

"Must'n mind him," said the shorter man dressed in overalls. His face was unmarred, although wrinkles pinched his tanned nose. "What is it, little Miss?"

"Where is Classroom 204?" The building had been converted from a missionary to a school piece by piece, without an overall plan. Consequently, not all stairways went to the expected places. Ling stepped further from the cart. One of the evergreens had been cut into the shape of a sitting rabbit. She patted the animal on the head. The soft needles bent under her palm.

Both men stared blankly.

"Those stairs." The shorter one pointed down the hall.

Ling thanked them and followed the direction indicated by the tan finger. Most classes were held on the ground floor. The second level housed science labs and religious seminars. On the very top, where she wasn't allowed to explore, were the residences of nuns and teachers. When she reached Room 204, she peeked into the dusty space, which was cluttered with boxes.

Ling's heart soared when she spotted Miss James in a corner. The space had been repurposed with the glare of sodium grow lights. Baby plants sprouted from tubes of water, warming under glass lids. A stained-glass window illustrated Saint Fiacre with an abundant garden and sunflowers. Green and yellow light shone across the repurposed classroom.

"I see you got my note." The teacher waved her closer. Ling looked curiously into the open boxes, finding everything from grammar guides to comics. Ling waited for Miss James to finish what she was writing. "Do you see this specimen right here?" she asked, not looking up.

Ling crouched, staring at the lighter underside of a leaf.

"A friend gifted me this from a faraway rainforest. It's carnivorous, reproducing with its own spores. I have been watching it for weeks. Move three inches to your right, and you'll see them better."

"What do they eat?" Ling gazed at the fleshy colored leaves.

"Small children," she chuckled.

Ling flinched before realizing Miss James had no idea that local children had been going missing.

"A long tube down the middle of the plant draws in its prey. At the bottom is sweet nectar. Flies and beetles crawl inside for a meal, but never make it out. Their bodies are slowly dissolved by the acidic walls." Her big eyes sparkled in wonder at the bulbous sores. Then she covered the plant with a glass lid. "No need to breathe in those babies when they hatch. Hopefully, I can propagate an entire field of them."

Ling wanted more time exploring the plants under the lights. They seemed so peaceful in their own dedicated space, away from the commotion of people.

Miss James stopped fretting with her notes and looked at her. "Ling, I am sorry about your uncle."

Ling didn't know what to say, so she remained silent. What details of Dabak's arrest were public knowledge? The circumstances of the crime could be easily misrepresented and whipped into a frenzy. Ling's eyes scanned the room for something else to discuss.

Miss James seemed to perceive Ling's discomfort. "Shall we confer about the blue petals?" Her teacher pointed behind Ling, where five stacks of texts sat near the worn writing desk.

"Is the information in one of these books?" Scanning the spines, Ling saw with some disappointment that she had already read most of these botany texts. She could not recall any reference to a petal with sharp and rounded edges. Ling had only seen a small portion of the plant. Flowers also had a stem, anther, ovule, and much more. People tended to fixate on the most visible and beautiful portion of the plant, forgetting about the essential anatomy, mostly hidden away.

"It might be. I gathered every book even remotely related to botany." Miss James put her finger to her mouth, and whispered, "even the manuscripts from the forbidden section."

"Sister Winters will not miss them." Ling parroted Emma's assurance from the day before.

Miss James smiled. "I figured you had have already read the common texts, so those are organized on the right side. The rare ones are to the left. Most of them are personal notebooks of gardeners and potion makers. A very interesting place to start, but most tedious, as they are not organized like books."

"And the middle stacks?" Ling couldn't control the excitement of her question.

Miss James smirked. "The middle two are written in other languages. Some we may understand and others we may not. By luck, if you find an illustration in there, we can ask one of the nuns to translate the pages."

Ling stared at the knowledge collected on the table. There was a lot of work ahead of them.

"Do not worry, Ling. We can do it together. In fact, you should consider asking Emma to join us." Miss James picked a book from the top of the middle pile. She gestured to a page with ancient symbols. "Is there any chance you know what this means?"

"I'll ask my un—" she began to say out of habit. A knot formed in her stomach. "I can inquire with the language teacher at lunch."

Her teacher didn't object and continued to organize her lessons for the day. Ling started copying the primordial signs into her notebook. This arcane language had been appearing unnaturally frequent. As she mimicked the narrow strokes, a low-pitched noise bellowed. Ling paused, holding the pen midair, and skimmed the edges of the room. It sounded like a monster was coming up from the floorboards. She gritted her teeth and started again. With every line, noises vibrated from deep inside of her. Verses crept out from her shadowy parts. Her teacher didn't notice.

"You should be present in your first class." Miss James scribbled on a piece of paper. The bells chimed downstairs, calling Ling away to scripture class.

"This is for Sister March. Tell her you were helping with sprouting seeds," her teacher said, handing her the paper. Ling gave a small smile. This was a lie, but the wrath of Sister March was much worse than a sin against God. Miss James knew this as well as she.

"May I borrow this?" Ling squeezed the spine of the disturbing book. A mildew smell seeped from the pages.

Miss James pursed her lips. "Better to keep it here. I do not want to get you in trouble again." She winked. Ling still had to return the copy of *Camilla* without her mother checking her bag. "However, you can come back any time to read it and go through the other texts. I will add a note about working on a special project. Call it categorization of the Lord's plants."

When she returned to the classroom, Sister March crossed her arms even after Ling produced the note. The nun read it with a tight lip.

"Better late than never...." Her eyebrows slanted deep into the center of her face.

Ling curtsied before sitting down, asking for grace from Sister March. Ling glued her attention to the wood pattern on the floor. At her desk, she pulled out the King James Bible from a lower compartment. Complying with classroom rituals deflected the wrath of the nuns.

Sister March cleared her throat, disdain bleeding from her glare. "Miss Shaw has a tolerable excuse for her tardiness. Let's return our attention to *Leviticus 26:29*. Recite." She held up a hand and upon bringing it down to her hip, the class started the passage:

And ye shall eat the flesh of your sons, and the flesh of your daughters shall ye eat.

"Class, can you tell me why this is so?" Sister March bellowed at the five rows of students.

Ling touched the three lines on the page. *Eat the flesh.* The holy words melted in front of her eyes. *Your sons.* A discomfort gripped her stomach. *Your daughters.* She rubbed her sweaty palms under the desk. *Shall ye eat.* The skin around her eyes burned.

When no one responded, the nun said: "Ling, you are in the apropos position to answer this question." She glared with a stern expression.

Ling disagreed. She was in the worst position to speak. Sister March was putting her front and center to prove a point.

"This should not be a trick question." The nun tapped her fingers on a desk.

Ling's hands clammed up. The verse referred to punishments for disobeying the Sanctuary of the Lord. It had been taught to her again and again. The right explanation seared into her throat, designed to confirm that God controlled all her decisions.

But this time, the corners of her mouth lifted. Sister March's scoffing remarks pushed Ling over the edge. The underlying message was supposed to be that locals deserved their tortured fates. Ghosts had arrived to show the savages how to reach the holy lands. If this was the case, then how had the emperors of eighty-three dynasties received their mandate from heaven to rule?

She answered: "The verse means vampires exist."

Collectively, the classroom gasped.

Emma shot Ling a nervous look. Her confusion turned to a smile. "Ling is hilarious." She laughed, goading the entire class to follow. She shot her friend a look, wiping her hand over her forehead, valiantly trying to defuse the situation.

But Sister March stormed to the middle row and lifted Ling by her ear. Ling hollered as the Sister jerked her into the hallway.

"I thought better of you. What did I tell you about reading the devil's stories?" Sister March said as her eyes turned dark. With a shooing motion, Sister March wished Ling away. "Off to the Headmaster's office."

Sister March glared at her through the classroom door as it closed, whispering, "Are you not the regular family of criminals?"

Ling seethed on the way to the office. Sister March's comment shouldn't have influenced her emotions so much. She was mad at herself for feeling a sting from the comment. What if she simply hid in the second-floor storage room for the rest of the day? She had the permission slip from Miss James. The idea was enticing. Somehow, Sister March's punishment would ferment with more time. Could she blame her distress on Dabak's arrest? Would the headmaster have any sympathy for her? Did he believe in vampires?

She did not know if it would be better if he did, or if he did not.

Twenty-Six

The headmaster pressed his chin into the phone receiver as his brows furrowed. Hair stuck out from his temples. A sheen of perspiration shone on his forehead. "Miss Shaw, just the pupil I needed to speak to."

She tensed at the sound of her name, stepping into the evergreen-painted office. A carpet with two tigers spanned the center of the room, swirling golds with honey yellow. She smoothed the ends of her pigtails. Had Sister March phoned him while she walked down the hall? Headmaster Lee waved her inside, wiping a handkerchief across his nose.

"I'll let her know. She's in my office right now...." He paused, glancing at Ling. She bit her bottom lip, bracing herself for a speech. He might ask her to go to confession or write out a Bible verse a hundred times before tomorrow morning. Either punishment would take valuable time away from freeing her uncle.

"It is your aunt."

Ling froze. Did she have news about Dabak?

"She says your mother needs to meet you at the stand. Be there by noon."

"May I speak with her?" The last-minute request puzzled Ling.

Headmaster Lee didn't respond. He placed the phone back into the holder. "I was not aware your aunt is Lord Langley's niece." He slid a pair of spectacles to the bridge of his nose and searched in a phone book. "Charles Langley is a great benefactor of this school. He provided the funds to expand the greenhouse. We should make a bigger fuss about the relationship."

Ling craned her neck to read the names too. She searched for Eggers and Stewart, which didn't seem to be on the first page. "Yes, he is my"— she drew a line from her to Aunt Marcella's uncle— "great-uncle."

"Well, he's a relation, to say the least." He paid no mind to his glasses, which were sliding down his sweaty nose. "Your fortunes are clearly on the rise. He's an asset in the antiquities trade."

Good fortunes hadn't flowed in with Dabak's marriage yet. Things were in fact going quite poorly for Aunt Marcella and now Dabak.

"Did she tell you the reason for my mother's request?" Ahma had never disturbed Ling's education. A strict boundary existed between home and school, one that would be broken today.

Headmaster Lee stiffened his lip. "She did not provide details. But I have a piece of advice for you. Close the shop on the first of July. Stay home, or better yet stay with your aunt on the island."

Ling lifted her chin. July first was in two days.

"The protestors have planned an event on the pier," the Headmaster said, his voice glum. He tapped a pen on his papers. "I am concerned for your safety, especially with your uncle away."

Enlai had mentioned the celebration. She hadn't given it a second thought until now. The local event was garnering attention. To Dabak, a large gathering was mostly an opportunity to sell more teas.

A soft knock drew their attention. It was the receptionist, bringing a note to the headmaster. She walked by Ling, smelling of roses.

At the desk, he raised his eyebrows. He glanced at the secretary in the red lipstick, at the note, and at Ling again. "You are quite popular today. The Police Chief has also phoned for you."

Ling jumped up. "He did?" Embarrassed by her rashness, she took a seat again and composed herself. "Apologies. It's been a long few days since..."

"Yes, of course. He asked you to call him back. It must be about Dr. Shaw." He extended the note over the top of his papers. Ling pinched the small square of paper between her fingers, her hand shaking a bit. "This is his personal phone number."

Sweat beaded on her hairline. She felt the hot glare of the two other people. Ling was a well-behaved student. Yet, the last few days had inspired a wildness from her soul. This part of her would outlive its welcome soon.

"Why were you here in the first place? The religion class has not ended," he said. Ling saw the secretary open her mouth to reply. Did she mean to give her away?

Ling hastened to speak up first. "To thank you...um, for your call to the police outpost. Mother would not be able to visit Dr. Shaw if you had not put in a word." She smiled, hoping the reason was enough to leave.

The Headmaster's expression softened. "I do what I can." He fanned his face. "As for classes, let's not fall too much farther behind. Sister March will have my head."

"I promise, I'll make up for these past few days." She stood up too fast, and the phone number slipped. It sailed from her lap and under the desk. The thin-armed secretary tried to grab for the swooping paper too. Her legs were hugged too close by the pencil dress she wore, which made it difficult for her to move quickly.

"Apologies for my clumsiness." Ling landed on her hands and knees, crawling under the desk.

Headmaster Lee shuffled in his seat. "Wait, allow me."

She had already spotted the paper by his feet. "Do not trouble yourself Headmaster. I found it." Snatching the note, she glimpsed a coin. It was engraved with the bronze symbol for snake. The same kind of coin as the one Kit had been given. Why did he have it? She retreated as fast as she could, holding her question in. Keeping her head down, blood drained from her face. She needed to hide her reaction. Ahma was right. He was not to be trusted.

———

Ling snuck up to the second floor. The classroom with the books to research had a working phone. Up there she had a modicum of privacy, away from the ears of the prying office staff. Thanks to her excused absence, she had carte blanche to craft the rest of her morning as she wished.

She checked the center stack selection of books, where the less common texts were arranged. Miss James's efforts had truly been above and beyond. Ling found several volumes which interested her in this pile. She spotted a beautiful floral cover with patterns of poppies with the title *Gospel of Mary Magdalene.* Why include a religious text? It wasn't a common chapter of the good book. She focused on a hand-sewn manuscript, stitched together with a heavy linen cord. Fishing it out of the pile, she gasped at its title.

Along a strip of white paper, *Bencao Gengmu* was written in thick ink. She bit her lip, not believing her eyes. A rare copy of the Great Pharmacopeia, written by a naturalist and herbalist, had found her. It held forbidden knowledge. From the first pages, it was apparent this volume covered the extraction and consumption of human body parts for healing. Ling's mind soared as she flipped through the pages. The issues of the day fell away. Side-by-side illustrations of male and female human bodies noted the gender's energetic differences. Life, the book said, existed on a continuum of yin and yang energies. Yin was the feminine energy of darkness, coldness, passivity, and nurturing. Yang was the masculine energy of light, dryness, activity, and strength. The human body was self-healing and held special properties inside each cell.

What were the medicinal qualities of eyes? This had been a burning question for days, since she had come across the strange purple orbs that showed her visions. She moved through the sections quickly, stopping on the one about sight. This chapter was shorter than the others, with a brief synopsis of the limited medical properties they possessed. Physically, eyes were soft and passive. Their yin form allowed for the absorption of environment and light. The text didn't recommend them for consumption. They were noted as a diagnostic tool for organs tied closely to the liver and lungs, windows to a person's mental and emotional state. At the very end of the measly two pages, the writer mentioned the possibility of ingesting the powder of healthy eyes to reverse progressive blindness.

There was no information regarding the collecting and preserving of eyes in saline jars. She was disappointed, but relieved that holding eyes prisoners wasn't advised in even the most obscure traditional medicine practices. The idea of hurting one person to heal another didn't sit well with her.

Ling transferred a stack of hand-stitched books next to the phone. She would keep searching until the last possible second. She felt that there was a good chance that the Police Chief would do as she asked. Then her family wouldn't have to engage with Wupo,

"Good morning, I am returning a call to the police chief. I am Ling Shaw, the niece of both Dr. Shaw and Lord Charles Langley." While referencing Langley as a relation felt contrived, she knew it added force to her request. The relation conjured up more prestige and privilege than Ling could ever imagine.

"Please hold. I'll fetch the Chief," said a man with a meek voice. There was shuffling on the other side and loud footsteps. Ling flipped through the first hand-written text as she waited. The cork cover crumbled between her hands. She struggled to open the damaged page. As far as she could glean, it had been a personal diary of a nun.

"Ah yes, Miss Shaw. This is Bartholomew Stewart. Thank you for your concern about my health."

Ling's mouth went dry. She cast the broken book aside. Her first instinct was to rattle off everything she'd read in his patient file. However, Emma had pointed out the flaws in Ling's reflexes. She could not blurt out what she was thinking. She had to speak in a refined and confident manner when addressing one of the highest-ranking ghosts on the island. He was giving her his complete attention.

"I am as dedicated to patients as much as my uncle. While Dr. Shaw is unavailable, I must step in for the care of his most... valued patients." Ling paused, putting weight on the last words. She about to list the medicines her uncle prescribed when Captain Stewart jumped in.

"Everything is fine." He breathed heavily into the line.

She waited until he spoke again. His nervousness came out in his pauses.

"Miss, if there is nothing specific, we shall conclude this discussion. I am feeling rather... satisfied."

Ling had no intention of ending the conversation until he agreed to free her uncle. Sensing his desire to hang up, she asked, "Did you know I started hearing voices two days ago? They recite many secrets in Kowloon."

"Excuse me? I—how—it's not my—" Small cracks started to show in the Captain's resolve.

Ling cupped the receiver and whispered, "What do the voices say to you?"

"Young lady, your questions are preposterous."

"Not to your constituents and to the legislative council. Once the medication runs out, they would quite like to know the nature of your phantom advisers."

"Inflammatory." The captain huffed. She heard his teeth grinding. Then he spoke tersely. "What do you want?"

"Apologies. I do not mean any offense." She lifted her tone. "My uncle should be released."

"Your's is an impossible request." She heard his heavy, pacing footsteps through the phone. He took three steps in one direction and then the other. The captain was working out a problem. Dabak did the exact same thing when he was stumped.

"Captain, nothing is impossible for you." She knew he fretted about her knowledge of his condition. Otherwise, the conversation would've ended a long time ago. Revelation of his corruption and immorality would end his career and destroy his reputation. Residents would go after him.

"He...I cannot do it," he protested.

Ling waited silently, steadying her thoughts. She could threaten to oust him again. But Emma had advised patience, not reacting immediately to each idea.

The captain exhaled. "Hold on." He put down the phone and the thumping of footsteps faded.

Ling tapped her toes. She rummaged in the stack for a viable book before landing on a dry manuscript she might've skipped but for the delay on the phone. The paper was unexpectedly thick and well-made, piquing her curiosity. She was taken aback by what she discovered within.

There were strange plant and flower drawings. She hadn't seen most of the life depicted in the pages. Was this a book of rare plant life? *Fritillaria delavayi*, the name for a shy green flower that lived in the high altitudes of the Himalayas. A place Ling had never even dreamed of. A description followed written in several dialects.

Perennis planta, Flos viridis quinquennalis, Bulbi pulverem contra tussim.

The Latin said it was a perennial that bloomed a bright green flower every five years. Its bulbs could be created into a potent powder for coughs. The language Ling understood was followed by ancient text that was reminiscent of the symbols at the police outpost. Regardless of the *lingua franca*, she knew medicine when she read it.

Ling touched the image of the mysterious green flower. Who was the author of the loosely bound pages? Was it another piece of the Great Pharmacopeia? She turned more pages, hoping this would be the solution she needed.

The captain picked up the phone again, winded. "Do you have the eyes?"

Ling didn't respond right away, still processing the contents she had stumbled on. She was taken aback by his question. How did he know?

"We can make this an exchange. Bring them to the outpost this evening." His voice was distant.

"I do not trust you." A knot turned in Ling's stomach. The outpost was the last place she wanted to go.

"You have to. If Dr. Shaw is not released tonight, then you will miss your chance."

"What do you mean?" Her hand was shaking. She heard the danger in his words.

"I cannot discuss this further. Eyes for the doctor. Period."

TWENTY-SEVEN

Pink sunlight beamed onto the desk. The hands on the clock inched closer to 11:30 a.m. Surrounded by books and quiet, Ling hummed. Each page of the unbound manuscript enveloped her in new species of flora. She almost forgot what she was looking for jagged petals. On the boat, the man dressed in the hunter's uniform had given her a clue within the image of Lady Tun. Danger lurked around her brothers. With the woman gone, deciphering the flower was the key. She marveled at the artist's hand and detailed notes on its efficacy.

What did she have to do at noon? She clenched her jaw, belatedly remembering that she agreed to meet her mother at the pier. She would be late, even if she sprinted down the long road to the docks. School didn't let out until three, so there wouldn't be any pulled cart drivers waiting at the gate yet.

Carrying out the most promising books in her bag, despite Miss James' warning to leave everything in there, she left the room at a run. Her shoes skidded on the tile as her arms and bare manuscript crashed almost immediately into the gardener with the marks on his face. The books in her hands to the items from her bag flew everywhere. The room spun. She was knocked against the plaster walls and fell onto the tiled floor.

Her head spun as the gardener approached her.

"Miss, my apologies. Are you injured?" His words were polite, but the cold expression on his face did not alter. She couldn't read emotion in his cloudy eyes.

Reaching into her pocket, she fished out Dabak's protective salve. The balm stopped the pounding in her head. Holding the container to her nose, she daubed the spaces between her eyes with cooling mint. The buzzing stopped and her vision stabilized.

The man was gathering up the scattered things. "Sorry, so sorry," he kept repeating. His eyebrows lifted as he approached her, seated on the floor where she had fallen.

"What is that smell?" He crouched in front of her, pointing at her hand. His crooked back tiled him forward. His gray pupils frantically moved from side to side.

Ling lifted the corners of her mouth. "Doctor Sh...." Her explanation was cut short when the gardener abruptly swiped the tin out of her hand. *You have to ask*, she wanted to say. Instead, her mouth fell open.

The man scooped a heap of ointment with beastly fingers. He inhaled a portion through his nose. Ling scooted to the side as far as she could, watching his pure delight with utter bafflement. He was acting as if he had discovered gold. She had never seen anyone act this way with any medicine.

He scooped the remaining glop onto his fingers and inserted them into his eyes.

"Excuse me...." The application shocked Ling. She jumped to her feet. Was the man hurting himself?

The man screamed and then laughed. Ling worried whether she should be alone with him at this moment.

Someone had surely heard the strange sounds. His noises morphed to whimpers as he convulsed on the floor. Ling's training made her want to help, even if he had done this to himself. No one else could ensure his safety. But why did he have to ingest the salve through his nose and eyes? Why did his body have such an intense reaction to it? The doctor in her needed to know.

"Keep your wits," she mumbled to herself, approaching the distressed patient. She inserted a hard stick in between his teeth and positioned him on his back. She had to deal with this herself. Going for help would draw unfavorable questions, including why she had been alone in this wing of the school. After a few minutes, he stopped twitching.

Ling pressed two fingers onto his wrist. A pulse beat fast under his skin. His heart was stressed. She lifted his eyelids to check the aftermath of his rash action. Grease from the salve still caked his lashes. To her surprise, there were now shimmers of green in his irises. The last time she had been up so close to such eyes, they had been her father's. However, Ba had been a Captain of a ship, always standing tall and enunciating his words. This gardener was nothing like him. She was grasping at straws.

Her things were still strewn across the hallway. Ling was overwhelmed by the mess. Shells were cracked in half. Coffee stained her father's journal. Emily's precious toffees were smashed into the tiles. She picked up only the red bow and fell to her knees. She couldn't even keep her smallest treasures safe.

Tears started to well under her eyes when she felt a tap on her shoulder. Ling jumped to her feet.

"Sorry to scare you." She was shocked to realized that his voice was different. The man held up a book, a page opened to an entry showing blue flowers. The exact ones she had been looking for. "Do you need this?"

Ling stared with amazement at the page. The word were written in an unfamiliar tongue. As the gardener's pink cheeks, she stammered, "I... thank you."

"My name is Wai. I can help you with the mess." His still-cloudy eyes met hers. "I appreciate you allowing me the ointment. It's strange to admit. That particular herbal scent had been in my dreams. And now, I feel like a haze has been lifted from my sight."

"Doctor Shaw has more at the shop," she managed to reply. She couldn't understand the difference in his manner and appearance. The application of the medicinal solution had completely changed him. What ailment did he have? "You may want to see him to follow up."

"Yes, I know your uncle well. I work with him at the Hong family estate." He held the book out again.

"I am Ling," she said, as the tower of the church chimed twelve times. She winced inside. Her mother would be furious with her tardiness.

"Oh yes, the budding young doctor. Your uncle is kind. I am indebted to him, and now even more for this miraculous medicine. The least I can do is help his niece. Is there anything you need?" He spoke in a remarkably flawless English accent. Even Dabak, who had studied at Oxford and whose English was excellent, had a trace of a countryside accent.

"I must meet my mother at the pier, I am late." Ling shoved her scattered items into her bag. Then hastily she asked Wai one more question. "I have been searching for the name of this flora for many days. Can you read the language?" It was clearly a grimoire, so she expected him to say no.

Wai lowered his eyes to the floral illustration then recited easily, "Moonflowers drink in the power of the dark, developing healing properties for yin deficiency."

"You know this script?" Ling didn't hide her surprise. She felt bad for assuming he had no experience with esoteric knowledge.

He smiled, bringing the text very close to his face. "Yes. It's one of the oldest languages."

Ling stared at the white spots dotting the blue petals like a rash. According to Aunt Marcella, these flowers treated vampire bites. But healing wasn't the flowers only trait; it had other uses. The petals had been stuffed into dead woman's mouth.

In a trance-like state, Wai moved his lips. He pressed his fingers into the book and uttered guttural noises. Ling shivered. English translations trailed his strange sounds. "This flower nourishes darkness. This flora, paired with Chrysanthemums or hot peppers, smothers the desire to feast on blood. However, as the blooms are temporary, so is the potency. Alone, with enough petals, it can snuff out physical embodiments of evil."

This explained the ingredient in Aunt Marcella's medicine. The petals provided nourishment like the men at sea who ate fisheyes. How did these petals also quell the impulses of the dead? What evil had Lady Tun personified?

He groaned, clenching his head. "Apologies, this text is more difficult than I expected. The knowledge in this book can bring about madness." But despite his evident discomfort, and the stated risk to his sanity, he continued scanning the page.

Ling was running out of time. She knew she had to go. Yet, she couldn't help herself from asking about the red flower in the following entry.

"*Papaver somniferum*," she said, naming the source of hallucinogenic tar, *nga pien*, imported by ghost ships. This was the poppy.

Wai shook his head but gave in to reading. "Harvesting

the flower at an immature stage will produce a sap to induce lethargy in physical and spiritual bodies when ingested. This product has a binding effect on those who voluntarily submit to any spell or curse."

"What are the symbols for curse?" Ling asked, trying to deduce the similarities between the two plants. Back-to-back entries usually meant something in a self-bound grimoire. The blue flowers released, while the red one bound people to enchantment. She had always thought it was odd for the poppy to produce such a hypnotic effect on its users.

Wai tilted the book toward her. Ling marveled at the drawings of two flowers that couldn't be more different. He pointed to a grouping of lines and slashes. In both notes and in their same language, they had the same form.

Ling raised her eyebrows. "Is *r'luhhor mgvulgtlagln* a specific curse?"

"From what I know in another context, the *r'luhhor mgvulgtlagln* is a force originating from the old ones. Ancients who existed before mankind. The closest idea that you know is probably Tao or the laws of physics. Where did you find this?"

"In a box hidden inside a storage room," she said. But she wondered. How had Miss James casually stumbled upon this ancient spell book? Did Miss James understand the contents of what she had found? "Why does the school even have a book with curses and spells?"

Wai pressed the book to his chest. By way of answer, he said, "How does a foreign church erect a marble building under the very shadow of Kowloon Mountain? It's quite a feat without the right blessings."

Something inside Ling clicked into place. Magic was involved. Magic pervaded the land. The events of the past several days had proved this to Ling. Had the church bound themselves to the ancients, or the other way around?

"I heard *Ny'ghft Zhro'khal* was the source of her suffering." The man on the boat used the term to explain Lady Tun's death.

"Summoning an ancient wrath." Fear flashed in his eyes. "A terrible thing to bring back to the world."

Ling let the interpretation sink in. The ancients wanted to punish excessiveness. Yet, Lady Tun's death hadn't driven the greed away. It had instead triggered chaos, surfacing secrets that threatened the status quo. Dangerous people were searching for a dead woman's treasures. All things Ling knew about. She realized that she and her family were in a most dangerous position. Worse, even, than she had feared.

Twenty-Eight

An odd stink seeped into the twins' bedroom. The streets had been cleared this morning in anticipation of the upcoming celebration, so it wasn't certain where the smell was coming from. Ling whiffed the scent as soon as she walked in the door. She had gone to the medicine stand late, only to find it abandoned. What had been so important that her mother abandoned the store? Ling managed to salvage the day with a dozen sales or so.

She pondered her upcoming discussion with Captain Stewart. Who would be a fitting companion? Ahma had to care for Aunt Marcella and the twins. Emma was a staunch friend but unsuited for conflict. Enlai was the only choice left, but his help was almost certain to come with strings.

As she inspected the bedroom her brothers and Ahma shared, her train of thought faltered. The twins' beds by the window were unmade, in contrast with her mother's neat and tidy mattress by the door. This was odd. It was routine to close windows and doors before leaving for the day. Their window was open a crack. Had it been left unlatched all night? She sniffed over the sill to locate the source of the rotting stench.

Then someone burst through the front door. "Nuer, are you here?"

"Ahma, where were you?" Ling rushed out to the common room.

"Your brothers. Have you seen them?" Her face was contorted with worry. Her shirt was drenched in sweat and her pants caked with dirt. Had she spent her day crawling through a gutter?

"I thought you picked them up at school." Ling was rapidly beginning to share in her mother's anxiety. The twins didn't go places on their own.

"They aren't... weren't there." Ahma wiped her face with a kitchen towel. "I forgot to pack their midday meal. I left the stand to bring it to them at the school yard. I intended to return but...." She put her hands over her face and sat down. "The teachers said they never arrived...."

Her mother's voice faded. She couldn't be saying what Ling thought she was saying. "Maybe they are with a friend. Got caught up in a game...." A few names popped up in her head. Unfortunately, Cili was one of them. The missing girl.

"I re-traced their steps and knocked on everyone's door." Ahma's eyes were wild. She was out of breath. "Nobody saw them."

Ling leaned against the wall. This couldn't be happening. "I am seeing the police chief later on. Perhaps, he...."

"He will not help..." Sobs escaped Ahma's throat.

Ling knew that time was critical when looking for missing persons. Less than a half day had passed; it might not be too late. "We have to ask everyone to help. We will have merchants and protesters to comb the forest, bay, and marshes." Ling spilled out a rush of ideas. "They might be in the Walled City."

"This is all my fault." Her mother cried into her hands on the circle table. "I never should have angered Wupo. When we did not go...."

"Why do you...Wupo? You think Wupo took them?" Ling cast a skeptical eye on her mother's ravings. Her mind raced. Was the monster who killed Lady Tun behind this? Distracting her with a request for William and instead going after her siblings? The cases of Mei and Cili had never been pursued. Was there just one person, or a whole group behind the missing children?

"It turns out Wupo commented on the virtue of all my children, not just one." Ahma fidgeted with her hands. What else was she not saying? "I thought they were safe at the missionary school. The secretary, Mrs. Lam, called the parents. She has no leads. What can we do?" Her mother peered blankly through the front door. Her demeanor crumpled into a pool of despair.

Searching under the twins' bed, Ling found a pile of their clothes. She tossed them aside. Perhaps this was a misunderstanding. They would rush through the door caked in mud any minute, unaware of having caused any trouble. It was wishful thinking.

She rummaged through their drawers. Far in the back, she fished out multicolored wrappers. There were toffee wrappers from the soda shop, and also some plain wax ones. The store candy wrappers had writing and logos printed on them. These wax ones were homemade.

They had told Ling that beyond the marshes, a witch offered Cili sweets. The truth dawned on her. Lady Tun had been the one responsible. The feat however would be impossible now that she was dead. Why did this woman's spirit continue to haunt Ling?

A thought hit her. Running to her room, she uncovered the jar with the eyes. They had intimate knowledge about the seaside shack and Lady Tun. Without hesitating, Ling dipped her fingers into the saline water. "Do you know where my brothers are?" The eyes had witnessed and shown her visions of a dead girl. They might well know other secrets of the universe.

Ling watched as the veins attached to her fingers and squeezed.

An image flared in her mind.

The eyes landed Ling in the middle of winding branches of a banyan. Only a little light filtered in through its lush leaves and intertwined roots. She tried to crawl out. Yet, the quicker she moved, the farther the light seemed. Until finally at the last branch, she spotted a clearing and a vast mountain range. As her face skimmed the dirt, the dainty feet of a woman moved into the clearing. In front of pink and white buds blooming on the trees, the woman turned toward the vines. Fresh blood ran down her face as her eyes glowed red.

"What are you doing?" Her mother cried from the kitchen, cutting off Ling's last impressions. It did not matter; the eyes had already confirmed Wupo as the kidnapper.

Ling set down the jar. The flowers had been blossoming tea leaves. As far as Ling could tell, the site was likely on the northern side of the mountain. The ocean was not visible at all from the angle and altitude in the vision. "I am going to the Walled City for help," she replied.

She hated to admit it, but there was only one person who would believe her and confront Wupo with her, and she would need his help, whatever strings may be attached.

Twenty-Nine

By the late afternoon, the winds had started to shift. Enlai was Ling's last resort. He could deploy his people to search for the twins and ensure her safety when visiting Wupo. These tasks were the least he could offer; he owed her that much. Her mother would begin a search with students and their parents.

At the entrance of the Walled City, an uneasy stillness stopped her. A worker pulling a cart full of produce threw her a fearful look. *Don't go in there,* his face said. A fresh gash sliced across his cheek, yellowed and swelling. She thought of Wai's injuries, never healing without the proper care. A simple application of pulverized ginger would nourish the man's broken skin. The wound caused the idea of the twins suffering to bubble up in her head. They were all alone. She had to hurry.

As she turned through dark and light, her eyes were slow in adjusting to the changes. Behind shuttered windows, people quarreled and cried. She didn't often venture this deep into the Walled City, and less than ten minutes inside the walls, she was lost. Stopping a mother with two young children in tow, she asked for directions to Cafe de Sourire.

"Are you sure you want to go *there*?" The mother tugged on the shirts of her kindergarteners. "Please, let's help this lady."

The children had dirt-streaked faces. One of them, a girl with short hair, stuck out her tongue. "The food there is dreadful. Eat at Nam Wan instead."

"I am afraid my friend insisted on meeting there. Anything I should not order?" Ling lifted the corners of her mouth, but a tightness gripped her chest.

"If you must, turn left. First ladder on your right." The mother frowned, pointing to the direction with a flick of her head. "On you go."

The family hurried away in the opposite direction.

Ling turned left, quickening her pace, so she wouldn't change her mind. Enlai was the last person she wanted to see, but he was the only one with the means and courage to help. First Street crossed White Street. The ladder spilled her onto the balcony of a private apartment. With no rails, the sliding doors had been taped over with newspapers. Was this really the right place?

From the balcony, she could see over the uneven stone walls surrounding the city. The stones alternated low and high with bump outs for archers and cannons. Up here the clouds appeared lower, touching the horizon like foam on top of a root beer float. Her mouth watered.

A voice inquired from the obscured entrance. "Who goes there?"

"I am looking for Cafe de Sourire," she answered in her best French.

Laughter erupted from the other side. "Enlai's petite amie."

Ling blushed without knowing why. "Is he there?"

Suddenly, her bag was yanked backwards. A white-haired woman in a grease-splashed apron waved her inside. "Food and drink through here."

Ling followed, scanning the vacant apartment with curiosity. The savory smells of fried garlic, roasted peppers, and potatoes drew her further inside. There was at least a promise of food.

The cook didn't wait to answer Ling's many questions and darted back to her station. Behind a curtain, a heavy cloth opened up to reveal a large space with metal tables and stools. Rowdy conversation buzzed through the room. This was the Cafe of Smiles.

Several groups played cards while others stacked tiles. People drank and smoked while a handful of waiters carted refreshments and plates in and out of the kitchen. Men had opened the collars to their traditional jackets. Women wore dresses with low necklines and tight bodices. Ling couldn't have been more out of place with her braids, navy blouse, and starched trousers. Where was Enlai?

Before she could think of a plan, a bulky man grabbed her by the waist. "Jie Jie, little sis, why are you standing there so fresh?"

She swatted at his hands, but he held on tight. Bile rose up in her throat. *Why was he touching her?* He was repulsive; his skin was slathered with beer and tobacco, and he smelled of regurgitated food.

"I am looking for Enlai," she said as he plopped her on a stool next to him without space between them.

"Dai Guo, leave her alone." A delicate woman in a light orange dress addressed the boss. She flashed Ling a sympathetic look.

"Why should I?" The big man fisted a handful of peanuts and shoved them in his mouth.

Resting a hand on top of his bulging gut, she said, "This

is Enlai's girl. Did you not hear her just say that?" The words were uttered calmly. Her lashes pointed downward. But the tremble in her voice said, regardless, that it wasn't her place to question this man.

Dai Guo's eyes widened. His expression soured as he pushed Ling off the chair. The woman in the orange dress took a step back, but he caught her wrist. He twisted her tiny bones invoking a silent scream. "Do not tell me what to do."

The entire place hushed, watching a man three times a lady's size show her who was in charge.

Tears streamed down the lady's cheeks. "My apologies."

Ling took this moment to escape.

"Go get more beers." Dai Lou boomed a command. A small whimper escaped the woman's lips. The ruckus restarted as Ling huddled by the stove.

The willowy dashed behind the curtain. She barked orders to the staff. "I need beers and the fish dishes for the boss." She turned her gaze down to Ling. "Listen, private school. Don't just show up expecting special treatment."

Ling looked up and nodded solemnly.

"Leave now. I will not be able to save you again."

"Enlai told me to come. I need help." Ling put her hands together.

The woman huffed. "That boy is an idiot. Hitching your house to that wagon is—"

"Go easy on her," said another cook cutting vegetables.

Orange dress tapped her fingers on a cutting board. "He's not here. Best I can do is give him a message." She pulled a container out and patted a white powder puff over the redness on her wrists, masking the marks of savagery.

"Hau Wang Miu? I'll wait for him there." Ling climbed out of her hiding place and went back the way she came.

"Good luck," voices said as Ling ducked behind the tarp.

On the way back, Ling didn't bump into a single soul. Cafe de Sourire wasn't open to the public. Who were all those men? Had she stumbled upon a band of Red Society brothers or yet another sort of hooligan? She walked uneasily, feeling a shadow lurking behind her. Dampness gathered on her skin. Could someone from the café have followed her out? She had taken only two steps out from the stone walls when two strong arms pulled her back inside.

She tipped backward, smacking her backside against the stones. Her vision blurred. A figure hovered over her.

Punching at the space above her head, she panicked. The man that had grabbed her in the café triggered something inside of her. She aimed at the legs of the attacker. A loud crack followed a well-aimed jab. She'd hit her target.

Ling clambered to her feet.

"A feisty one," Brother Tam choked. He wiped his face with his sleeve. His large hands grasped her shoulders.

Blood throbbed in Ling's ears. "What is this?" Blood leaked from a cut inside her mouth. Flavors of iron and sand coated her tongue.

Tam twisted his lips. "Where is Enlai?"

Ling was startled. "I thought you might know." She swiped at his face, gritting her teeth.

"I knew he was a liar." Tam's lips curved in a smile.

"No...he is my caller. We had a fight. I am looking for him."

"Lover's quarrel. Let me see." Tam pulled her closer, scanning her face. "I heard Wupo was looking for you." He frisked her pockets then ripped the canvas bag away from her.

"Stop!" she shouted into his face. "My uncle paid your

fees. This is my medical bag for sick patients." She frantically lunged for her possessions.

He struck her in the chest with the back of his hand. It stunned her. "Excellent. Da Lou will be pleased with these eyes. Wupo asked us to find them. Lucky day for a fortune to fall into my lap." He adjusted the black cloth around his head.

"You are a fool." Ling backed away.

He grabbed a handful of skin on her waist. Her leg lifted on impulse. Bringing the edge of her heel down on his foot, she tried to sprint away. He yelped but twisted her wrist tighter. "On second thought, I don't care about Enlai."

Ling tried to wriggle free. "Everyone wants the eyes. The police captain. A vampire. They will be after you now. Give them back."

He laughed. "I am not a child. Vampires are a fantasy of the ghosts."

"You have been locked inside these stone walls for too long." Ling was getting desperate. She needed those eyes for her uncle's freedom. "The Red Society should protect locals, not extort them." She glared at him through half-lidded eyes. She allowed a darkness to seize her words, giving them strength. "The eyes are cursed."

Fear flashed across his face, and he loosened his hold for a second. Ling dashed free and scrambled down the street. But in a flash, he was back at her side. "Wild thing." A haze clouded his face. "You are mine." He pulled her hair.

"I am not anyone's!" Hot pain permeated through her scalp. She hated being immobilized, not able to fight back. She hated how quickly he caught up to her.

He licked his lips and pressed them against hers. She thrashed with all her might. His touch was abhorrent. Her body tightened as he forced her lips apart. She didn't have the strength to fight him off indefinitely. A slippery tongue crept into her mouth. The back of her throat heaved. Tasting his cigarette ash and grime, she bit down. Blood filled her senses, a flavor she preferred over his putrid kisses.

He pushed her roughly to the ground. His hand was over his mouth, crying inaudible obscenities.

Ling ran for a hiding place with hair over her face. "Enlai!" she called out to the only person who could help her in this dark place.

"Do not make this harder than it has to be." Tam grabbed the back of her shirt, dragging her from the street into a building. Her shirt collar choked her. She couldn't breathe, and before long, everything went dark.

———

Ling woke up in a shed. Light filtered through the broken glass of a small window over her head. She panicked, patting down her shirt. Her bag wasn't on her. Thankfully, her clothes hadn't been disturbed.

"It is right here." Tam smoked from the back corner of the room. The dim red glow of his cigarette marked his location as far from her as possible in this small space. She was relieved. "I need to check if this is the real thing before I deliver it to Da Lou. Then we can play."

Ling flinched. She had only been kissed by Enlai once when they were kids. It was pleasant, but not fiery. She hadn't felt the tingles, jitters, or butterflies other girls talked about. Enlai was better than Tam. But who said it was a choice she had to make? "I need to leave. Give me...."

Tam cut her off. "Where I go, you go. Do you hear me?" He stepped into the light and spit. Ash and tar landed near her feet.

Ling tensed, catching the darkness in his cold eyes. It was the same glimmer from the vision when Lady Tun had taken the oracle child's eyes. She realized that he enjoyed watching her struggle. Fighting him wouldn't work. She needed a different approach.

Softening her tone, she asked. "We should take the eyes to Wupo ourselves? No need for middlemen. You should get all of the money."

Tam inhaled until his cheeks puffed up. A thick smoke spilled out of his nostrils on his exhale. "I knew you were something else." He pointed the cigarette at her. "You are too smart for Enlai."

The next drag lit up his sinister smile. "That entanglement business is more lucrative than selling tonics to laborers." His hands rustled inside the bag. "The strike is preposterous anyway. The ghosts are here to haunt us, regardless of the number of signs anyone holds up. Waste of time." He spat onto the dirt floor again.

Ling balled her hands into a fist. He didn't deserve any luck or fortune. But she forced herself to exude calm, so she could wait for the right moment.

Tam whistled a long, surprised note. "I might negotiate for more territories with these beauties. See the purple?"

He held the jar up to the light, pointing to them. Even in the dim light, there was a hint of violet gleaming from within. Ling couldn't get her head straight. The fresh scratch across his nose was a satisfying sight. What was he rambling about? "Wupo is paying more for purple ones. I mean, she's not *the* oracle. Not anymore. Replaced by a ghost."

"You speak nonsense." Ling replied, unable to process his foolish conspiracies. He was speaking to her as if she cared. All she wanted was to leave. "Give them back."

"Gullible Ling. Good and bad does not exist. The Red Society has its hands in everything. Sometimes we make moral judgements, and sometimes decisions are made for the money." He lifted the jar again, squinting uncertainly at the ghoulish orbs. "But you are correct. These eyes are for a sinister purpose. Too bad I am not well versed in magic myself."

A longing vibrated in Tam's voice. Ling realized she had found a weakness. "I understand the spells. Keep me as your own oracle. Then you will not need to kowtow to others. You'll have the territories of your choosing."

Tam squinted at Ling. "In due time. Overturning an empire does not take a day. Now, time for fun." Tam stepped toward Ling. "How does your hair taste?"

Ling tensed. There was only one exit. The pocketknife was in her bag. Not that running or fighting had worked before. Would he kill her if she didn't submit? She lifted her hands. "Not here." While her whole body was shaking, Ling used her most authoritative tone.

Tam raised his eyebrows. "I was not asking."

"My powers." She fought back tears. Ideas were her only weapon. She had to believe every word and put the weight of her soul into them. She cleared her throat. "If you desire to embody my enchantments, we must be initiated *willingly*. Power blossoms in beauty, not violence." She smoldered the trickery into Tam's forehead.

His eyes narrowed.

"How many oracles have you been with?" Ling lifted her chin. The most likely answer was zero.

He cocked his head to one side. It looked like he was thinking.

Ling didn't know how long she could put him off. But every second provided a chance to alter his motivations. Her survival was being counted in minutes.

Tam shook off his hesitation and came at her again. Her heart leapt into her throat.

Suddenly, overhead, what sounded like footsteps

rumbled on the steel roof like thunder. Ling lifted her chin, tracing the noise from one end to another. A large crack startled Tam.

He turned to the door. "Who's there?" he shouted. Ling picked up a rock and drew back her hand. Stepping outside, Tam rotated his body, pointing his finger on the roof. "You...."

A boom and then a crash. Tam wobbled back and forth before his eyes turned blank. The light left his gaze. First two drops of blood fell from his hair, then a red river flowed down his neck. A large piece of concrete toppled from his head. It had somehow fallen from the sky. His forehead was cracked open. Tam fell onto his back. Ling relaxed her stance.

She ran outside as Tam convulsed in a pool of his own fluids. The walls of the shed shook. Ling turned to see what stroke of fortune had delivered her. Enlai gazed at her from the roof, his gaze unreadable.

Thirty

Ling stood motionless next to the fallen man. Tam's skin had turned white. Gray sludge flowed out from his forehead. He was beyond saving. She didn't even try.

Reclaiming her bag, she gripped the straps. Enlai climbed down and whisked her away to an empty studio apartment on an upper floor. Inside the four walls, they sat in the dark. Newspapers taped over the windows blotted out the disappearing daylight. Ling's body trembled. The blood had drained from her appendages. Their breath filled up the hollowness in the room. She was hidden and felt safe for the first time since the full moon.

"How did you find me?" Ling asked. Her head throbbed. Today had been a cruel introduction to the reality of life inside the Walled City.

Enlai didn't look at her. He walked slowly to the window, peeling up a piece of the paper to look outside. "I saw you leave from the cafe. It's not usually occupied with Zhong and his men. Kali told me what happened."

"Was Kali the woman wearing an orange dress?" Ling had wanted to ask her name, but there had not been time.

He nodded. "She was worried. Aren't you supposed to be in school?"

"I...I..." She shuddered. Enlai had saved her once already. "I was coming to see you. You gave me your card. I need your help."

Enlai fidgeted with a pocketknife, turning the blade around his knuckles. He turned to her, lifting his eyebrows. "Well, what is it?"

"The twins. They are missing. Ahma thinks Wupo has them." Ling's leg started to shake. Her nerves. She stood up and squeezed next to Enlai at the window. "There is more. Dabak was arrested for a murder. He's innocent. I have arranged to meet Captain Stewart at the outpost up the mountain this evening for an exchange."

"You have more problems than I do," Enlai admitted. "I am not without troubles however." He pointed out the men patrolling in the alleyway. "Tam was important, and if anyone saw what I did, then I am dead too. They'll torture me first though." He bit his lip.

Ling felt a pang of regret for creating such troubles for him. Enlai could lose years of his hard work.

"You however don't have to be caught up in this mess," Enlai said.

"You only hurt Tam because of me." Emotions welled inside of Ling. She wasn't sure if she should give Enlai a hug or slap him. He didn't have to use such a heavy hand. But there was no sense in dwelling in the past.

"It wasn't right," Enlai objected. "He was disrespecting you and undermining my authority. If I didn't stop him, then I wouldn't be your man." His eyes reddened.

Ling flinched. He had killed a man for her, but she hadn't asked him to. And she couldn't ignore the real reason he had come at Tam with such incredible force. Tam had disregarded Enlai's claim on his property. Her old friend hadn't helped her out of compassion. Even with his endearment, she was still an object of value to be owned.

Enlai chewed on his fingernails. "How will they explain Tam's death? What can I say to divert suspicion from me?"

Ling had an idea. Everything had to be carried out quickly for it to work. Dabak's escape had to be handled like a hooligan, not a lady.

"Enlai, trust me for a second. Do you know the symbol of interconnecting eights?" She traced the shape on the ground.

He made a tsking sound. "The symbol belongs to a brotherhood pledged to the dark gods. We call them the loyalists. A network of ghosts who trade in souls. They are who the Red Society works against." He raised his voice as he spoke. "What dealings do you have with them?"

"I have business with them tonight. We may be able to work out benefits for both of us, especially in light of Tam's death," said Ling. This plan had to work.

Ling took his hand. She spilled the details about her brothers, missing children, and Wupo. "The island's Chief of Police agreed to trade Dabak for a pair of eyes. I believe it is a trap. Why would a ghost keep his word to a local girl?"

"Tonight is too quick," Enlai objected.

"No," Ling responded. "We need to do something right now. The ghosts have amassed weapons. Guns, ammo and explosives. They are planning to end the protests with violence. The captain said Dabak needs to be freed tonight or else..."

Between Enlai's eyebrows, deep wrinkles folded. "This will be a hard sell."

"Show them this." She fished out the bullet from her trouser pocket.

Enlai froze at the sight. "How?"

"I picked it up at the station while visiting Dabak," Ling

said. "A lot of strange things have happened over the last few days. Rest assured. I am not out of my wits." Since the full moon, Ling had learned about magic and had a very different perspective of her hometown. It was a lot for Enlai to take in. She hadn't even attempted to explain the moon-flowers, curse, and vampires.

Enlai tilted his head.

She could sense his gears turning, making sense of the offer. She continued. "I can get inside the outpost armory and open the back door for your crew. They can collect whatever they need. The remaining stock will have to be destroyed, or else it will be used to hurt the residents of Kowloon."

He shook his head. Doubt crept into his face. He folded into himself. Ling was losing him.

"Is dying more palatable? You can at least try to talk to the Society." She placed her hand on his forearm. "I must try to free my uncle, with or without you. Plus, you need to do more than steal trinkets to become a boss. You don't need to be more ruthless, but smarter. I can help you."

Enlai straightened his posture. "We have a chance to bring the ideas to the brothers. Soon, at teatime, the leaders honor the Guan Gong at the center square. There'll be food and drink for the start of the spirit's holiday. I'll tell them there. We will form a search party for your brothers and Cili."

"But before we go, you have to promise me something." Ling waited for Enlai to nod before continuing with the request. When he did, she added, "I must keep the eyes. I need Dabak and my brothers back with me."

———

Enlai led the way to the Walled City's center. They crawled through tight spaces and shimmied across thin ledges. It was uncomfortable, but the best path to avoid confronting any of Brother Tam's men.

"Be careful, there's a gap." Enlai stopped in the middle of a rickety staircase. He hopped from the step to another landing, pointing to the open hole. Ling looked down into the mess of wiring and held her breath. Her knees locked.

"I...is there another way?" She thought of being tangled in the wires like a fly in a web. Inside the mesh of electricity, she was sure that death would be slow. Clenching her teeth, she pressed down the spiraling thoughts about the potential end of her life.

Enlai shuffled on the other side. He rearranged himself, wrapping a telephone wire around one forearm. "You can do it." His other hand reached out as he leaned over the gap.

Ling steadied herself. She paused, locking with Enlai's patient eyes "Not much further. We are almost there."

She shook out her shoulder and jumped. One foot landed on a step, while the other missed the ledge. Her stomach dropped. Expecting to fall, she closed her eyes. But she was suspended, one foot dangling over the ledge.

"Got"—Enlai grunted and pulled her up—"you."

His breath smelled like peppermint, warm against her cheek.

"I cannot believe..." Turning to observe the distance from the other side, she let out an exasperated laugh. "I made it."

She turned back to Enlai.

Their faces were so close, his lips grazed hers. It was like they were again playing marbles and giggling about comics. For a second, they were carefree again.

Neither of them moved. A rock dropped from above, ping ponging down the walls and metal roofs. From four stories up, the noise rattled, giving away their position. Enlai put Ling back on her feet. His face was flushed.

"If we're going to pretend to be together, then we might as well try to be nice to each other." Ling felt her body warm from the proximity to Enlai. It felt nice.

Descending a ladder, Ling could see the entryway over the heads of queued people, patiently waiting their turn for blessings. A gate was painted in red and gold paint. Blessings adorned the pillars. Fresh flowers and an abundance of home-cooked plates filled the table in front of the altar. It was the most reassuring thing she'd seen in the Walled City.

When Ling set her feet onto solid ground, she had extra appreciation for being alive. A patch of twilight sky hovered over the center of the enclosed city. Sandalwood incense and burning paper drifted into the alleyway. Vendors sold food and trinkets similar to those at Queen's Pier. She had never visited the Walled City's temple, though she knew it had been built over a hundred years ago.

When they were almost to the entry way, a man jumped out from the crowd. His hair was wild and his cheeks were smeared with grease. Ling stumbled backward while Enlai grabbed onto the stranger's arm. It took her a second to process that instead of fear, Enlai's face registered joy.

"Nice to see you!" The dirty-faced man shook hands with Enlai. His accent was reminiscent of the central regions, brusque yet clear. "Don't mind my messiness. I am having stove issues. Here is a small thank you for acquiring an engine for the truck." The man handed Enlai two *jong*, rice wrapped in bamboo leaves.

Her stomach grumbled. Hunger hit her like bricks. She hadn't eaten since the morning.

"No problem. Glad I could help." Enlai handed Ling the food. He whispered in her ear. "Yanked the motor straight out of a policeman's car." Ling smelled the aroma of steamed rice as Enlai gave her instructions. "The residents will not give you trouble. If anything happens, you can go back the way we came or escape down the main alleyways."

As Enlai turned around, Ling grabbed his hand. "Wait." He looked at her with concern. She slipped the bullet in his hand. "Be careful." What more could she do?

Enlai moved from the gate to the podium, weaving through the crowd. People greeted him, allowing him to float to the front. From his pocket, he produced a black bandana. Tying it around his head, he stopped before a row of older men who were smoking heavily. Some of them wore sunglasses while others rubbed old scars on their faces with ointment. Each leader carried an aura of prestige, having earned their positions with cunning, violence, or both. They watched as patrons bowed to the statue gods and then to them, without giving Enlai a second look.

Ling bit into the warm glutinous rice, chewing in suspense as Enlai lit incense. He offered himself to the golden busts of the Guan Gong and Wong Dai Sin. Laid out on a long altar to the Goddess of Compassion and Godfather of Health were rich offerings of fruit, long life noodles, and roasted duck. Enlai reached far over his head then extended down to the ground. The bosses turned toward Enlai's full body prostration. After three intentional bows, he repeated a prayer and assembled the incense into the community cauldron.

"Big brothers, I bring news." He turned and saluted to the dignitaries. "Wupo is a fraud, replaced by another who plans to infiltrate our walls. The ghosts plan an attack on the strikers with a stockpile of weapons and bombs," Enlai bellowed for everyone to hear.

People turned to each other in shock and repeated his words to those that couldn't hear. The leaders were drawn in too. Around her, conversation buzzed:

"Aiya, Wupo isn't right, I believe it."

"Poor Mei. Really a tragedy."

"Stop the ghosts!"

Over the murmurs of the crowd, she lost the rest of Enlai's story. A man in a striped shirt, wearing thick gold chains, waved Enlai forward. They continued in a side conversation. The boss rubbed the stubble on his chin. Then an older man opened his palm. Enlai placed the bullet in his hand. The proof.

The leader's expression lit up. Enlai turned in Ling's direction and flashed a smile.

He was in.

Thirty-One

W hile the deal with Red Society leaders was still in negotiations, Ling inquired about Wupo's location. The oracle never stayed in the same place. Locals said it was for her safety. It also meant that nothing could ever become familiar.

Wupo's abilities to cure ailments, locate objects, and sleuth out unfaithful husbands were legendary. Several versions of the women existed: a truth-seeking beacon, willowy soothsayer, or collector of souls. Yet in recent times, Wupo delved out mostly bad predictions and faulty invocations. The people thought she was lying. Individually, they had allowed shame and unworthiness to overcome them. But as a group, they demanded justice.

"We are all frustrated. Too many of us approaching her will scare her away. Who knows, maybe she's heard the ruckus and has already left," Mata, a woman in a construction uniform reasoned with a few dozen people congregating in the alleyway.

Ling understood the unwieldiness of a crowd's strength. On the docks when too many people queued for the boats, they stopped listening to the captain's instructions for boarding.

She could only steer the group's intention. The group handpicked two women and three men skilled in combat. They would fetch the oracle back to the temple for questioning. Everyone else would wait for the interrogation.

Ling followed the condensed search party that lived among the winding lanes. The noise of construction was constant, muting their voices. Stone and mortar walls gave way to bunkers—scrap-metal structures. If the Walled City was a monster, it would have been Frankenstein's creation, a patchwork of things born to a different life.

"The oracle is higher up this time." Mata consulted a piece of paper in her palm. She was a heavy-set woman, built like an ox.

They walked through the back of a busy restaurant, passing cutting boards with stretched out animal parts. Stripes of raw tendons glimmered in the dim light. A tangy smell blanketed the air. Ling heaved, swallowing hard against the disgust crawling out of her throat.

"Watch yourself," Mata said as Ling's shoes licked mysterious murky pools.

They weaved through the amalgamation of old and new. Glows from cooking fires and oil lamps lit the way up staircases and rusty warped ladders. The passageways narrowed with leaning shelves and discarded furniture. After a few more turns, the group stopped at a door with a red square paper cutout. The bone script character for *wu* was drawn in the middle:

"Shaman" in ancient bone script.

Transcending time, this had been the designation for an oracle for thousands of years. A coiled snake was also carved into the wooden frame, signaling protection by the Red Society.

Ling's left ear rang. She opened her mouth, attempting to clear pressure in her head. As Mata knocked, Ling became more and more uncomfortable with the idea of detaining this woman. Despite all she had seen, Ling didn't condone violence. Would she talk willingly, or would she struggle all the way down the hall?

"Come in," a voice croaked from the other side. Opening the screen door sounded like clashing pans. Ling gestured for the rest of the group to wait out of sight. The door would remain open as Ling reasoned with the person who presented herself as Wupo.

Inside, a lady sat at a table overflowing with tins, jars, and stacked cups. A handful of candles flickered at the far end of the room while everything else was blanketed in darkness. Shadows obscured the woman's face.

"I am here as my mother promised." Ling bowed, entering into the amber glow. Wisps of darkness reached toward her.

The oracle slanted a bandaged head. "Not a child." The words were spat. Deep wrinkles flowered from her grimace.

"Ahma said you once offered me the apprentice position." Had she addressed the same Wupo so many years ago, or was this the corrupted one? Ling shuddered at the idea of growing up in these rancid quarters, having to cater to the whim of this one and only taskmaster. This fate would have been worse than marriage.

"Before little Mei? Heeei, so you were the one that got away? How old are you now?" Wupo bent her neck too far forward. Gray and brown spots stained the covering over her left eye. A word was written across her forehead in red.

"Nineteen." The number barely made it past Ling's teeth when the old lady squealed. Her age was off-putting to the rotting woman.

Wupo licked her lips. "Too old… yet maybe still viable… hmm. You were here at nine. Your mother should have brought you sooner, especially with your father so far away."

Ling froze. Why bring up her father now, except as an attempt to trigger her emotions? "What could you know about him?" She narrowed her gaze. Her father was much more than anyone ever admitted.

"Come closer. I'll tell you." The woman's voice was laced with jagged glass.

"I will not agree to anything until you return my brothers." Ling backed away as she made this statement. It would be simple for the group to charge in and pick up this frail woman. "I know you have them."

"Where are you *Leng Mui*?" The woman darted her head wildly from left to right. The shape of her hunched back was oddly familiar.

A force tugged at the ends of her shirt. She resisted, sank back in her heels. But against her will, her shoes were pulled over the greasy floor. Inch-by-inch something dragged her toward the burning candles. The flames flickered black.

Ling yelled for help. Women clamored outside the unit as a crawling sensation inched up her throat. She brought her hands to her neck. An unseen hand pulled her to the table. Candlelight dyed the imposter's skin orange. Now clearer, the ancient script for oracle was painted on her forehead. The same symbol she'd seen on the young girl in the vision in the cave. Ling's pulse stumbled and raced in alarm.

Cracks splintered Wupo's lips. "Give me your hand, if you know what is good for you." Warts and boils trailed down her neck.

"Where are my brothers?" Ling cringed, extending an arm. She was doing this for Kit and Gou.

Wupo pounced on it. Rubbing Ling's palm with her scaly fingers and smelling of over-ripe bananas and soured milk, the oracle uttered foreign guttural noises. Droplets from her mouth landed on Ling's skin.

Ling's fingers tingled under Wupo's grip. Blood stopped flowing to her fingertips. Ling felt light-headed. As she peered into the dark stone, the snake with green eyes stared back. Was it trickery of the candles? A sharp pain burned her skin. Ling yanked her hand back. The ringing inside her head turned to a scream. She only could respond with a loud screech. Agony seeped into her bones. She smelled her own burnt flesh. Looking down, smoke smoldered from the hole in her palm.

"What have you done?" Wupo hissed. Her bulbous nostrils flared. "Who granted you protection?"

Ling frowned. "I will not say until you answer me." Her eyes watered. Wupo must have meant her tattoo, bestowed by a friendly sea witch with braided hair.

"Your brothers are alive." The old lady flashed her browned teeth and bruised gums, reminding Ling of the purple eye's vision. A nasty woman had carved out a young girl's eyes. Could this Wupo have been working with Lady Tun? "No wonder I could not find you for so long. Your father...."

"Take me to the twins." Ling snapped. One thing at a time. The oracle was trying to provoke her. She told herself not to react. Stay calm.

"You are too much like him, you know. Always wanting adventure, an easy target for entanglement." Wupo smirked. The blackened and yellowed gauze on her wounds stared back at Ling. "He was punished for refusing me."

"What do you mean? That was not you!" Ling protested. But she was not sure. Did Wupo send her father away? Had she given him faulty advice, or had she given him an offer he could not refuse?

"Grudges transfer. If I ever want to be beautiful again." Wupo ran a broken finger down Ling's cheek. "Perhaps...? You are here now, so it is fated."

"Will you take me in exchange for my brothers?" Her whole-body shook.

"Are you sure?" Wupo jerked her head.

Ling didn't want to go. In her gut, she knew not to lie. Instead, she asked, "Where are your eyes?"

The oracle twisted Ling's wrist. "Nosey girl. You were watching under the moonlight. *Zhul'guth* stole mine." She exhaled a putrid breath.

This was impossible. Ling had watched Lady Tun suffer. A pit widened in her stomach as she remembered Brother Tam's blame: "Another ghost feigning as a savior." He hadn't been guessing or repeating rumors. Could Wupo and Lady Tun be the same person?

She studied the woman in front of her. One eyelid was encrusted in thick green and black mucus. The other was bandaged but a watery secretion leaked out. These injuries were consistent with Lady Tun's. And the ring on her finger looked like the one she had seen on the corpse. No one had mentioned a body. It was in fact possible Lady Tun had survived, but how?

"For an exchange, I need to know where you have markings." Wupo licked her chapped lips.

Revealing this would surrender the layer of protection with which Ling had been endowed. Her choices were few however. "What of my brothers?" She tried to be smarter, not giving up anything without something to gain.

"Dear, tell me now before it's too late for them." Wupo grinned, showing her nubs of wooden teeth.

She surrendered to the urgency of retrieving her brothers. She didn't matter as much as they did. Ling pointed to her arm.

Wupo pushed up her sleeve. The fabric wouldn't cooperate. It bunched up over Ling's shoulders. The old woman grabbed a pair of scissors, impatiently cutting the fabric from her shoulders down to the cuff. "They have descended to the Dreamlands," she said, tearing apart the sleeve. "In between sleep and waking, you will not find them, unless...."

Her group crashed through the door before Wupo could finish. Mata screamed Ling's name.

Wupo stood up. Flames cast shadows under her chin. Behind her, twisted faces flashed with glowing eyes. She dropped Ling's arms and put up one hand. Her companions crashed against an invisible wall, unable to reach her. The same force had pulled Ling forward and pinned her in place. Phantom appendages grabbed at her feet.

With a flip of Wupo's wrist, five people fell to the ground. They moaned and rolled in pain. Panicking, Ling punched at the oracle's shoulder, but the woman didn't flinch. Wupo cemented her fingertips around Ling's eyes. "I shall have my parts. No matter the source."

Sharp fingernails bore into her flesh. Ling went limp. Nails broke through her skin. Her body quivered as blood spilled down her cheeks. With her shaking hands, Ling ripped off the soothsayer's bandages. A bloody socket met Ling's gaze. It pulsed and reeled her into the abyss.

"See with me," Wupo whispered.

Then a hard object was lobbed at Wupo's head, knocking her backwards and over a chair. A terrible rottenness burst into the air. Tin pieces flew past Ling's face. Bits of spoiled meat splattered against the walls. She felt herself able to move again. Two people carried her to the door. Another bloated can went flying as Ling struggled to stand.

Wupo laughed, sending a sharp pain into Ling's heart. "It's going to take more than a rotten can... enough of this nonsense." Brown sludge oozed down the oracle's neck. Her pustules squirmed as her fingers flitted. A sound jeered in her ear.

Ling numbly reached into her pocket, retrieving the bundle the old woman had given to her on the ship. The power in the room needed disruption.

She held the protective herbs over a candle, and the dried leaves immediately flared up. Smoke billowed from Ling's fist of herbs, splintering the unseen forces assailing them. Inching closer to the table, she paved the way for the group to pounce. One man grabbed the old woman by the shoulders while another tied her hands behind her back. Wupo's thrashing stopped when someone placed a Gwun Yin pendant necklace over Wupo's head. Her head fell backward as the women carried her out.

Thirty-Two

Ling and Enlai observed the police outpost from the edge of the jungle.

The Walled City bosses had assured Ling that, by any means necessary, the twins would be returned by the time they returned with weapons. Wupo was still unconscious when Ling left with Enlai for the jungle outpost. She could not be everywhere and do all things; Ling had to trust progress could be made by her temporary allies. Her uncle and the village depended on her.

The police outpost had changed in the days since she had seen it. Canvas tents now covered the bare landscape. A long trench of embers warmed large pots. Steam wafted out of the cauldrons with smells of boiled onions and tomatoes. Men wiped sweat from their brows and picked at their scabs, languishing to the strum of guitar chords. The group was waiting for dinner.

Enlai grabbed Ling's hand and kissed it. Then he placed his pocketknife in her palm. "You may need this."

She lifted the corners of her mouth in an acknowledgment. The knife was reassuring, small weapon though it was. The consequences of her mission weighed heavy on her heart. If she failed, Dabak would vanish. The attack on the strikers could destroy the countryside. Without her, the search for the twins may end before they are found.

Thunder sounded down the road. Several carts rolled up the hill like an oncoming storm. As the eyes and ears of the Walled City, the Red Society had learned of several large orders for fermented grains and cow's milk. The local vendors had just begun their journey when they caught up with them. Ling convinced them to take Enlai, herself, and ten men on the errand.

Of course, these bakers didn't know the police planned a raid against the protesters and hadn't balked at the offer of gold. While the ghosts smuggled weapons between worlds, they couldn't conceal the hunger and thirst of two hundred military men.

Ling prepared herself, dotting her phantom points with the sacred ointment. She handed Enlai bay leaves and wished them to efficacy. "*Sit possessor custodiri*. May the holder be protected."

"This is all I need?" Enlai rubbed the dried leaf between his fingers.

Uncomfortable ringing confirmed her decisions. The plan would work. She had to believe it. Soon, she and Dabak would be with Aunt Marcella, and the twins would be safe. "Be silent. Wait for my signal."

Ling maneuvered around the sprawling roots of the banyan trees. Draping branches shielded her body like curtains. As the men turned their attentions to the carts of beer and bread, she crawled out of the jungle. She easily reached the fire undetected. Crouching behind sacks of potatoes, she readied two fistfuls of senna leaf powder. The delicate yellow flowers sprouted from a highly potent diuretic plant. Ling stood on her toes over the bubbling cauldron. Flames wrapped around the girth of the cast iron, lapping at her shoes. The hot stones scorched her cork soles as she released the powder and mixed the concoction with a long stick.

Three more times, she dropped in the additive and stirred. Even with her nimbleness, heat burned the bottoms of her feet. She hobbled back into the banyans, hugging the burns on her arms. The cool dirt soothed the swelling, but it didn't take long for curious insects to nip at her sores.

Within an hour of ingesting the food, the men would grab their bellies and become incapacitated. For the men who didn't eat, Ling had already added the powder into the beer.

As she waited, she wrapped long strips of bamboo around her feet and crept into the building through the front door. A clean-shaven guard was sitting at the desk, slurping soup. She smiled, knowing the discomfort would soon arrive.

As before, she circled his desk unseen by his beady eyes. A ring of keys was fastened to his hip. The phone rang.

Ling gasped.

"What are you doing here?" the officer asked while the phone kept ringing. Did he address her? She pressed her back into the pillar, out of the officer's line of sight.

Another voice replied. "Inflammatory. Officer Brands, is that how you greet your captain?" In person, the captain's voice was full-bodied. It simmered with disgust.

"Sorry, sir. Did you eat?" The officer spoke crisply and respectfully now.

"The phone's tolling," said the captain, his footsteps receding down the hall.

"Yes, sir." He picked up the receiver and mumbled a greeting. "This is Officer Brand. Yes, all the men are having dinner. The vendors came with the bread and extra beer. Units will be ready at 0500 hours."

After the officer hung up, his legs started to shake. Ling was a little surprised; his symptoms were manifesting sooner than she had expected. He slouched, holding his stomach. Sweat gathered under his neck. His hand trembled as he reached for the telephone, but before he could dial a new number, he ran outside.

Ling dashed out of hiding to the back door so she could open it for Enlai's men. More ancient symbols were whittled into the timber. Their power beamed into her, and she welcomed them, whatever the source. She struggled with the metal crossbeam, stirring up dust and sand. It was very heavy. She squatted and hoisted up the rod over the two brackets. The metal bar slipped out of her hands and bounced. The clanking noise vibrated through the quiet.

She cringed as she worked on the second one as quickly as she could. Someone could come sprinting down the corridor at any moment now. As she lifted the other one, a man bellowed.

"Who goes there?" Captain Stewart asked from around the corner. His footsteps echoed in the empty space.

Drat. Dropping the first bar had alerted him of her presence. Ling grimaced, finishing the task. Did she dare turn around? The second bar smacked against the existing one.

She turned, finding her uncle slumped beside the Captain. Shadows encircled Dabak's eyes, so she couldn't see his pupils. A long, styled mustache curved from the corner of the Captain's mouth to his cheeks, swooping in a neat curl. He was dressed for a party.

Squinting at the ground, Captain Stewart then scanned the walls. "Do you see her?" He bent over, shaking Dabak by his shoulders. "Is your niece here?" The strange powers cloaking Ling held fast.

Dabak groaned. Ling wanted to clobber the Captain over the head, but staying out of his sight was more advantageous. Ling instead tiptoed toward her uncle.

Captain Stewart sniffed the air. "I smell you." He stepped toward the doors and steel bars.

Ling stopped behind the man. He hadn't tracked her movements. However, with one wrong move, and she could be captured. Should she walk out the front door and into freedom? She stared at her uncle on the floor. The side of his face was bruised. His breaths were shallow. He couldn't fend for himself. She couldn't bear to leave him.

"No need for formalities." The captain rotated with two steps. He spoke to where he thought she might be. Red veins spread to the edges of his pupils. His skin was much paler than her uncle's. "I imagined meeting under different circumstances. I sense your presence. You smell like a mint julip."

"Do not attempt escape." Captain Stewart unsheathed a knife and swiped at the back door. He leaned into the metal frame. Sand fell from its edges as he pushed it open. As sounds of insects and upset men flooded inside, Ling crouched down and untied the bindings on her uncle.

After a long inquisitiveness look, the captain scoffed. Ling swept a glob of ointment across her uncle's upper lip, hopping the herbs would restore his energy. "Wake up, wake up," she whispered as a prayer.

As far as the Captain was concerned, Ling was a spirit haunting him. Her uncle didn't stir. Out of ideas and feeling the time slip away, she tucked the pocketknife into Dabak's trouser pocket. Unless he woke up soon, there was nothing more she could do. Perhaps Enlai and his companions could carry Dabak out.

The door slammed shut. Ling froze as footsteps rushed

toward her. A white dusting fell onto her arm. Before she realized it, Captain Stewart grabbed her.

"Did you ever hear of curiosity killing a cat?" He gripped another handful of white powder and rubbed it on her face.

She couldn't move fast enough to escape. "A cat has nine lives."

He wrinkled his nose. "Your manners are repulsive."

"Opportunity only knocks once," she said, quoting a traditional proverb on reflex.

The captain grumbled, scanning her smug expression. "It's only baby powder. I could certainly make this worse. Now, young lady, the eyes? No time for games."

"What did you do to Dr. Shaw?" Ling nudged her uncle with her foot. *Please wake up*, she pleaded to him in silence.

"I have kept my part of the bargain," he said, not answering her. "He's alive. The eyes?" She yanked on her uncle's shirt. Captain Stewart's face scrunched. His eyes grew frantic, searching the room. "Did you arrive empty-handed?"

Ling said nothing.

"This is not a game." Captain Stewart's voice boomed. "Inflammatory!"

When wind blew the door open, the captain let go of Ling. He turned around and whipped out his knife. Ling took the chance to sprint down the hall and out the door. She was on her way. However, in her panic, she didn't notice Office Brand returning to his post. She ran straight into him.

"Are you making trouble at camp?" Officer Brands said, red in the face. He had a tight grip on her arm.

"Hand her to me," said Captain Stewart from behind. The men exchanged glances. "Why were not you here? She entered on her own. Where are the men?"

"My stomach...." The officer started.

"I am not interested in personal issues. Return to your station at once." Captain Stewart stomped his feet. "I'll be in to reprimand you once I decide what to do with her."

Officer Brand clutched his torso, lumbering inside.

"You are as plain as day outside." Captain Stewart pinched the ends of his frayed mustache. Rolling the hairs between his fingers, he curled the ends back into place. He studied Ling with uncomfortable intensity.

From the corner of her eye, shadows moved along the side of the building. Knowing Enlai and his men were progressing with the plans brought her relief. This could be over soon. Her eyes found the writing on the arch again. The ancient letters were also written in the grimoire at school and in the books on Dabak's shelves. The herbs hadn't made her invisible, she now she knew. It was these symbols that shielded her from the evil eyes of men.

"What sort of folkcraft....?" His face froze for a moment. "Where are your shoes?" The captain tied her wrists together with rope and dragged her into nearest tent. The closer to the encampment, the more horrible the stench became.

"I thought it was dinner time." His face contorted in repulsion. He secured the rope to a stake in the ground. When he walked outside, he flagged a soldier returning from the woods.

"Wh—what has happened here?" the captain shuttered. His silhouette stood tall next to a person bent in the middle. Ling sat on the dirt floor, struggling against the restraints. She reflected sourly that if she had not given her knife to Dabak this would be easier.

"The food," a solider answered in a labored tone. He wretched, spilling his insides. A horrible smell seeped through the burlap fabric of the tent. The commotion esca-lated outside.

"Well...make yourself useful. Do—do not...." The Captain clenched his jaw in frustration.

"Captain, are you okay?"

"Shut up! Watch her." The captain stomped away. She wiggled and twisted her hands free. It was easier than she had expected. Between Tam and Stewart, she'd had quite enough for the day.

Chaos ensued in the camp. There wasn't much time to think, or was there?

She raised her arm. Touching the star at the top of the tattoo, she gathered inspiration. Then, dipping her fingers into a bowl of dirty water, she mimicked the writings from the outpost's walls and arches on the cloth over her head. Drawing from the wounds on her feet, she drew the runes she memorized over the past few days. Mixing scripts from the bronze age and language of the old ones, she invoked the cover of protective magic.

People screamed. Tents collapsed around her. Not a single person tried to enter or force her into something else. She remained grounded until it was the right time. She had escaped several terrible situations through timing and luck. It wasn't in her nature to fight. Her training was all in healing.

Then someone called her name. It was first a whisper. The sound crawled up the nape of her neck. She hugged her knees together, hoping Captain Stewart wouldn't return and soldiers wouldn't demand justice for their poisoned soups. Instead, Enlai stuck his head in.

A sigh of relief escaped her lungs.

"Where have you been?" He blinked quickly. "We must leave. It's time."

She believed him and took his hand. Night had faded.

They raced to the bottom of the road, jumping into the vendors' carts. Two men each towing at the handles like oxen. Large crates had replaced the previous stock of bread and vegetable baskets.

"Where's Dabak?" Ling observed the outpost as it shrank from their view.

"We got him out." Enlai lifted the cloth next to them, showing her an array of weapons. "The men and I carted out what we could. The rest... well...."

Before he finished, the outpost lit up like a candle. When she turned back in amazement for a second, the scalding heat smacked her in the face. A magnificent array of colors streamed from its melting walls. The blaze engulfed the windowless building. The men hauling their treasures sped up. Then an explosion sent the entire structure tumbling down.

Thirty-Three

The blast resounded through the mountains and down to the bay. In the dim morning light, fisherman and farmers witnessed the smoke billowing from the jungle. The haze brought Ling back to the Dreamlands. The faint cries of the twins twisted her heart.

By the time Ling arrived at the pier, the black cloud had dissolved into gray. While Enlai returned to the Walled City to speak with his bosses, Ling headed to the docks. Smoke had settled over the shoreline.

Ling approached the stands, suddenly conscious of her appearance. Torn clothes, punctures around her eyes, and scratches down her arms. Ash and dirt covered her face. She was sure she was a sight to behold.

The merchants stared, dumbfounded by the fire on the hillside.

"Did you come from there?" the fruit seller asked her.

She nodded.

"Another fight?" he asked, getting ready to leave.

"Hopefully, this is the end of one." A crowd gathered around Ling as she shared the events of the previous night.

A crazed woman with a cloth over her head pushed herself through the crowd. She wore a linen smock stained by sweat and dirt. The hole in Ling's hand throbbed.

Lunging at Ling, the woman screamed. "What of the twins?"

Ling jumped backwards. Others in the crowd tried to block the raving woman.

"Ling, I am your mother." The exhausted woman untied the scarf around her head.

For a moment, Ling couldn't place the person with the sunken eyes, papery skin, and streaks of white hair. Her features resembled that of the decrepit oracle more than her mother's. When Ling realized her error, she rushed to the woman's side.

"It looks like we both have been through hell." Ahma produced a meek smile. "What of the twins?"

Ling hung her head. Now that Dabak was free, she still had to find them. She looked up, noticing a black car approach the docks. A short list of possible people came to mind: Headmaster Lee, Captain Stewart, or Emma.

Instead, to her surprise, Dabak stepped out in clean trousers, joining the cluster of merchants, strikers, and local residents. They cheered for him. He was taken aback by the greeting.

Ling squeezed around a dozen people and hugged her uncle. "You are safe."

"All thanks to you." The corner of his eyes crinkled. "I am still not out of the woods entirely. But at least now I can help with the twins. Have you heard anything?"

Ling stepped back, shaking her head. Her uncle looked better but bore signs of his ordeal. His glasses sat lopsided on his black and purple nose. Bald patches dotted his scalp. Bruises stained his face. He was in worse shape than her.

"Thanks to you both." Dabak bowed. As Ahma rested

her hand on Ling's shoulder, Dabak reached over for a handshake.

Ahma didn't extend her hand. "Why did you not pay your way out of jail?"

Ling felt her mother seething.

He shook his head, brushing off the awkward moment. "I apologize for the inconvenience. Your daughter has gone out of her way to help me." His brow wrinkled as he lowered his head. "I will make this right."

Ling preferred not to question him in public. More than a dozen pair of eyes stared at them. "We cannot waste time on quarrels. We must focus on the twins." She turned to Ahma. "We have waited ten years for answers. What's a few more days?"

Her mother breathed out. "What do you need me to do?"

Ling was at loss for words. If only someone could tell her where Wupo had taken her brothers. Had the Red Society determined the twins' location? Would they be able to enter Dreamland? Did an enchantment conceal her brothers, preventing them from being found?

As if she had wished him into existence, Enlai ran up next to Dabak. He was breathing hard and bent over with his hands on his knees to catch his breath.

"Pray, step back," Dabak bellowed. The center of the crowd opened up.

Enlai narrowed his eyebrows, coughing between words. "Wupo... brothers... did not... gone...."

"Take deep breaths. It is difficult to understand you." Dabak fanned Enlai with a handkerchief. As he waved the cloth back and forth, Ling spotted embroidered initials: "WSL"

"Wait." Ling pointed at the cloth midair. "Where did this come from?"

"These pockets." Dabak unfolded the fabric, smoothing out the letters with his fingers. "Initials of Langley's son. William Samual Langley. He went missing eight years ago. A sad tale that I hope is not repeated." He choked up.

WSL also matched the initials etched under a jar in Lady Tun's secret cave. Another missing child? It was a mystery she hadn't wanted to solve. The desperation of the creature on the boat came back to her. It had begged for the whereabouts of a William. Finally, she realized who the creature had been. It was her step-uncle, Lord Langley, William's father. He was right. She did know the location of his son.

"How did you get in contact with Langley? Has he returned?" Ling asked. Aunt Marcella had sent Langley a message about Dabak's arrest.

"His staff answered the phone," Dabak said as Enlai regained his wits.

They turned to Enlai as he spoke. "Wupo escaped. She has disappeared into the jungle."

"Did they find out anything else about my brothers? Where are they hidden away?" Ling's chest heaved. They had lost a crucial opportunity.

"One man said she mentioned the mountains." Enlai lowered his head.

That was not much help. The wilderness was a large place. Tracking them would take days. Ling needed more information.

"The women from the rescue party found only a silver coin in the oracle's possession. Wupo refused to respond to questions. After I left, no one would go near her. She threatened them and their families with an everlasting curse. Her chants sounded like a demon drowning, spitting and sweating everywhere." He handed her a round metal piece. It bore the serpent symbol. Kit had handed something like this at the kitchen table. The day she had learned that a woman was enticing children with candy.

"Can you repeat the words?" She might recognize the phrase, even if recited in an ancient language.

"Ask Mata, she transported the cart from the Walled City. She heard the chanting." Enlai pulled Ling to the edge of the road.

Mata emerged from behind a tree. A bold red scarf was wrapped around her shoulders. "Sir, ready to go?" Her vehicle was partially covered by a bush.

"Mata, do you remember the eerie chants?" Enlai asked. "Ling might be able to understand the language."

Mata nodded and let out a guttural roar. "Wupo made that noise over and over again. She bowed and bellowed: *rrr-lou-lok-kiu*. People ignored her, as they ignore most things. I jotted everything down." Mata unfolded a piece of paper from a pocket on her chest. "I tried to find a pattern. It was a strange and awful worship."

On the note, Mata had approximated the phrases with Tangwa characters. There was no direct translation. To anyone else, the sequence was nonsense. But when Ling repeated the prayer under her breath, her fingers tingled.

"I found a gardener who taught me the ancient symbols in a text. He may be able to translate Mata's observations." Ling motioned down the pebbled road in the direction of her school. "It'll be a quick trip by trishaw."

Dabak caught up to them. He addressed Ling. "The shopkeepers told me what you did for me." He patted her on the back.

"We must be going...." she started to explain, but Dabak cut in.

"Let's first see someone at your school. The church has a printing press. Wai may have more information about the twins."

Ling nodded. She would explain that the salve healed Wai. He had a connection to her family through the moonflowers. He could read ancient writings, but was he also familiar with ancient practices? Had he learned all this in the Guianas?

In her many days of searching for answers, Ling found only more questions.

Thirty-Four

Sitting together in the rear of the three-wheeled cart, Dabak squeezed Ling's hand. Mata breathed hard, pulling them uphill through a path cut through the jungle. On one side, insects screeched, while the other side featured sheer drop-offs.

Enlai had stayed behind. There was room in the cart for only two. He took over calming the crowd of local residents and protestors and kept Ahma from losing her wits about the twins. His Red Society men were combing the hillside for Wupo. Ling still had hopes of finding the twins alive.

The road jostled them in the un-cushioned seats. Rubbing ointment into bruises on Dabak's arm, she broke up the congealed blood under his skin. The technique sped up healing.

His voice trembled. "I am out because of you. This is what I know: the police discovered a pool of blood at Lady Tun's shack. Traditional herbs were scattered along the path. They pressured me to confess to a murder even though there was no body." He whispered the last part.

The body had gone missing entirely. She recollected Lady

Tun's hollowed-out stare. With her uncle's information, there was a real possibility that Lady Tun was the Walled City Wupo.

"First, the police accused me of throwing her into the ocean. I swore on Wong Dai Sin I hadn't done anything wrong. Lady Tun had many enemies. However, to control damage to the family's reputation, the police wanted to pin the crime on a local. During the process, officers changed the narrative. They instead invoked my skills as a surgeon, claiming I had butchered the body in the Walled City. That was when I knew they had nothing solid." Dabak looked blankly out into the bay. "The Police Captain was determined to put me away at any cost. He has secrets."

Ling nodded. Her head hurt. "I used those against him." The captain's weaknesses had been Ling's advantage. She reached in her bag and showed Dabak the jar of eyes.

"What are those?" He was taken aback.

"They found me. On the night of Lady Tun's death. They must have found their way into my bag. I am certain they belonged to the previous Wupo, the one mentoring Mei. I can ask the eyes questions, and they show me visions." Ling had much more of her story yet to tell.

Dabak held onto his stunned expression. "Did you ask it about the twins?"

"It did not have much. I glimpsed a clearing next to a massive camphor surrounded by flowering tea trees." She closed her eyes, remembering a warmth glowing from the other side of the roots. The kidnapper would be there too.

"The camp must be on the South side of the jungle. It's a relief that it's not over the peak." Dabak wrote down a note. His eyebrows flexed with agitation. "I do not know the location of all the camphor trees, but farmers might know. You have suffered much." He patted her knee. "I am ashamed to have put you through this. Your father will be angry."

Ling's mind flittered from one thought to another. She could not even process the fact that Dabak had confirmed his belief that her father yet lived. The most important goal right now was the twins. "Can we focus on finding Guo and Kit?"

He dabbed the handkerchief over his brows. "Wai, the gardener, with whom I gather you are already acquainted. Well, he has a powerful sense of smell. I should have asked earlier; do you have an item belonging to the twins?"

She rummaged around in her bag. Her brothers often hid things. Inside, rolled in one of their bunched-up shirts, was Kit's slingshot. She touched the handle. The toy edged her to tears. She missed them so much.

"That will do," said Dabak. "The blue flowers I use in Aunt Marcella's medicine will help as well. There is a batch of them at the school."

"So, Wai the gardener is from the Guianas?" She recalled a letter from this country in Ba's paperwork. Had her father visited there?

"You read the letters." Dabak leaned back. "He is the only person in the world who can cultivate moonflowers. He is blooming them in the greenhouse until Langley builds our own atrium."

Ling fidgeted with the strap of her bag. "Did the medicine man ever meet my father?"

Dabak stiffened. "This gardener, he is not able to recall his life prior to the island. Marcella and I have been working to recover his memories. Rishi mushrooms, ginseng, and special formulations.... Marcella and he came about the same ailment. Wai, regrettably, ingested too many petals. The antidote eats away links in the brain, or at least that is the hypothesis."

Her uncle described Wai as feeble-minded. He'll be surprised that Wai was no longer this way. "How does his memory relate to the safe return of the twins?"

"His senses were heightened by the ailment. That stayed with him, while Marcella lost all of the powers gained from turning...." Dabak writhed his hands.

"Aunt Marcella told me the story. I am aware of the meaning of turning, at least the medical symptoms."

Dabak sighed. "Did you read the *K. Hoopers* manifest?"

Ling blinked as the school came into view. "No, I have not," she lowered her eyes. Why hadn't she looked harder for the documents?

"The manifest differs from the captain's notes. There is a mention of stopping on a small island in the Atlantic Ocean. This entry is the key to your father's whereabouts." Dabak adjusted his glasses again.

"My father is still there?" Hope surged in Ling. They could commission a rescue ship with the money from the safe.

"This is how I was able to file for the technical completion of his contract." He lifted the corners of his mouth. "If the captain left him on an island, then it was not your father's duty to find his way to North America on his own."

The answer was satisfying. The notes proved the shipping company had acted in willful abandonment. Ahma had the right intuition. Wai must know her father and had attested to him living in Guiana. He and the moonflowers connected her father, Aunt Marcella, and Lady Tun.

She still had a lot of questions. "How did Lady Tun find you?"

Why had she gone to him? And why had Langley stuffed the blue flower petals into her mouth?

"She came to me as an ailing grandma after your father

left on his voyage. I prescribed herbs for arthritis before she revealed her more savage urges."

The swaying of the ride jostled sour notes in Ling's head. She recalled a cacophonous nursery rhyme from the twins. They sang it the night before they had been taken. *Three Blind Mice. They have no eyes. They ran away from the soldier's wife, who gouged their eyes with a carving knife.* The rhythmic savagery conjured up the correspondence with Lord Eggers. Paired with Dabak's assessment, Ling now had no doubt that Lady Tun was responsible for the missing children. "What else did Lady Tun ask for?"

"Longevity. I prescribed *wong kei* and *ling zi* to replenish her energy. Dried plants easily attained from any general merchant." He removed his glasses. "However, the remedies escalated to jade and cinnabar shavings. I do not know if she always knew or had researched the *Bencao Gangmu* in the course of creating her new demands." His voice trailed off. "I am a doctor, but that type of medicine plunges one into the dark side. In that pool, I do not know how to swim."

"I read it. The medical text." Ling swallowed.

Dabak lowered his head. "You did?"

"The school had a copy of the Great Pharmacopoeia." She turned away, not wanting to see the disappointment on her uncle's face. "I was researching reasons for someone to keep a set of eyes. I could not find any medicinal value." She had also read the text to face the darkness head-on. There was no need to confess this fact now.

As the pebbled road turned into pavement, a steadiness returned to Ling's thoughts. Dabak pointed Mata in the direction back to the pier.

"Have you visited the greenhouse?" he asked Ling.

———

Ling marveled at the lit-up glass structure. It glowed like a pearl. She had never taken the time to appreciate it during the day. Always late and dashing between school, home, and the shop had prevented her from enjoying the landscape. The moon's reflection from the radiant panes hypnotized her.

After walking fifteen paces from Mata, Dabak stopped on the path. "I must add something important," he turned to her with quiet urgency. "I preferred not to share details in front of Enlai's people."

"Wai is a special relation." Dabak approached the entryway. The wrought iron gate surrounding the greenhouse was two heads taller than her uncle. The metal roses had been forged into mesmerizing curves and patterns.

"You have already...." she started to say. Her uncle had repeated several times his role as Aunt Marcella's savior.

He pulled on the door handles, but chains secured by a padlock thrashed against the metal. "Confound it. This is never locked." He stepped back with his hands on his waist. "Time is dear. Boost me over."

Ling put her hand on Dabak's shoulder. "We must make haste. You are injured, and I am not. You head to the printing press. I will speak with Wai."

Dabak threw up his hands. "I was saying...." He crouched down. As she stepped onto his thigh, she hoisted herself to the top of the gate. "Wai may not have the words. He's...."

"He's recovered," she said as he stood up, giving her the distance to seize the topmost bar.

As she swung her leg over the top, he encouraged her, "*Gaa Jau*. Add Oil."

She whimpered, searching for a spot to steady herself. Using the decorative curls between the bars, she lowered herself down. Little by little, she concentrated on her footing and where to put her hands. She ignored the additional advice by her uncle.

When she landed, her hands felt raw. "Dabak, do not fret. I am fit to climb over fences and walls. What did you say?"

"It is not that... just be careful." He gave her hand a pensive squeeze through the gate.

It dawned on Ling. If Wai and Aunt Marcella shared the same disease, then could the gardener act erratically? She had no way of knowing if he required medicine. "Is it dangerous to meet Wai this way?"

"Wai is not expecting us. Don't let him mistake you for a trespasser. He may be able to sense the location of the twins. He is familiar unfortunately with the witch—Wupo or whatever she holds herself out to be. And who knows? Perhaps you'll manage to trigger his memories. I will meet you inside as soon as I can."

"Dabak, the headmaster is not to be trusted." There was little time to say more.

He nodded and hurried into the main building.

She was alone again. Dabak's advice was odd. In truth, who was Wai? Why would she succeed in triggering his memories when her uncle could not? But if he could save the twins, it didn't matter who he had been.

The door to the greenhouse creaked as it opened, spreading the scents of jasmine and salt. To her relief, it was unlocked. She headed toward the glow of candles. Through a serrated pattern of outstretched branches and variegated leaves, the night sky cast twisted shadows across the stone terrace. Humidity pressed into her skin as she glided through the aisles.

"Mr. Wai." She didn't know his last name. "I am here at the behest of Doctor Shaw."

The stars guided her around planters and pots. She

stopped to smell the colorful roses and perky lavender as a way to calm her nerves. But deeper to the center, shadows closed in. Shrubs scraped the sides of her legs. She gasped when her shirt was snagged by a branch.

As she pulled away, her sleeve ripped. "Mr. Wai, I have an emergency." Her voice squeaked. If he was here, then he would find her. The greenhouse was small enough that she could always see an exterior wall. Yet from certain positions, leafy tropical plants obscured the immediate surroundings. Without stars above, it felt like she was stranded in a wild place.

Out of the corner of her eyes, a cerulean glow caught her attention. She turned down a row and passed sun-loving roses. Reds, pinks, and yellows were planted like a rainbow. Under a retractable canopy, a new breed of plants shimmered purple and red. Flowers that loved the moon. Could this be the radiance of the moonflowers? Her steps quickened.

Around a far partition, her heart leapt. Clusters of blue-headed flowers opened toward the moon, almost visibly gulping in the nocturnal luminescence. She staggered forward, her hand extended with enthusiasm. Before she could come close to the delicate petals, a gust of air pushed her backwards. The unexpected momentum stole her breath. A cold, invisible force skimmed the side of her neck, and her pulse sped up as invisible fingers wrapped around her neck.

Thirty-Five

Ling clenched her jaw. Fear thickened on her tongue. Could this be Wai or the creature Langley? From her pocket, she produced the healing salve. The pressure on her neck loosened. Her offer was snatched from her hand.

She coughed from the pain as fresh air circulated in her lungs. Her eyes refocused on the fracturing lights, glowing white and cerulean. A man in a beige uniform cowered in the corner. It was Wai. His hunch hadn't altered.

"Sorry," he huffed. "Thought you stealing."

Ling rubbed her throat. Wai's speech had devolved. "My brothers are missing."

He grunted as he scrubbed the balm over his tongue. "I heard the forbidden prayer." Pain trembled between each of his words. "Others heard too."

"Was it *Rrr-lou-lok-kiu*?" She noticed Wai shake from the phrase.

He grunted. "Why you say?"

"Wupo stole my brothers. How can I get them back?" Ling backed away from Wai, hoping he would change into an articulate gentleman again.

His shoulders shook, raising the throaty phrase: "*r'luhhor mgvulgtlagln.* It's an invitation to the ancient ones."

Ling shuddered from the vibrations. The call was for retribution. The goddess had shown herself in a dream. A snake-bodied monster had consumed a deity of light on a hilltop. Had this vision been a metaphor for Wupo's disrespect of the gods? Ling wasn't interested in the details. "What does this mean for my brothers?"

Her logical mind screamed for her brothers to be alive. Her heart clung to hope.

Wai grabbed the sides of his head. "Whoever initiate chaos need energy by rite, bite, or blood." The cadence of his speech smoothed out. "Those are the way to connect with power from the ancient ones. You must convert."

Ling was sure Wupo needed innocent flesh. The scars around her eye proved this fact. "Does Dreamland mean anything to you?"

Wai stepped into the silvery moonlight. His white hairs had darkened to purple. "It is *diyu*, a realm between the dead and living. After I was bitten, I could freely come and go from it. It feels like the last moments of a dream or the second before you wake up."

"Doing so requires reconfiguration into another form?" Ling was anxious for the next step. Standing in a greenhouse seemed a most unproductive use of her time.

"As I said, one can become both living and dead." Wai spread more salve down his arms. "By rite, bite, or blood."

Ling looked into his murky eyes. Was he a monster who would save her brothers? The scar across his cheek extended down the side of his neck. She or someone else had to fetch her brothers. "Can you go there again?"

Wai picked up a dried moonflower. "I am afraid I

consumed too much of the antidote." He turned the stem between his index finger and thumb.

"Dr. Shaw or I must find a way to the Dreamlands. What will this cost us?" She didn't mean the price.

"Ah. The doctor has not been to the Dreamlands like you. The eyes in the jar have altered your perspective. You smell a little rotten with an aura colored in mischief colors," he said, appearing concerned.

She gasped. How did he know about the eyes? "Sir, tell me a person may go there again." Ling didn't think his assessment of her health made sense. Wai wasn't a doctor, at least not by training. Then his words sprang into clarity in her mind. "By bite, rite, or death?" Ling lifted the grimoire from her bag. "Is the ritual in here?"

She flipped through the pages. The illustrations were a blur as she passed over the ancient verses.

He stopped the motion of her hand. "*Mgvulgtlagln* is borne and nourished through sacrifice. Power from the curse is exchanged by flesh. Understand that once the call from the ancients takes root, it will never let go. You will be forever bound to the ancients, and I cannot always tell you which one."

"What is your advice?" Ling plopped down on the bench.

"Rescuing your brothers is one thing. The ceremony is not in this book. *Dho-ur tuhgnacg'moq* is the text with the strongest binding rites. The instructions are inside the school, I can feel it." Wai started to fill a sack with dried moonflowers. "We will need these too."

"Where can we find it?" Ling's mind raced to the basement library or in Miss James' plant room.

Under the moonlight, Wai's face was softer and kinder. He had a familiar look again. In another life, he must've been a neighbor or a friend.

"I know you have made up your mind. The ritual is not easy. You may still lose yourself like I did." Wai's warnings were sympathetic. Ling would not be turned from her path though. The truth would not dissuade her from trying to save her brothers.

———

Wai and Ling split up. It was the best way to avoid suspicion. On the way out, Wai said, "Look for a green cover." He drew the ancient symbols and left a note for Dabak. "You will know when the ritual is near. As with the grimoire, the prayer will find you."

As she walked out, Ling gathered a bunch of roses. She would leave a few for Miss James as gratitude. When everything settled down, she could gift some to Emma too.

The school clearly kept secrets, which felt counter to their teachings of morality and righteousness. Yet, in Book of Corinthians, taught to her by Sister March, verse 11:14 said:

"And no marvel; for even Satan fashioneth himself into an angel of light."

Nothing was just black and white. The school was a shade of gray, like her life. She didn't see the contrast until now.

Wai had given her special keys to unlock the side door. Ling ran up the service stairs. Frayed edges of wallpaper guided her up to the third story to the Saint Fiacre window. She stopped when echoes of additional footsteps followed behind her. As the steps drew closer, Ling pressed herself into a corner. Her ears buzzed loudly.

"I heard the incantation." A dark figure stood at the floor above her. "It was uttered from the lips of a woman who is supposed to be dead."

"My brothers have been taken by her...." She had been waiting for this creature since the full moon. It was Langley. It was his fault. His violence had caused this. "You must help find the twins."

The man hid his face behind the lapel of his long coat. Black nails stuck out from the bottom of the sleeves.

Why? His eyes blazed with the question. He clearly didn't feel the same way.

"I'll trade you the location of William's eyes," Ling offered.

He lifted his neck. His beady eyes glared down at her. Parting his lips, white canines poked out of his mouth. *No,* he rejected the demand.

Ling clenched her fist. "And why not?" It would be simple. He had already murdered her once, so why not again? "Finish the job."

"You seem to think the task is easy, like baking a cake." The creature's mouth grimaced. "If I go, your brothers will be dead within the hour. Even before I cross the bay, the horrible witch will perceive me." He opened his hand, displaying a handful of waxy leaves. "These will assist you. I went as close as I could to their camp without arousing suspicion. She is already alerted to my vendetta. I erred, did not complete the rites of absolution to end her life. I was distracted... thinking I heard William's voice."

Ling could tell that the leaves had been plucked minutes ago. A strong smell of camphor eased her mind. "What are you?" Ling asked, putting the foliage in her pocket. He was a puzzlement. He wore the armor of a holy warrior, but he carried the features of a monster.

He spoke through her mind.

I have been searching for my son. His knotty fingers grazed Ling's lacerations.

"How do I save them? Are they far from the school? Can I reach them by sunset?"

He plucked a single stream of Ling's consciousness, threading his knowledge into hers. She became aware for the first time that he was saying nothing, that he communicated with only thoughts. Like jolts of electricity, she watched ideas and questions form and transfer to the creature:

Where did you come from?

Where are you headed?

He bestowed knowledge. Told her his identity. This creature was indeed her uncle, Lord Langley. William had been her cousin. For a moment, their minds bonded. He shared with her slices of his elation and sorrows.

I was trained to vanquish inhuman foes and beasts. My purpose was to extinguish their taste for innocence. Now, as one myself, I am both hunter and hunted.

Is your form forever? Ling projected to him. He had willingly mutated to recover his child. In the end, he had been too late. *Was it worth it?*

My son is my duty. His wholeness is worth any effort.

Parenthood shaped into a form inside her head. His identity and life were linked to his child. *Could nothing else help?*

Only a monster can subvert the primordial mother, Langley shared.

She looked into his unyielding gaze.

He drew her into his vision. *I wavered in my decision. Do not hesitate or else regret lives forever.* There was a time when he second guessed the path to saving his son. His remorse were now paper cuts over raw and salted skin.

When Wupo is dead, will it expel the curse on the island?

Langley laughed. *The curse extends beyond one entity. Even the order, in hundreds of years, has not extinguished its hold.*

Ling pulled out the jar of eyes. "These eyes will guide you to William."

He reached out his bony hands to accept the grisly gift. Dark blood ran through his veins. He held the container, muscles twitched on his face. "I should not have let these out of my sight."

"How do we end the curse?" she persisted. Even if Ling saved her brothers, the misfortunes of children would continue. If the curse continued on, her efforts could be for naught.

"*Dho-ur tuhgnacg'moq.* A forbidden truth," he uttered the words in defiance. The walls shook. With a hand, he touched his fingers onto her skull. Symbols and ancient knowledge tumbled into her mind.

The loyalists need flesh. Once they entangle with the curse, they need souls, essences of natural life to preserve their human parts. Eyes become a potent energy source. This knowledge from me and my predecessors is written in the books I bequeathed to Marcella.

When Langley had given all that he wanted, he fell backwards. Vigor surged in Ling. During their meeting, Ling peeked inside Langley's spirit, the little that remained, and asked: *Will your guilt ever dissolve?*

She had hoped she could convince him to stay. He wouldn't hear of it.

He pressed the jar to his ear. *To the end of the earth, so William may live again.* Then Langley was gone.

Thirty-Six

Inside Classroom 204, bulbs lit every corner of the room. Ling had to look hard for the magnificent green cover she needed. The *Dho-ur tuhgnacg'moq* was pivotal to freeing her brothers.

She sniffed at the shelves, boxes, and piles of dusty books. If winning required searching every nook, then she would surely run out of time. She had to be strategic. Closing her eyes, she enchanted her senses.

"See with me," she said from the back of her throat. *llll mgr'luh ya.* Langley had transferred to her ancient knowledge. A ringing sounded in her ear. This time, it was a comfort. The hairs on her arms stood up. Instead of shutting them out, Ling invited the voices from the shadow to her mind. The twanging morphed into a purr, thrummed somewhere in the room.

Opening her eyes again, her pulse raced as she realized that an aura now surrounded each book. It was as if the pages retained a bit of their owner's spirits. Some spines were silent. Others screamed. The sensations were amazing.

She passed the tall shelves and stacks of texts. A peculiar smell rose up and out from the back of the room, drawing her attention. Colors and foreign scents guided her to a wooden trunk. She knelt down, exploring the hand-carved warships engraved into the four sides of an antique chest. She touched the closed clasp and heard the cries of her brothers.

Grasping, she fumbled with the mechanism. The terrifying noises were trying to convey a message.

"Please," she pleaded under her breath. But the echoes faded. "Stay with me."

Flinging open the lid, she picked out a thin book. Chips of green paint speckled the cover. Pages spilled out from its damaged binding. The book's ancient appearance caused her jubilation and concern. What secrets did it hold?

Cryptograms in the pages reminded Ling of ancient stone age scripts. Bizarre diagrams sprawled in grotesque tangles, engulfing the meticulous handwritten text. There were drawings of human parts cut with unnatural shapes. Ling closed the book. It was difficult to be in such close proximity to the unspeakable procedures for binding. She needed the forbidden texts but could not bring herself to continue reading. Placing it back into the box, her fingers were sticky, and her eyes were coated in a film of grit. She turned to run, and bumped into Wai, right behind her.

"I loathed to intrude upon you. You were immersed in the reading." His hands gripped her upper arms.

"I found a book but... horror dripped from it." Ling felt disappointed at not being able to read more. How did she expect to keep going when she couldn't even finish reading the text?

"Where?"

Ling pointed to the open box.

Wai nodded. "Cleanse your hands and return. We shall

alchemize the words to prepare for your journey to the Dreamlands. To save your brothers." He walked to the box as Ling left the room.

In the ladies' room, she scrubbed her hands so hard that she took off a layer of skin. If the cure had troubled even Langley, then how was she going to overcome its immense power? She splashed water onto her face. The ice-cold water washed away her fear, reminding her to the importance of her perseverance. She had to try.

When Ling returned to the room, Wai had laid out the terrible book on a table and lit a black candle. A pot burned over a fire. He looked up, expressionless, and spoke, translating from the book.

"Entanglement is for binding to a purpose or person. It is the initiation. If a loyalist has your brothers, then the curse will answer. The danger is that you can be pulled in yourself. Any interaction with the curse brings you into its focus." Wai's face twisted in discomfort. "Once begun, this cannot be undone."

Ling pushed aside concerns for herself. "But you are still alive, no?" Why would the powerful curse concern itself with her?

Wai replied, "Evil always wants to make itself known, because only then can it flourish. It desires to be seen. Call its name and be prepared. Steel your nerves for the truth."

"The truth is what I am asking for." Ling looked away from the pages. "By rite." She confirmed her commitment to move forward.

"When did the twins disappear?" Wai asked in a steady tone.

"My mother saw them in the morning yesterday. I found some candies hidden in their desks, possibly from Lady Tun, and a coin...." Ling bit her lip.

Wai turned a page. "Let us start with the purpose." His

fingers moved over the open binding. "What are your brother's names?"

"Shiu Yi Gou and Shiu Yi Kit." Tears welled in her eyes. "They are only nine years old." Their faces appeared in her mind, calling out with fear.

"Write down your brothers' names on separate pieces of paper." Wai chanted elongated series of consonants. Guttural noises escaped the back of his throat. He dropped his jaw and extended his mouth until his voice resembled the one plaguing her from the full moon. The noises pierced her skin and scratched behind her eyes.

He finally wrote out four characters in her native language. "This is the incantation to move the twins out of the Dreamlands and grant you passage into the realm. Memorize these words." Reciting a clash of vowels and consonants, he waved his hands over the book.

She repeated after him:

Lei mung jin jing

l'yha fhtagn

Come forth from the veil and make known your form.

His hands passed through dark candle's flame, changing it from a bright yellow to orange. She added the twins' names to paper scraps. If only the rest would be this easy.

He curled his fingers in a gesture for the names. "The fire will tell us your siblings' future. The color and the speed at which the paper burns will divine their paths."

"What color would your name burn?" Ling asked curiously as she handed him Gou's paper.

"Not yellow. Perhaps the hue of a cloudy sky. The curse clings to my blood." Wai dipped the name into a bowl, coating the paper with a viscous oil. "Purple is sacred. Red is cursed. Yellow is pure. Black is death. The book describes the significance of each part of the light spectrum." When he held the soaked name over the heat, the paper sparked pink and evaporated into ash. The fire licked Wai's fingers orange. He yelped, rubbing his hands with a wet rag.

What was the meaning of that color? Ling steeled herself to peer into the text again. Disgust climbed up her throat.

"Rose means he is alive, red diluted by white. But the curse is close. This brother will be harvested before sunrise." Wai shook his head. "We need more time."

Ling wrapped her arms around herself. They could be anywhere. The men combing the shoreline and town homes weren't enough. Her brothers were slipping through her fingertips. The mountains housed infinite hiding places and even more beyond consciousness.

"Should we light the second one?" Wai asked Ling through her tears.

"Not merely for location. What else can we find out?" Kit maintained his anonymity.

Wai scratched his head. "What is Wupo's name? Do you have anything belonging to her?"

Ling frowned. "Lady Tun or Lady Winnifred Eggers from England. Is she still alive?"

When Wai burned the lieutenant's wife's name, the flame charred the paper black. "She is alive and held by the curse." As the fire flashed an unnatural red, Wai leaned in so close his eyebrows singed. He didn't flinch this time. "The brothers are with her. She must die in order for your brothers to be freed." Ling smelled his burnt hair.

He looked up at the stained glass. "In Guiana, monsters regularly snuck into the huts to consume the blood of the laborers. I escaped after one bit me." He breathed out. "To kill a creature entangled with the curse, you must remove any stolen parts and drain their blood. The woman stole your brothers in the open. That is actually good, because this means she is weak. Not able to call upon powers from the ancients."

"My brothers are innocent. Does the book say how to disable her abilities?"

"This is exactly why she needs them. I don't have the answers, but the book... perhaps with more study...." Wai collapsed in his chair. "You must realize that even if you kill her, the curse will continue. I do not mean to alarm you."

She had a sinking feeling. Why did losing her brothers feel inevitable? "Then let us finish it."

Wai stood back up. "One of the keys to initiation is invitation. Despair or stagnation can encourage someone to invite the evil in, driving them toward darkness." Wai's voice trailed off. His eyes moved left and right. "Before the creature bit me, I wanted to destroy it and the people that held me there. Even though my bite had not been a choice, there was a part of me that sought power. I invited it in." He handed her a knife.

She unsheathed the instrument. The blade was sharp, tinted with gold, engraved with writings from another time. Tracing her fingers over the characters, she embodied their meaning justice and strength. *Ji Lik.* Two words she clung to with her soul.

"This is a pure weapon which has not killed. After it is used, it will turn black," Wai said. Where did the knife come from? This was no time for questions. "I will make the offering by rite. You must prick your finger and put three drops of blood in this tea. Say the incantation, accept the offering, and pour it over soil." He pointed toward the open window. "The tea must touch the earth."

Ling gathered her courage. The gardener placed a key onto the table and walked toward the stone wall. She became uneasy when he cuffed one of his hands to a set of rings fastened into the foundation. "Whatever are you engaged in?" she called to him.

"I do not wish to alarm you. The key to the cuffs is on the table. I am doing this for security. I do not trust myself around fresh blood. Please understand." He lowered his head and said the words.

Ling felt a burning sensation rise from her stomach.

Thirty-Seven

Each word held her in place like a link in a chain. She groaned from the ache in her muscles. Her whole body vibrated with pain. Her head fell backward as her muscles strained. The wound on her hand throbbed as the pain crawled into her heart like a centipede. There, it twisted her blood. When her fingers could move again, she grabbed the knife. Wai was slumped over on the ground. He hung from the metal ring around his wrist. Her own body was feverish and weak. Instead of giving her strength, the curse had sapped her energy. She pricked the end of her thumb. As her blood colored the contents of the porcelain cup a bright red, her knees shook. Parts of her felt like they were dying.

With clumsy steps, she lumbered to the window. Each breath scorched the inside of her lungs. Her stomach twisted and cramped. At the ledge, her exhausted and sweaty arms dropped the entire cup out the window. She heard a *plink*, and the tinkling of the cup shattering over a rock.

Soon, she regained a little more sense of herself.

Standing over the now bluish flame, she touched it with the intention to see. The world inside the storage room hadn't changed. However, she could now stare into the forbidden book and not feel eviscerated. The lessons from Langley intensified as she burned the leaf. He had been telling the truth. Inside the ultramarine flame, she could see her brothers.

Guo and Kit were in a clearing next to a giant banyan tree which gripped them like a monster from the ocean deep. Snaking roots turned and twisted around their small limp bodies. Dirt covered their skin, as if the earth was swallowing them whole. How long had they been there? A wind rattled the hanging vines, shaking loose large waxy leaves. Her vision was narrow, unable to see beyond the dense vegetation. Was this the present or the future? Their flushed cheeks at least told her they were alive.

"Wake up," she whispered through the flame. Their eyes fluttered. Guo sighed. She looked up into the night, adjusting her sight to the galaxy above. From the docks, the same stars twinkled up high. Spinning and turning into the starry patterns, she spotted a pointed triangle with four stars dotting a tail. In Greek astrology, this was the head of the *Serpens* constellation. Her father had written in his journal about a celestial marketplace called Tonshi. Today, the sparkling markings showed her the way to save her brothers. As the fire charred the stem of the leaf, the scene faded.

———

"Ling, are you in here?" Dabak bellowed from the stairwell.

She jumped up. "Here, Dr. Shaw. I am with the gardener." Wai looked up with a dreary expression. She had taken care to stop the flow of blood before unlocking Wai from the shackle. Her finger had clotted and was covered by thick herbal salve.

Her uncle rushed through the door. "Everything is set up. Mata will wait for the print run then take the fliers to the dock. Wai, what of the twins?"

Ling related an account of what had been revealed by burning their names and the leaf. She detailed the interpretations of colors, the speed at which they burned, and fragments of her vision.

"Divination is not reliable," Dabak said. "While your intuition points to the jungle, the logical choice is combing the beaches. There are enough men to handle the mountain side." Dabak rubbed the side of his face. Ling was not surprised to see that he was able to inspect the spell with no obvious repulsion or curiosity.

"Dr. Shaw, the twins will die before sunrise." Ling spoke fast and clear, wringing Guo's shirt in her hand. If he had only seen the colors for himself, then there would be no need to convince him of the proper next steps. She nudged the gardener with her arm.

"Wai, what say you?" Dabak flipped the pages, not looking at either of them. She could see that ideas brewed inside his head, and Ling was afraid his conclusion would be incorrect.

"Sir...um...." Wai's words petered out. He shook his head. Why was he holding back?

Dabak continued when Wai didn't answer. "Wai is a man of magic, and I am one inclined toward science. We must adopt a strategic approach. If the Red Society is searching in the jungle, then we must seek them in the coastlines and even the swamps."

Ling knew in her gut the twins were not there. Yet, logic did dictate a more spread-out approach. "Divinations do not provide more information than the candy wrappers in the twin's bedroom. The stem of the leaf you burned appears to come from a Longan tree, which thrive near the water. Wupo is old and has little chance to fight against two rambunctious boys. And it's quite impossible to pluck out eyes intact without surgical tools."

Ling looked at Dabak with her mouth agape. In one mouthful, he cast doubt on everything that had happened to her in the past few days.

"Niece, do not take it personally. I am only trying to do what is best for the twins."

She tried one more time to urge Wai to come to her defense. But he remained in a stoic posture, unspeaking.

"I am sick of the fantasies of vampires and monsters. I had a long time to think while locked up, and my conclusion is we must live a purified life. Your Aunt Marcella's stories are indicative of this. She's sick, and it has gone straight to her head." By the end of the sentence, Dabak was yelling. His calmness had cracked and scattered to a million pieces. "This is not magic—but bad luck."

Ling felt the floor fall from under her feet. Adrift in her thoughts, she shifted from despair to resolve. Despite her uncle's speech, she didn't doubt what she had seen in the last four days. If the recent events showed her nothing else, it was the impact of her own strength. Listening to others would only lead her astray, even mentors she respected as much as Dabak. This was the moment where she broke free from her uncle.

Dabak stormed out of the room. Neither of them followed him. She caught her breath. When she turned back to the book, Wai stood over it. "Why did you not speak?" She asked him.

"Based on the constellation you gleaned and the angle down the mountain, the site of the twins is a six-to-eight-hour hike or more. Every step would require a machete to cut through the tangled and wild vines. If we do not die of exhaustion, then we will collapse from heat." He traced grains of wood on the desk. "The distance is not something we can overcome through spells. Correcting your uncle is one thing. Giving him hope would be worse than allowing him to carry on. If there is a modicum of a chance to save the twins, he should pursue it."

Her legs wobbled. Everything seemed hopeless. The more she tried to reason out of the situation, the more her head hurt. When her body lurched forward, Wai caught her. He smelled of grass and cooked fish, both land and sea. She extended her arms at the same time, grabbing onto his sleeve. The sound of tearing cloth in the background felt detached from her surroundings.

He helped her to a chair. From her tin, he applied a cold compress to her forehead. "Miss, please take a rest. I am sure you have not slept."

"It has been at least a day and a night since I put my head down." Her eyelids were heavy, but she didn't want to sleep. "But I cannot stop now...." She pushed back the tears. "It's not yet too late." But she felt that she was only deluding herself. She forced her eyes open wide. She saw that a circle had been inked on the back of Wai's arms. A star shone over a triangle and faint lines. Just like hers. She did not understand how someone else could have a tattoo like hers. "What is that marking on your arm?"

Wai looked at the rip on his shirt. "Pardon, I am so sorry." He turned to leave, not answering.

"I have the same one." Ling pulled up the right sleeve of her cardigan and lifted her arm. "It was from when I was small, from a traveler on my father's boat. He... you have one too."

They both looked at each other stunned.

Wai lifted his chin. "What does this mean?"

"It means...." Ling didn't care that she was jumping to conclusions. His tattoo was in the exact location as hers. This wasn't a coincidence. "It means you are my father."

They stared at one another.

"This cannot be." Wai studied the shapes on Ling's arm.

"How many people do you know with the exact markings as you?"

"None," he admitted. "Although, I never really searched for them. I thought... I was once a sailor. Every seafarer has some ink, even the proper ones. I don't remember where...." He scratched his head as his voice trailed off.

Ling remembered, as clearly as if it were yesterday, an enchanted woman poking their skins with a sharped sting ray barb. The mixture of squid ink and tar tingled on her skin. Bonding daughter and father together with the signs of protection.

She could tell Wai was overwhelmed. "The person who gifted these markings to us said it would help us find each other." Joy burst through her heart. While this wasn't the reunion she had imagined, it was enough. Without thinking, she wrapped her arms around Wai, accepting that he must be her father.

Wai cleared his throat. "If you are my daughter, then that means the missing twins are my sons?"

Ling let go and stepped back. In a matter of hours, she had gained a father, but risked losing her brothers. The facts were sobering. She nodded silently.

He bit his lip. "I am sorry, I do not remember," he said, sobbing into his hands.

Their relationship required more time. Like growing apples from a seed, warmth and nurture were keys. Ling felt the distress from her father's cries. "Father. I mean, Wai. Let's take our time. We can ask my mother, too."

Wai wiped his sleeve across his face. He smiled and

nodded to the proposal. "We will be reunited. And your mother, my wife, is still alive?"

"She is." Although Ling wondered what Ahma might think. Would she be furious at her for defying Dabak? If she was mad about redeeming the wage money, then her father's return was a death sentence for Dabak. However, right now, they needed to get to the twins.

Wai spread out the moonflower petals and filled separate satchels. "We will both need these to stop Wupo."

"I saw the creature push flowers into Lady Tun's mouth." Ling only cared to dictate facts. The things she had witnessed with her own eyes. "What does it do?"

Wai found the entry in the secret book. "Death is elusive for those bound to the spell. One must disinfect their physical energy."

Over his shoulder, Ling read the long list of natural sources purported to snuff out the curse's hold: garlic, oregano, and saliva of fruit bats. The solution, however, ended abruptly. Pages had been torn out.

Ling stared out of a clear pane of glass. She looked out into the nothingness of the ocean. Lights on ships dotted the dark horizon. If only Langley had been able to stay and teach her about the ancient ways. To be prepared for this moment, she needed time to study. A glimpse of the power that lingered in Ling's mind. Of course, two men counseled against her seeking unlimited powers. What could she do? She would still be a struggling healer with the responsibility of caring for her family.

"If the flowers do not cure, then why bother to dampen the powers?" Ling had seen the spectrum of the effects of the blood disease. Langley had ability beyond her imagination. Aunt Marcella, in comparison, had voluntarily become a sad and feeble version of her former self. Ling thirsted for the bolder of the two options.

Wai sighed. "Death is the only cure, and as we read, even that is hard to come by. You say power or *li*. Power by the curse has no comparison to what you know. It requires deep and dark suffering. By the end, you will rip out your own eyes. Pardon the analogy. I learned to appreciate my humanity, and this is what I want."

"Can you still pass it on?" Ling studied the stem of the rose. Every plant protected themselves, especially the most beautiful ones. Yet, the sharp thorns couldn't prevent it from being plucked from its bush.

"By rite, bite, or blood. *R'lyehsan, Xh'algh, Vhul'tak.*" Wai shook his head. "Not every bite turns someone into a beast. Vampires were once human. Their bite infects a person with a bacterium, which then must be re-activated by drinking the host's blood. To turn into a beast yourself, a victim must allow the evil to flourish willingly." He closed his eyes. "The curse's full effects will give you anything you wanted. You will also gain everything you did not want."

It was obvious Wai was trying to warn Ling. She recalled the famous quote: *Power tends to corrupt, and absolute power corrupts absolutely. Great men are almost always bad men.* But what would power do for a woman?

Ling dipped her nose inside the head of the rose. Breathing in its sweetness, she recalled the soda shop and her best friend's smile. She walked into the most shadowy corner of the hall. Crushing the velvety petals between her fingers, she forced the stem deep into her wrist. Tears streamed down her cheeks as the thorns cut through layers into her soul. The twisting motion slashed deep valleys along the underside of her forearms.

The earthy tinge of copper spiced the air. Instantly, Wai's eyes shut. "I don't want to do this."

"If I turn, then I can save my brothers. And you can regain your memories." Ling pleaded. "Don't you want to know your home again? After I rescue the twins, I can take the moonflowers and attend medical school." Warm blood dripped down Ling's arm and pooled on the floor.

A longing flashed across his face as he bowed his head, still for a moment. Then there was a horrible blur of motion. In an instant, everything turned black.

THIRTY-EIGHT

Wai drank with a tortured expression. Ling's head went back as her veins pulsed. She felt her body become jelly and then concrete. Her eyes fluttered and closed. She sank into her regrets. Her goals were modest, to live on the island and become a doctor. She didn't accept gentlemen callers, hadn't concluded her studies, and never strayed too far from her mother's advice. She was a flower collapsing into its center, like the millions that fade at the end of each spring. Beautiful colors wilting into decay. Her mind suspended over her roots as darkness swept over.

Wai released her. "What have I done?" He wiped his lips. "I am sorry, Ling. My... my... *neoiji*." Her body convulsed, and he held her head. "You were correct."

Wai stirred. A part of her stayed with him in the unlit corridor, while another part was plunged into nothingness. She could see him from her mind's eye on another plane. Yet, she had no way to respond right then.

Wai ran back to the room and returned with garden shears. He sliced into his own wrists with the muddy blades, then wrung the bitter drops into Ling's mouth. The thick liquid collected on her tongue. Her heartbeat quickened; each pulse carried in new sensations and otherworldly memories. Pieces of bones and broken flesh came apart inside multiple lives. Her sluggishness metamorphosed into weightlessness.

In her mind, she saw a boy. He cried over a pile of ashes. Only a brick fireplace remained of a once two-story building. *Was this a dream?* This boy transformed into a skinny teen who ran barefoot through the nine-dragon mountain range with all the courage in the world. Not once being scared, not once calling out to his dead mother. Longing replaced the happiness on young boy's face as he morphed into a man. She realized that the child was her father.

Her father grilled catches from the Pearl River Delta coastline. The memories this time brought her face-to-face with a little girl in pigtails. With a detached surprise, she realized that this was her. Sometimes Ling had accompanied her father on his voyages. His captain's quarters were clad with oak panels. Intricate stories were carved into pictures telling of heroes who sailed into storms and wrestled monsters. Ling shifted through more memories. The pigtailed girl hugged her pregnant Ahma while her father grilled shrimp and sardines. The girl played with Enlai, still innocent then.

Turning to a specific feeling or thoughts was like skimming the pages of a book. The index was intuitive. She changed scenes on command, moving between people and time.

Where had her father been for so long?

The rips on her wrist burned. Heat radiated from them, transmitting the tactile and ephemeral. Like her father, her body was unwilling to die. She forced her mind onto the hull of a ship. One she had never seen. The name *K. Hooper* was painted on the ship's bow. Trepidation filled this memory. Her father was peering through an opening under the deck. In the distance a verdant coastline came into view. *Would they land here?*

Tension crowded the hull. Battered and bruised, the men's hands were bound; they were squatting next to a pile of rotting corpses. An oily stench of spoiled meat lingered in the tight quarters. She was looking at this horrific scene through her father's frantic eyes. She was seeing him and feeling his fear. He had wanted to go home. He had longed for his family. She felt awful for him, but a part of her was also secretly elated. Ling hadn't been discarded.

This wasn't the end of the story.

Anger seethed inside Ling. To the soldiers, sailors, and captors, her and her father's lives didn't matter. They were cattle. These were her foes. He had not returned because a slaver had held him against his will.

Now, Ling had the same ailment that coursed through Aunt Marcella and her father. The idea of turning into a monster had once scared her. With her new knowledge, she realized these were childish fears.

"I know you are in there." Her father patted her face.

His touch radiated warmth on her skin. It grounded her. The gentleness of his words exuded care. Most of her life had been borne from his absence.

He tested her breath and pulse. "Find your brothers. Your mind can take you anywhere. Do not be hasty. Remember that the protective herbs can hurt you now. To stop Wupo, drain her blood and remove the stolen eyes from her sockets." He gritted his teeth. "I believe in you, Ling. I saw how you have kept our family strong."

Sensation returned to Ling's fingers. She wiggled her pinky and opened her eyes. Her mouth and cheeks were still numb, but she could see his face clearly in the dark. His face was now a composite of all the ones in her memory. From the little boy to the sullen prisoner on an island, he was much more than her father.

"Cut her throat with the golden knife. Not your bite. You must not drink her blood." Her father placed a sheathed dagger in her bag. "Wupo's blood will only bind you deeper to the curse. You will inherit her entanglement."

Once again, she heard Dabak call out their names. "I am sorry." Footsteps vibrated against the floor. Ling pulled herself against the wall.

Dabak turned the corner and yelped. "Ling, what's wrong?" He pressed two fingers against her neck. He turned to Wai. "Did you slip?"

There was a long pause.

"Her lips are pale." He stood up in an aggressive stance. "What is the meaning of this?"

"Why didn't you tell me she was my daughter?" Her father's voice shook. "Brother."

"I couldn't... you were... How did...? What happened?" Dabak turned to face Wai. They embraced. "You couldn't even recall your birth name in the morning." Her uncle cried into Ba's shoulder.

Away with you. Ba mouthed the words while holding onto Dabak. *I'll explain it all to him and your mother.*

Ling slid to an open window. She concentrated on Aunt Marcella. She was at Queen's pier. Ling chose there. Her body floated, every muscle and hair enlivened by the change. She couldn't believe it until her feet left the ground. She hovered over the two men. Being untethered to the floor took her a few seconds to comprehend. It felt like climbing swiftly up on a ladder, forever.

The higher she lifted, the easier it became. She elevated herself and slipped outside. Under the dark sky, the stars and night enveloped her. Winds from every direction carried secrets from other lands. She drifted over the tops of buildings, first the school and then the foreign mansions. Even from Kowloon, she could see across the bay.

Aunt Marcella sat on a bench with gas lamps flickering. She flinched as Ling touched her feet to the ground.

I came to see you. Ling said nothing aloud, projecting the thought.

Aunt Marcella craned her neck. Her head darted from one direction to another. She was aghast. "What have you done?" Their minds connected, seamlessly sharing their histories.

Ling touched her aunt's quivering hand. She heard blood pumping from Aunt Marcella's heart to her fingertips. Between them, different paths were illuminated. *Why did you ever give up this power?* Ling was certain now; her destiny would no longer be forged by others.

"Love. I was young and foolish." Aunt Marcella spoke to the wind. A forlornness spread across her face. "Where are your brothers?"

Her brothers were nearby.

Smells from the sea engulfed Ling. With her new senses, she observed creatures moving under the waves. Past the salt and seaweed, she inhaled the fragrant turmeric, ginger, and pepper inside the passing ships. A mosquito buzzed over flowers. Ling focused on the bug's wings and then further into its belly full of blood. She caught a faint scent of Kit.

Where have you been, little mosquito?

Aunt Marcella pulled a blanket across her chest. "Be cautious of the sun."

Ling kissed her aunt's cheek and then launched from the pier toward the mountains. Her feet grazed the cresting waves, tickling a poem in her.

Darkness settles on roofs and walls,
But the sea, the sea in the darkness calls.
The little waves, with their soft, white hands,

And the tide rises, the tide falls.

She first stopped at the medicine stand, smelling the twins sitting under Banyan trees. Kit's and Gou's location was miles away, more than halfway up the side of the highest cliff. The brigade would never have found them. At least not before their captor mutilated and gutted their bodies.

Ling was cautious when projecting near the twins; she knew that Wupo was near. She must be subtle and not allow her presence to be detected. Dirt clung to their sweaty skin swollen from mosquito bites. They were alive. Wupo sat on the other side of a fire, digging into the belly of a calf. She had plucked out the poor cow's eyes. Mixing with the raw intestines and burning of manure in the center of the fire, the oracle's physical form rotted.

As quiet as she could, Ling sang the rhyme:

Three Blind Mice.

You will have your eyes.

First, run away from the soldier's wife.

Who stole two boys from their bed.

Did you ever hear a snake in the woods save the little ones?

Her brothers' ears perked up. They were bound to a tree at the edge of a clearing. As tears fell down their cheeks, Ling crossed her fingers.

They have no eyes. They have no eyes. The boys gazed into the dark forest, waiting for a creature to pounce.

They all ran away from the cow-eating witch. The brothers looked at each other in surprise.

"Help?" Gou whispered. His eyes puffy from crying.

Yet, a bird will pluck out the wretched eyes.

Kit and Gou bit their lips.

What else is to gather about the fire site?

Kit covered his face with his hands. "Water hurts her," he mumbled into his palms.

The bird will be there. Chirp Chirp.

Ling quieted her mind just as Wupo started to listen.

"Shoo birds," Wupo yelled toward the trees. Innards clung to the side of her face. "Or I'll barbecue you for breakfast." She cackled, shaking tree branches. The sound grated Ling to the bone. But Wupo had only caught the very end of her message, and did not understand it.

Every fiber in Ling's body wanted to race into the forest. But she paused. Consulting the book of secrets, she read the pages in lightning speed, no longer struggling with the obscure meanings. She learned that smoke from bay and mugwort leaves weakened the entanglement's hold. Then, she gathered ingredients, pulverizing them to a fine powder, careful not to touch the herbs herself. Her training served her well here. She poured the mixture into a glass jar.

Passing Emma's house, she couldn't resist peeking inside her friend's bedroom. She had only intended to check in on her, take a moment to quell a curiosity burning inside of her. Make sure her best friend was safe.

From the window, moonlight reflected off Emma's porcelain skin. Ling's heart fluttered. Ling leaned against the opened windowsill, observing Emma's gentle breaths behind a set of chiffon curtains. An unfamiliar passion stirred inside. She yearned to caress her friend's parted lips. The sudden urge to burst through the window scared her. Her finger reached out to touch the drapes, but a barrier held her back. Her fingers dissolved upon touching the barricade, searing a warning into her blood. Even in such a powerful form, Ling couldn't go everywhere. She realized it was because she hadn't been invited.

Emma rolled over, away from Ling's desperation. Her thirst for blood scared her. Knowing the effects of a bite, the hunger frightened Ling. Voices compelled her to feast. The desire burned with a greater intensity than she had ever felt. The disease regressed her to a carnal state. Her father had resisted, hunting only a few animals; he had taken the moonflowers before tasting human flesh. The beast that bit her father had acted many times more wicked.

She had witnessed its memories too; On an island in the middle of the ocean, a cadre of blood eaters tore out the throats of babies, hung a wreath of human fingers in the trees, and engaged in bodily pleasures even the devil would question. The curse, without keepers, could destroy the entire world.

Thirty-Nine

Ling rubbed the burn scar where Wupo had tried to first capture her soul. Following the fading scent of the mosquito, she also used the stars to point her toward the clearing. A flame dancing at the top of the next mountain range beckoned Ling deeper into the jungle.

Getting closer to her camp, Ling moved slow and low. She slithered around the tangled roots of sprawling camphor trees, dropped pinecones, and fragrant incense leaves. She could sense every creature's beating heart for miles. Ants crawled under the spongy white bark of tropical evergreens. Resting birds tucked themselves under their wings. She outstretched her tongue, tasting the air. The twins were beyond the next tree.

From behind a wall of vines, Ling watched. Branches encircled Wupo's head like a twisted crown. She sharpened a knife. A calf lay on its side, entrails spilling from its open belly. Its eye sockets were dark and hollow. As metal grated against rock, Ling's teeth vibrated. The back and forth polishing of the blade sounded like the second hand of a clock. The fire in the middle of the clearing illuminated the determination on the soothsayer's mutilated face.

Gou groaned behind the dead cow. Kit whimpered, secured only by a loose knot. His blindfold had already fallen to his chest.

She suppressed an urge to leap forward. Every muscle in her body wanted to fight and pull her siblings out. But Wupo was old and experienced, and more deeply entangled with the curse than Ling. The element of surprise was the most important aspect of the plan. Weakening the curse's protection improved her chances of rescue. Even if the oracle was blind, she was skilled and powerful.

The one bulbous eye clung to the side of her face, scanning the dark. Ends of the branches on her crown protruded from her head. She had arranged for minimal protections. No child had ever escaped her. No parents had ever identified her as the culprit.

Inching toward Kit's tree, Ling hissed.

"Snake?" Kit whispered, shuffling his feet over the dirt. She heard his heart pounding faster.

"Ssssshhh... *ma lou*." Her little monkey had to stay calm. She slipped a slingshot into one hand and round stones into another. He calmed, gripping the wooden handle.

"For your enemies." Ling whispered the plan into his ear. Kit smiled with his eyes lowered to the ground.

When Ling untied his hands, a yelp escaped from him.

"What is the fuss over there?" Wupo jerked up. Orange flames cast crooked shadows over her broken face.

"Snake." Kit spoke into his knees.

"Bah." Wupo mashed the swelling bovine eye back into her socket. "I can barely see, and I know you're lying." The unnatural eye wildly probed the surroundings. "Blasted vermin, you must be glad that you taste like decomposing garbage." Her laughter shook the trees.

Kit howled at the top of his lungs. "It bit me." His body convulsed and foam leaked from his mouth.

"You meddlesome twit." Wupo hobbled toward him. Her overgrown body lumbered over rocks and fallen trunks. A dark liquid leaked from her crown. "Better death by snake than by my knife. I still need eyes. Better to get them fresh." She licked her lips. "Before the poison reaches them."

Kit shot up. Thumbing his nose at the old lady's threats, he stuck out his tongue as he bolted into the forest. She couldn't move fast enough to catch him.

"Foolish. You cannot hide." Wupo bared her blackened teeth as a stone flew through the air. *Splat*, the rock landed on the side of her head with unexpected force. She wobbled on her uneven legs, trying to cover herself.

Ling readied herself to pounce on the oracle. The evil woman wouldn't lay another hand on her brothers again. Wouldn't sour another innocent life.

The next hit caught the side of Wupo's lumpy eye. The orb fell to the ground and started rolling down the slope.

"This damned cow's eye! I'll have new ones soon," Wupo spat. She struggled to her hands and knees then groped in the dark. "Once I get you again, I'll do more than eat your flesh. I pull out the precious seeds of your life." Her knotty fingers flicked up grass. "Delays. Delays... the precious seed be mine."

Ling crouched further in the shadows, relieved her brother had moved away from the camp and distracted the old lady.

The eye tumbled away until Kit stopped it with his foot. He picked up dirt caked body part.

While the soothsayer was distracted, Ling untied Gou.

Using a leaf, she smeared salve under his nose. A bit of the ointment splashed onto her skin and smoldered. She was sad to realize that the protective herbs shielded others from her too. Her head now throbbed from the once-comforting aromas. Kit had climbed up a tree, unreachable by the blind old lady.

But Ling was overconfident. Before she could hide, Wupo lumbered out in front of her. Ling could see much that her eyes did not, and so could Wupo.

"Almost, Ling almost." The soothsayer flung her hands forward in a quick motion. A sharp pain pierced Ling's chest. She teetered backwards. Her chest burned. Looking down, she saw a metallic shard sticking out from her breast. Venom spilled into her veins, weakening her. She tightened her hold of the satchel of herbs. The plan must continue. Both Gou and Kit needed to escape the Dreamland, a circle of protection laid down by Wupo. But Ling's legs gave out.

"Girl. Did you think you can stop me? With childish tricks?" She pointed the end of the long knife straight at Ling's heart. "This is ready for you."

"Snake." Kit shouted from the branches of the tree.

"Give the eyes here." Wupo turned, heaving another thin metal shard. Ling lunged for the lady's feet, pulling down to disorient the oracle's aim.

The needle missed Kit as he let go of his slingshot. The orb flew straight into the fire. The flames changed to black, the same darkness that burned with Lady Tun's name. While Wupo readied another sharp projectile, Ling spotted the serpentine ring adorning her finger again. Kit had already gone. Pain continued to radiate from her wound.

"You destroyed my enchantment! Nobody does that and gets away with it." Wupo pulled at her scalp, shoving her hands into the fire. "You cannot stop me." The fire ate away her garments, spewing a bright red. It was the curse's color.

Ling gritted her teeth, running full speed into the witch's backside. The oracle fell face first into the hot coals. Heat licked Ling's face, searing her brows. She was beyond ready. With one hand holding down the oracle, the other smashed the herbs over the embers.

Ashes set free the power of crushed bay leaves, basil, and mugwort. The cloud knocked Ling backwards. It entirely engulfed Wupo. Her screeches rang into the valley as the fire glowed a brilliant purple. Animals dashed from their nests. Flocks of birds vacated the trees. The very sky rumbled with anger.

Kit sprang out from his hiding place. He ran to his sister, gasping as he noticed the needle embedded in her chest. Ling squeezed out the poisonous thread soaked in the poison of raw *wutou*. Then she and Kit dragged the unconscious Gou behind a tree. Ling could complete the detangling alone.

"Wait here." Ling showed Kit how to tend to Gou's wound. "Press this cloth firmly. It should stop the bleeding. Do not look at what's happening to Wupo."

Kit nodded. His eyes fixed on his brother's shallow breath.

The fire raged on, lighting up the sky. Ling had freed her family from this woman's torment. But even Langley couldn't rid the world of the unholy. The order of vampire hunting monks lived on for a reason. At least Langley had tried.

She crouched down, watching the witch's blackened flesh twist and crack. The silver ring still sparkled on her bony finger. At the ring's center, a black stone cracked into two.

Between Wupo's teeth, Ling inserted bay leaves, careful not to touch them with her bare hands. She referenced the book of secrets in her bag and recited the last rites.

With flame in hand, to darkness send.
This wicked heart, no chance to mend.
By earth and water, fire, air, bind her below, forever there.
Nulla spes emendandi,
mo fu dai sou bou,
No chance to mend.

Ling had shackled the words to the disfigured body. The spirit could now no longer return to the living realm. Langley had omitted this step with Lady Tun. It was a ritual for trapping the curse inside its physical form, hence prohibiting a corrupted soul from inhabiting another body.

Lady Winnifred Eggers would never steal another pair of eyes again.

One last thing to do. Ling grabbed the skull, staring into its empty sockets. Flesh dripped off the bones. Then, she pressed her father's golden knife into the neck.

We are the same, a faint voice echoed inside of her head. The body croaked when the blade severed the head from its body. Blood splashed onto the stones, sizzling and burning away with the rest of her legacy.

After she drained the corpse of its fluids, Ling collapsed onto the ground. She was coated in sweat and blood. Even with this witch dead, she didn't feel safe. More loyalists in the form of humans fueled the curse. More eyes remained in the sea cave. Bringing her missing siblings home was the least she could do for the lost.

The idea of leaving them alone racked her with guilt. When she inspected her hands, she noticed blood splattered over her knuckles. For a moment, she wondered what Wupo had seen. Both the curse and the woman had invited her into a new world. Their power must have been grand. The curse had absolute control.

But what if she could learn yet more? After all, she had beaten the oracle at her own game. Against her better senses and her promise to her father, Ling touched the back of her hand to her mouth. The blood tasted like toffee and broken glass.

FORTY

Ling stared at the back of her hand. A whole world swirled inside of the red. Unlike with the tinny aftertaste of a *mantou* soaked in human blood, memories jabbed into her thoughts. Her breath grew labored as a rush of sensations fought every cell in her body. On the smoldering pile of coals, Wupo's corpse laid silent. A sinister smile still stretched across her charred face.

See with me.

Wupo had lived many hundreds of lives before the Walled City. When Kowloon was still raw and an uninhabited place, she was sent by the mountain gods to balance good and evil. With the body of a snake and face of a human, she sowed plants and regulated the tides. On her journeys, she fell in love with an ashy-haired soldier. But he couldn't love a monster like her.

The darkness consoled her and whispered the ways she could transmute into a beautiful lady. Each transformation entangled her further with the curse. She soon learned that the only way to hold another form was through human parts. So, she stole them.

From women and to unsuspecting men, she had maintained the desired shape. Children had the most enchanting souls. Their innocence perfected her physical form.

As the curse had done countless times before, it beckoned Ling. The taste of blood brought her closer to its purpose. But she knew she could use it for good. This power could save every child on this land.

She didn't fight the curse's suggestions. The orphan eyes in the cliffside cave had weeping fathers and mothers. They deserved to have their souls returned. Ling's eyes rolled back as she allowed the curse to tell her more.

I will see with you.

Her body shook. Blood drained from her fingers. The dirt swirled around her body. Ancient voices came alive.

Ymg' ah geb

Nei hei dou

You are here.

It was the answer to the question at the start. Was this her destiny or a scheme of the curse? Either way, Ling could no longer hide.

Before she fell completely over a cliff, small hands pulled her back. She had willingly agreed to invite evil in. Her shoulders shook. She heard someone calling her name. Ling regained her balance and opened her eyes.

"Jhe, what's wrong?" Two small faces stared into hers. Dirt walls surrounded her. The ground had tried to eat her up. It wasn't a dream.

"Gou? Kit?" I am not well." She shivered uncontrollably. The curse had drawn her very close. Her brothers carried her out of the pit. They hugged her until warmth returned to her bones.

"Jhe, how do we get back?" Gou wiped Ling's face with the end of his shirt. Slivers of dawn shone through openings in the canopy. The sunlight would not touch Ling in the forest. While she could never run from the curse, distance from the witch's body offered a reprieve. And she still had at least one more place to go.

Ling found strength in her legs and carried her brothers to the foothills. At the edge of the woods, she stopped. If she took them back, she was risking the people she loved. From her father's and Wupo's blood, hunger coursed through her veins. It was part of her.

She set down her brothers and pointed to the village. "You can make the walk to the temple. I know you both can do it." In the distance, she heard Enlai and Dabak shouting their names. This morning, only two of three of them would return.

"But why...." Gou whined.

Kit made a face.

"I cannot explain now, but I'll be back...." She wanted to say soon, but she had no idea if that was true. She didn't want to break a promise. "I will see you again. Listen to Ahma. Be good." She had much more to say about life and finding Ba. Yet, the sun started to flood the valley. She kissed them each on the forehead and watched them scurry away, into a sunlit world that was no longer hers.

Forty-One

Ling returned to the site and wrapped the remains of Wupo. Having a body was important to the ghosts. This burnt body would absolve her uncle of wrongdoing. Her family wouldn't need to wallow in the shame of a murder accusation. Just as the sun reached the summit of the Nine Dragon Mountain, Ling entered the shadows of the Walled City.

The blood-stained canvas slammed onto the edge of the roof at Cafe de Sourire. The movement was meant to be quiet, but her hands slipped from a slickness on the fabric. The streets of the Walled City were still. Customers hadn't yet awoken. The cafe was empty.

Kali walked out sleepy eyed, shuffling in slippers. Curlers bounced in her hair as she collected empty beer bottles. Looking up, she was startled.

"Ling, I did not see you there. You should leave," Her mouth stretched open in a huge yawn. With each table, Kali got closer and closer.

"Do not come near me." Ling shielded her face with her sleeve.

"Hold on." Kali lifted one finger, checking the ground. "Sometimes people leave things here. Money. Weapons. Paraphernalia." She looked up. "Well, you are a proper mess."

As Kali took one step toward the body, Ling flashed her teeth. She had hoped to keep to the shadows, but she couldn't have anyone else moving Wupo.

"You are one of them." Kali gulped. Her expression crumpled with disappointment.

"Them?" Ling didn't know what she meant. With a stranger, Ling preferred not to intrude on their thoughts. Asking questions was an old habit she didn't want to lose.

"Loyalist." Kali's face flashed an annoyance. "I used to entertain them on the island. Hell, most of them consider plundering and enslavement a right."

Ling clothes and face were in disarray. "Do you have extra clothes?" She no longer wanted to be covered in other people's blood.

"Do you want something to eat?" Kali asked. The whole time Ling had held back the hunger vexing her. Kali understood Ling could not be satisfied by simple cooked meats or sweets. She required raw materials—blood. Kali glanced at Ling's desperate expression. "A man brings us fresh chickens every day. You can have one of those."

Ling closed her eyes and thought of Enlai.

I am at the cafe, she whispered.

Kali nodded. "Wash up inside. Not sure when Enlai will show up."

———

Soon, Enlai arrived. "I swear you told me to come here. I heard your voice in my house. But obviously you were not there."

Ling smiled, sitting at a table with a cup of hot coffee. He scooted into the chair next to her. She had cleaned up and changed into a purple silk blouse with yellow cloth buttons. The outfit hung loose on her body. The airiness of the fabric was refreshing. "I need you to do something for my family. I am hoping this will clear my uncle as a murder suspect. He must maintain his practice as a healer."

Enlai glanced over her shoulder at the end of the landing. He recognized the body wrapped in canvas. Without a second thought, he agreed.

"Not in the usual way." Ling transferred an image to Enlai. The picture was of Wupo's charred body laid across the statute of Sir Thomas Jackson in Royal Square. The square had been built before her lifetime over a plot of reclaimed land. She meant for every ghost to witness the death of one of their own. Only a few would understand the meaning of the way she had died. Those who did would be warned of a future where the world could be free from the curse.

"I know what to do." Enlai winced. "We must deliver the body, but in a public place, so no one may deny Lady Tun's death. Which of course is not by the hand of your uncle."

Ling must retrieve one of the woman's dresses.

Enlai bit his lip, removing a plain box from his bag. "I have something for you." Ling purposely didn't peek inside. He handed her the heavy box, the width of his palm. Leaning forward over the table, she pulled off the paper lid, revealing a brass plated compass. Her father's compass.

Tears welled in her eyes.

"After yesterday's events, I became a boss and manage a neighborhood in the Walled City. The position comes with perks." Enlai reached across the table, touching the top of her hand. "Should I ask Kali for a blanket? You're cold."

She shook her head, feeling heat evaporate from her wet hair. He ordered a drink with Kali as a phrase repeated in his mind.

He placed another hand over hers. "We make a great team." His eye wistfully looked into hers. "We should...."

"Continue the partnership." Ling interjected. She knew what he would say. She didn't want him to feel embarrassed for proposing a union. In a way, he appreciated her value.

Enlai furrowed his brow.

"I am grateful, and so will my father." Ling replaced the lid over the box. "What do you want in exchange?"

"As I was saying, a more permanent partnership...." Enlai's eyes sparkled. Perhaps Ling, before last night, would been flattered by the attention and even considered the proposal, despite Enlai's unsavory work. But after her change, it no longer made sense to have ties to any place or anyone. She wondered about her feelings and leaned over the table. Touching her lips to his, she felt the pleasantness of their friendship. In his passion to show her his worth, he had lost the purpose of love. He didn't even know where his desire came from.

"I'll give you what you need," he said when she pulled back, not thinking of Ling's best future.

Ling smiled. Enlai did believe in his abilities to fulfill her. Love, status, or stability were purported benefits of marriage. But in her observations, marrying a man offered a weak representation of those things. A man could love only in certain ways. A wife was forever trapped under her husband's rule and his whim. In Ling's blood churned echoes of many unhappy wives, both aristocratic and low-born. Most of them died the same, with thankfulness that they were letting go.

"You have done so much for the Red Society, and me." Enlai fidgeted with his hands. She could see he had envisioned a scenario in which Ling accepted his marriage proposal.

Ling placed Wupo's serpent ring onto the table. It shimmered in the shadows. His eyes grew wide. "This is ancient and once belonged to a goddess. You can have it for your lifetime."

As his fingertips grazed the metal, his mouth watered. Twitching, a new power surged into his body. "How...?"

Ling opened her mouth, flashing the tips of two pointed teeth. "Last night I ended the lore of Wupo. With this, you will be the most powerful man in the Walled City, and maybe even the island. The curse rules on the other side of the bay. Unless you want to become like me. Gather all the riches that you desire, but you must protect the people who live here, most importantly children."

"But you do not want to stay here? Not with me?" Enlai slumped back is his seat. "What does this all mean?"

He had never been her first choice, but she wouldn't speak this truth. If they were to be allies, he couldn't hold any ill will against her. She couldn't wound his ego, so she recited the ending verse of her favorite poem:

The morning breaks; the steeds in their stalls
Stamp and neigh, as the hostler calls;
The day returns, but nevermore
Returns the traveler to the shore,
. . .And the tide rises, the tide falls.

Forty-Two

Inside the cave, water lifted during high tide, submerging the opening. The ancient writing etched onto the stones hid the sheltered space. The moon was waxing. Where the light from the small opening above couldn't touch, tiny eyes watched her. Small creatures made their home in this underground hollow. This morning, they sacrificed themselves as Ling's breakfast.

She cracked the mice's skulls to cease their suffering and thrashing about. Their rancid-tasting meat produced the most satisfying blood. More pleasing than any dish Ling had ever tasted. The red elixir warmed her like hot black tea. She now understood the reasons the ghosts killed for leaves and spices. They had urges beyond their control.

Ling stretched. Her ravenous thirst was quenched for the moment. But she was soaked in blood and her fingers matted with fur. She was repulsive. Inhaling the scent of carnage, she started to regret her choice to turn. Whiskers, bones, and tails were strewn about the corners of the damp cave. Would this be the rest of her life? A hermit in a cave?

She washed herself in sea water. In the reflection, her

eyes sparkled with gold. She hissed, lifting the corners of her lips. Sharp teeth mirrored back a menacing grin. She slapped the surface of the pool of water. Why hadn't she steadied herself? She was usually rational, not an impulsive idiot. Both Dabak and her father had warned her. Regardless, she had stepped into the curse's trap.

Her father and Aunt Marcella functioned fine in society. They weren't totally themselves in every sense, but they functioned. With the right support, she could continue her previous life. But did she want to become a shell of her former self?

Life would figure itself out. She always had a plan. Even before Ba's return, she'd had determination. When Ahma had to fend for them, Ling figured out where to register for schools and scholarships for which she could apply. It had been her idea to sell herbal remedies at the smaller port.

As the water lifted, she scribbled protective symbols onto the walls. This cave was her place now, trapped between the sea and earth. It was her own Dreamland.

A thread of sunlight radiated through an opening. She had many hours to think before she could crawl out again. Ling made good use of her situation and explored the boxes.

She no longer needed tools to open them. Ling simply dug her fingernails under the hardwood, prying open the containers. New strength had changed her bones and muscles. She even moved differently. Four days after the full moon, Ling had transformed into someone else, someone stronger. Stamped inside the crates was the figure eights, tucked close to each other like a tight spring bud. It was a mark of ownership; one allocated to people, places, and things.

Lifting the lid, Ling was delighted. The first crate overflowed with silk ball gowns and shiny shoes. The second one was filled with precious jewelry, gems, and gold. She daringly tried on an emerald dress. The bodice fit snugly and curved along her hips. Her bare legs rubbed together as she danced along a dry ledge. A warmth traveled up her stomach to her neck. The feeling was new. She imagined the places these clothes might be worn. Her almost twenty years of life had been filled with hard work and personal sacrifice; she had never attended a ball, while her classmates regularly celebrated in mansion parties on the island.

Next, she picked a teardrop diamond dangling from a gold necklace. She couldn't imagine how much these jewels were worth. If she gave a few to Emma, would she have enough resources so she would not have to marry?

Even in low light, the glassy stone sparkled like the surface of the ocean. The cool pendant fell between her breasts, stroking the delight flowing inside of her. Between the caress of the soft fabric and the diamond's sparkle, Ling felt like a full-bodied person again. Hearing blood beat in her heart. Life coursed from her toes, womanhood, and to the top of her head.

Bejeweled and beset with power, she approached the shelf of eyes. They had been forced sacrifices. Ling had started this journey to garner favor with people of influence. Her fate had different plans. How much more would she change? She was still mostly herself. Would she eventually become like Wupo, obsessed with long life or beauty? Ling ripped away the wood planks nailed to the wall, meeting the row of eyes. An empty place sat where William's had stood.

She chose the most intense pair. The red color glowed as its tendrils laid bunched into one corner. The iris pulsated as it registered her presence. This time, Ling spoke to them. She brought the eyes close to her face. She detected a hint of dried peppers and cinnamon.

"The spice trade," she whispered, reaching her fingers inside of the jar.

The orbs inside her palms stirred. *See with me.* They transported her to other places.

One-by-one, Ling absorbed messages from the seven eyes. Each had their own story. Tears flowed down her face as she visited the images of lost friends, siblings, and parents. She vowed to reunite them with their families, free their generation from the despair of never knowing.

When she touched a fresh-looking pair, she pulled her hand back in shock. She knew them. They belonged to the little girl who went to school with her twin brothers.

"Cili, is it you?"

The yellow eyes bobbed, accounting the moments right before her death. Lady Tun had promised candy and food for her family. She was woefully unprepared in dealing with monsters.

As the light from above dimmed, Ling readied her return to the surface. She dressed in clean clothes and had gathered enough treasure for a voyage across the sea. Cili and the red fiery eye jars went into her bag. The darkness would be hers tonight. She had plans to seek justice and pull out the roots of the curse, one story at a time.

Epilogue

Coming home wasn't easy. Xie found a box of his old things in the pantry. These things captured his life before he boarded the *K. Hooper*. Ling had hoarded the remainders of his life like precious stones. He found old pictures and trinkets from their boat. In the margins of his journal, she had scribbled notes about her own experiences, making it her own as well. What would he give to hear Ling's words again?

He read about her good and bad days. He read about times she had feared doing poorly in school. In other entries, she raved about botany as her favorite subject, her excitement about becoming a doctor, and the simple glee of soda shops. Ling had even asked when Xie would fulfill his promise of returning home. He had thought of her almost every day.

Because of her, Xie committed one more to the practice of writing down his thoughts. However uninteresting or frivolous, he wrote to his daughter, no matter what. He was certain one day they would meet again. Although, time seemed to fight against them.

———

June 12, 1926

My Daughter Ling,

It is almost a year since our meeting. I had arrived much earlier, but July was the first time I actually remembered my past. Because of your sacrifice, I have most of my memories back and a family. The twins sorely miss you. Every week, Ahma brings dim sum to the forest, where the twins parted with you. Are you getting enough food? They said you weren't hurt, a little disoriented, but still yourself. In whatever life you choose, we will support you.

Will you not leave us a note?

Because of the information you exposed about Wupo and Lady Eggers, the community and Red Society banded together. This helped the strike succeed, pushing once-powerful institutions into debt and uncertainty. The foreign companies yielded to labor demands. The rents are down, and schools are accepting residents. All children now wear the mark of protection like the tattoo on our arms. This new school will do wonders for Gou and Kit, but I wonder if they will keep their rebellious streak.

Your Father

———

A few months after Xie wrote this last entry, he found a note written below. His heart soared.

———

Dearest Father,

I am well. Tell Ahma that I partake in her treats. Gou and Kit also leave notes and stories. They need to be careful, for Wupo's spirit haunts the shadows. Enlai has reached the rank of boss. You may rely on him. He will help the family, when you need him.

I hope to return soon. The exact timing, however, is uncertain.

The Ling you knew remains within me. The innocent and loving soul fights to return sometimes, but the old Ling is not quite strong enough to overcome the sights from my travels and knowledge of human nature.

Yet, I don't see it as a loss. For innocence is always lost, and I at least was able to choose my path. I am in my own power. I will write more. I can't wait to share my discoveries with you, mother, Aunt Marcella, and Dabak.

Your loving daughter

Acknowledgments

Writing requires tension. Whether tension is invented or found in awkward juxtapositions and eerie spaces, it still drives your story. Struggle makes writing powerful and at the end of the day worth the sweat, tears, and sleepless nights. It helps to have support, guidance, hugs, and commiserate with fellow writers and artists along the way. There are states after tension, after finishing the draft: release, rest, and reintegration.

Chasing Moonflowers has been an amazing journey. It wasn't the first manuscript I wrote, nor the last, but it was the first ready to be shared with the world. Along the way, I learned so much about storytelling, publishing, and how to be comfortable with my own thoughts. I was lucky to have formed and deepened connections with real people. And yes, there were *a lot* of buttons to press to bring this book into being. I think... I got maybe 80% of them right.

This book would not exist without the people who helped me believe in stories and my ability to bring them to life, especially the haunted, grotesque, magick-fueled delulus.

My family and ancestors shaped the roots of me and this story. Their love, struggles, triumphs, and joys are stitched into every part of this novel, and upcoming series.

I'm especially grateful for the mentors, critique partners, and early readers who redlined the text with me. Angela Yuriko Smith guided the early drafts into deeper weirdness, a hero of creating your own story in fiction, nonfiction, and independent publishing. Giuliette Nardone offered generous feedback and a willing set of eyes. Kathleen Palm provided amazing notes and motivation for Ling's character interiority. The Pick Your Potion Writing Coven's notes were crucial to Ling's blood-laced transformation, along with a perfectly timed class on cannibalism and vampires. HOWLS and WHADs continue to keep horror alive in my heart daily. These spaces have created an amazing way to boost your reading pace and keep your TBR list on point.

The cover was created by my partner, who knows that my love languages include beautiful book covers and copy-editing. He supports my artistic pursuits wholeheartedly, and shows it through his many hours in Photoshop. My kiddo is my number one hype-fan. She remains the inspiration for my hope for a brighter future.

And finally, to the reader. Thank you for stepping into Ling's world. May you find your power in the places you least expect.

Pauline Chow is a writer, coach, and ancestral magic practitioner, crafting alternative histories and optimistic futures. Not your average data scientist, she once sued slumlords and advocated for affordable housing in Southern California. Now, she lives in the woods and is planning her next trip to a historical (hopefully haunted) hotel.

She is a Pushcart Prize nominated author with words in *Cosmic Monthly Horror, Space and Time Magazine, Apocalypse Confidential*, and more. She is co-editing the forthcoming anthology called *Coven of the East: Reimagining Asian Women's Magical Histories*.

For more stories and updates:
www.paulinechowstories.com

 x.com/@itspaulinechow
 instagram.com/paulinechowstories
 goodreads.com/paulinechow